COUNTRY CAT BLUES

Alison O'Leary

**RED DOG
UK**

For Norah Agnes O'Leary

CHAPTER ONE

THE SWEAT DRIPPED into her eyes as she pushed the hair back from her face. The small blue ribbon that he had tied into her hair so carefully earlier that day unravelled and trailed across her neck. She swiped it away and looked up at him. He stared back as the blood ran down the inside of his arm. He dropped the knife to the floor. But there was something wrong. It was pink. The ribbon was a pale satiny pink. She only had one ribbon, it was the one that he had bought for her and it was blue. And he was smiling. But he hadn't been smiling. Neither of them had. She clutched her fists upwards and began clawing for air as she struggled her way back to consciousness.

In the kitchen the first faint streaks of dawn threw a promise of light through the uncurtained window. On the draining board the smeared wine glass which she had used to empty the best part of a bottle of wine the night before stood unwashed. She filled the glass with cold water and gulped it down before reaching across and picking up her tablet from where she'd dropped it earlier. The image showed local village residents celebrating the re-opening of a steam railway line in some place called Fallowfield. The picture was slightly blurred but it was him. She was sure of it. She pinched the screen to enlarge the picture. For nearly twenty years he had never been very far from the front of her mind, and now by complete chance, when she had been randomly searching for something else, his image had appeared. It felt weird, beyond weird, to be actually seeing him. She'd imagined it for so long, pictured every line and every contour of his face, rehearsed everything that she was going to say to him, and now here he was. Before her very eyes. She peered down at the screen. The hair showed threads of grey now and there was less of it, and he had a few folds of fat tucked under his chin that hadn't been there before, but it was him. She would know him anywhere.

A slick of nausea trickled across the back of her throat and she choked it back down. For a moment she held herself perfectly still, swallowing hard against the urge to vomit. Pushing the tablet away she stood up, her dressing gown flapping open. Reaching out for the back of the kitchen chair to steady herself, she pulled the robe more tightly around her and grabbed her stick. She didn't need it so much now, in fact she didn't really need it at all, but she had got used to it. She liked the feel of it. It was, literally, something to hold on to. And when she'd been in prison it had come in very handy.

"HONESTLY MOLL, IT could be a real opportunity. If things work out, it might be my route out of Sir Frank's. And they're only running the scheme as a pilot. It might not happen again. It's a good school, great Ofsted reports. And the house is in a really nice village," he added.

"What's it called?"

"Fallowfield."

From the other side of the room where he was squashed up beneath the radiator, Aubrey watched Molly's expression. Whatever it was they were talking about, it was sufficiently serious for them to be sitting down and facing each other across the kitchen table. Difficult to tell whether that was good or bad though. Could go either way. He rested his chin on his paws and listened harder.

"Fallowfield? Why does that ring a bell? I'm sure I've heard of it in some context or another."

Aubrey watched as Jeremy hesitated before responding, his index finger tapping lightly on the surface of the table. When he spoke, his tone was flat.

"There was an unsolved murder there about fifteen years ago."

"Not that nice, then." Molly thought for a moment. "Wasn't it a teenage girl? I seem to remember reading about it at the time. It was in all the papers."

"Moll, it was years ago."

Molly remained silent. Jeremy continued.

"According to the websites it's a very desirable place. There's been lots of development. In a good way," he added hastily. "Easy commuting, good facilities, all that. And it's got a village pub."

Molly smiled.

"Well, that clinches it then." She paused for a moment. "I'm not saying that you shouldn't accept. It's just... well... it's a big step. And there's my job to think about as well."

She stood up and walked over to the window, staring at the light rain pattering against the panes.

"Molly, it's only an exchange. It's not permanent. Just for a year. An academic year, so not even a whole year. We'll be back before the end of next July. And you've said yourself you fancy a change from Donaghue's. You could see it as a kind of gap year, a sort of breathing space to think about what you want to do next."

Molly turned back to face him.

"I guess so. But we need to think about Carlos, too. He's starting his final GCSE year in September. He's had enough disruption as it is, he doesn't need any more."

Jeremy picked up his empty wine glass and twirled it round by the stem before speaking.

"True, but you know as well as I do, at Sir Frank's he's always going to be known as the kid whose mother got killed. He could do with a fresh start, too."

Molly nodded slowly and bit her bottom lip. Although they rarely actually mentioned her name, the image of Maria seemed to suddenly spring between them, filling the space and almost as vivid in death as in life. Aubrey tucked his tail more tightly around him and drew into himself. Once encountered, never forgotten. Cat-hating Maria, with her fat little legs bulging out over her cheap sparkly flip flops, her sharp dark eyes that had the unfailing ability to winkle out a cat in a place he ought not to be, and her big mouth that could induce sonic shock even at a whisper; every inch of her had seemed to pulsate defiance and belligerence. And much good it had done her. Born in the back streets of Sao Paulo to an underage mother and a witless father, and then found strangled in her own home before the age of forty, her life had ended as it had begun. Ignominiously.

For a moment both Jeremy and Molly remained silent. Although it had been over a year since the dreadful discovery of Maria's lifeless body flung across her bed, the memory of that terrible time and all that followed in the immediate aftermath was never far away. Molly spoke first.

"We'd have to get approval to take him. We're only his foster parents; we don't really have any rights. What will we do if they say no?"

As if on cue, the low, insistent throb of Carlos's music began to pulsate through the ceiling. Jeremy reached across the table and re-filled his wine glass.

"Well, I don't think that Zanna is going to object. She's got a case load longer than both your arms and she's off sick half the time. She'll probably be delighted to lose him. She's only visited once and even then she could barely remember his name without looking at her notes. Don't you remember? She kept calling him Christopher."

Molly nodded and then glanced across the room. "There's Aubrey to think about too, don't forget."

Aubrey sat up abruptly and hit his head against the bottom of the radiator. What? Why did they have to think about him?

"It's fine. We can take a small pet; it was one of the first things I checked." They both looked doubtfully at Aubrey as he spoke. While Aubrey was indisputably a pet, whether or not he could be described as small was rather more open to debate.

Aubrey settled back down again and breathed a sigh of relief. That was all right then. Wherever it was they were going, he was clearly going with them. "And," continued Jeremy, "Ferndale is a good school. Carlos stands a much better chance of getting some decent grades there. And even if it wasn't such a good school, it has one huge advantage."

"What?"

"It's not Sir Frank's."

Jeremy tapped his thumb against his wine glass and frowned down at the table.

"The trouble is, I've been there too long. This exchange could be a real way out for me. You know as well as I do that the last five jobs I've applied for, I haven't even made the short-list."

"Well, I still don't understand why not. You're as well-qualified as anybody else and your results are good, everybody says so."

"Yes, but they're only good by Sir Frank's standards which is a pretty low starting point. When they're judged against the results of other schools, they look sick. Let's face it, when less than half the year achieve grades A–C and some manage, rather admirably when you think about it, to achieve no grade at all, it takes a bit of explaining. The truth of the matter is, everybody now is judged against the stats. It's no good trying to explain to an interview panel that half the class were being detained at Her Majesty's pleasure for the majority of the academic year, while the other half saw school as a place to borrow a few fags or somewhere to hang out when it was raining." He clutched the stem of his wine glass more tightly. "Moll, I have to find a way to get out. I don't want to end up like old Ned."

Aubrey agreed. He'd heard all about old Ned and seen him in the previous year's staff photograph. Only five years older than Jeremy but prematurely aged, with thinning hair and scrawny neck, he had been wearing the kind of ill-fitting jacket which suggested that although it had been hand-made, it hadn't been hand-made for him. Ned had been found by the school cleaners early one morning muttering gibberish to himself in the corner of the staff room. Managing to rouse himself, he had eventually staggered off to start his first lesson of the day only to be stretchered off five minutes later. Within two months he had retired early on the grounds of ill-health and dropped dead of a heart attack six months after that.

Molly smiled. "I don't think that's very likely."

"Moll, even old Ned was somebody before he was old Ned."

Aubrey stifled a yawn. Sometimes he had absolutely no idea what they were talking about. Anyway, wasn't it about feeding time? A cat could starve to death at this rate. He toyed with the idea of flopping onto his back and feigning illness. It had worked a couple of times in the past.

"The thing I don't understand though" Molly continued, "is why on earth anyone would want to swap a school like Ferndale for Sir Frank's?"

From beneath the radiator Aubrey paused mid-flop and pondered the question. Molly had a good point. Who in their right mind would willingly teach at Sir Frank's other than the certifiably insane? It was a question that he had frequently heard Jeremy ask himself, usually on a Monday morning.

"I know, I've thought about that myself." Jeremy considered for a moment. "I think that he's probably ambitious. I've come across his type before. I suspect that he wants to get in as full a range of experience in as short a time as possible. Like collecting stickers." He paused and stared ahead of him. "Actually, that's not a bad idea. Give every new teacher a sticker book and when they've got enough, they can get promoted. It's as good a way as any. They could have nice little stickers of licked arses. Anyway, I bet you this bloke will be a head teacher before he's thirty-five. And let's face it, there's no real risk to him. He's only got to stick it out for a year at Sir Frank's and then he's got an urban comprehensive in the bag."

"Jeremy, a year can be a long time. Remember Peter."

There was a moment's silence while all three of them remembered Peter.

"The kids did say sorry." He paused. "Some of them," he added.

"Yes, but honestly, hanging him upside down from the goalpost and building a bonfire under him..."

"They didn't actually light it, though, did they? Anyway, it's up to him. He must have checked out Sir Frank's before applying for the exchange. All the Ofsted reports are publicly available. He knows what he's getting into. Although," he paused for a moment and then continued. "I checked him out on Facebook. I must admit, he does look a complete dick."

"What's his name?"

"Quentin."

CHAPTER TWO

"SO IT'S DEFINITELY on then, is it Aubsie? No getting out of it?"

Aubrey shook his head. The late May sunshine was warm on his thick fur and he closed his eyes for a second, luxuriating in the heat. He'd miss this manor. He'd especially miss this garden. He didn't even know whether the new place had one. He might end up being an indoors cat, which in his opinion was only one step up from being in a rescue centre. He opened his eyes again. Ah well, time enough to worry about that later. And who was he to start getting fussy? There had been moments in his life when just not being dead had seemed like a pretty good result. Out of the corner of one eye he watched as Moses dabbed at a butterfly, his tiny paws flailing ineffectually at the air as it floated away from him.

"No. There's no going back. They've started making lists."

At least Molly had. Insisting on something that she'd called an inventory, she had spent the last two days itemising everything in the house. As she'd said to Jeremy:

"It's all very well just doing a straight swap but we don't know anything about this Quentin."

"I'm sure he's fine. Anyway, he's trusting us with his house too, don't forget. And at least we know that he's got a cat so he can't be all bad."

Aubrey had looked up, interested. He'd better let the lads know that there'd be a new cat on the block so they weren't taken by surprise. It was only feline friendliness to give a new cat a fighting chance.

Vincent continued.

"Ah well, look on the bright side. It's not for ever. You'll be back before you know it. And," he added, "at least they're taking you with them."

Aubrey nodded. Vincent was right. He was more relieved than he liked to admit that he was being included in Molly and Jeremy's plans. While he didn't really think that they would desert him, you could never be sure. Only last month he and Vincent had discovered Clyde, the black and white that had formerly lived at number twelve, desperately hungry and scavenging round the bins. His owners had divorced, the house had been sold and when everything had been divided up there was no place for Clyde. They hadn't even had the decency to place him in a rescue centre which, while an appalling prospect in itself, at least would have meant that he would be safe and fed.

After that first sighting, Clyde had simply disappeared. They had all looked for him, even the Siamese Rupert, and his twin Roger, had taken a break from their plans for world domination to help with the search, but there had been not a whisker. Clyde seemed simply to have vanished from the face of the earth. Aubrey sighed to himself. The fact was, they were all at the mercy of their owners, even Vincent. In terms of currency, former rescue cats had less worth than a pocket of loose change. It was how it was and they all knew it. It was either that or take your chances on the street and as he knew only too well, independence and the romance of the road wasn't all it was cracked up to be. He pushed the thought away and turned back to Vincent.

"One thing, Vin. This place we're going to, they keep calling it a village."

Vincent stared back; his expression blank. "Got me there, mate. A what?"

"A village," Aubrey repeated.

Vincent shook his head.

"No idea, mate. Never heard of it."

They both jumped sideways as a sleek lithe body dropped from a branch of the apple tree under which they had been sitting. Roger. How long had he been up there?

"Morning Aubrey. Morning Vincent." He nodded towards Moses and sat back. His piercing blue eyes swept from each to the next. "All well, I take it?"

"As ever, Roger. As ever." Vincent arched his sleek dark back and assumed an air of innocence. His gold neck tag sparkled in the sunlight. He lifted his left paw and studied it for a moment. "No Rupert this morning?"

Aubrey looked away and choked back the laugh that was threatening to erupt. Everybody knew that Rupert, Roger's twin, had been well and truly duffed up two days previously. Foolishly venturing out without the protection of his brother, Rupert had come across some of the Burmese mob who hadn't been able to believe their luck at finding Rupert alone. Rumour had it that he'd needed five stitches across his right ear, to say nothing of missing great clumps of fur. Word had spread among the cats like wildfire; someone had even suggested throwing a party. It was only the fear of Roger hearing about it that stopped them.

Ignoring Vincent, Roger turned to Aubrey.

"Hear that your lot are on the move."

Aubrey suppressed a shrug of irritation. Was there anything that Roger didn't get to find out about? It could only have come from Roger's grass, Lupin, whose sole purpose in life was to keep on the right side of Roger. It was a feat which he managed with spectacular success by the simple expedient of listening at cat flaps and passing on everything he heard. He glanced over at Vincent. They'd both been feeling quite happy until then—a feeling that had evaporated the second that Roger had dropped from the tree. Roger had the ability to lower the temperature by his mere presence. Oh well, at least the move meant that he'd get away from him and Rupert for a while. Rumour had it that they were already planning another scrap with the cats over the railway bridge.

CHAPTER THREE

AUBREY SAT ON the window sill and stared out across the garden. His big green-gold eyes swept the landscape, drinking in every inch that he could see of the great outdoors. Inside he felt a gnawing desperation. For two days now they'd kept him in, for fear, apparently, that he'd do a runner. Like that was ever going to happen. Apart from the fact that he was genuinely fond of Molly and Jeremy, he knew when he was on to a good thing. Where else was he going to get food bowls regularly re-filled and warm laps to sit on, to say nothing of the prospect of lounging around on one of the beds when they were out? He knew only too well from his enforced incarceration in Sunny Banks Rescue Centre that big male tabby cats weren't to everybody's taste. It had been the best day of his short life when Molly and Jeremy entered it and he wasn't about to mess things up by going off on unauthorised walkabout.

He comforted himself that, while they hadn't let him out yet, at least they hadn't done that weird thing about buttering his paws, which Vincent had assured him had happened to at least two cats of their acquaintance. He didn't even like butter. He'd licked some off some toast once when he lived with Raj and it had made him feel sick. Although that also might have had something to do with the fact that the butter was rancid and the toast was burnt, as was almost everything else that Raj ate. Raj hadn't so much cooked as incinerated. He pushed down the customary wave of sadness as the image of Raj's kindly, gentle face rose before him. He loved Jeremy, Molly, and Carlos with all his furry little heart, but Raj had been the first human to show him real kindness and he still missed him, even now.

He turned back and watched as Molly leaned over and, for the third time in as many minutes, inspected the controls on the cooker, a slight worry line creasing her brow. She looked up as Jeremy came in.

"I still have no idea how this thing works. I can turn it on but I can't see how to set the temperature. Only we can't keep cooking everything on the hob, we're going to want to use the oven at some point."

Jeremy strode over and stared down at what looked like a black glass plate set into the work surface. "In his email, Quentin said that he'd left all the instructions and everything in one of the drawers." He flicked one open as he spoke and began rummaging around.

Molly straightened up and looked around her at the high-backed, black leather kitchen chairs and the mirror finish units.

"How on earth did Quentin afford all this? It's like something out of a magazine."

Jeremy shrugged. "No idea. But he's a single bloke. Nothing else to spend his money on, I guess. Either that or he's a part-time drugs baron. In which case he should go down a storm at Sir Frank's. Where's Carlos?"

"Upstairs in his room."

"What's he doing?"

"He said something about his GCSE project. He's taken his iPad up with him, anyway."

"Do you think he's ok?"

Molly nodded. "He seems fine."

"Has he said anything about starting at Ferndale?"

Molly shook her head. "No, not really. I asked him this morning if he was looking forward to it and he just said yes. He looked happy enough, anyway."

Aubrey regarded them both, momentarily distracted from the tantalising prospect of the garden. If only they knew. Although officially he wasn't allowed upstairs, in the other house it was just a hop up from the garage roof to the window sill outside Carlos's bedroom and only the faintest of scratching was needed for Carlos to get up and let him in. That last night, the night before they had moved, Carlos hadn't even been in bed when he'd turned up. Instead he'd been hunched on the little armchair in the dark, knees tucked up under his chin. The armchair was the one item, apart from her handbag, that he had brought back from the flat he'd shared with Maria. It had been an afterthought and Jeremy had driven back to the Meadows to collect it. After a lot of seat folding and swearing, he had eventually somehow managed to cram it into the back of his car. Now it sat in Carlos's bedroom, a small, fat little chair with the kind of scratched woodwork that looked as if a dog had been allowed to gnaw on it, and sorry looking shreds of stuffing hanging out of the back like a botched operation. Maria had got it from the only furniture store that she could afford, i.e. the local tip, along with her mattress and anything else that she could scrub clean.

Carlos had stared dolefully at him.

"The thing is Aubrey, I've been thinking. What am I going to do if nobody likes me? Like, they'll all have their own friends and that. There won't be no room for me. And what if they start calling me Pedro like they did at Sir Frank's?" He paused and swallowed; his gaze fixed straight ahead as he dropped his voice slightly. "What if they know about Mum and... and what happened, and... stuff?"

Aubrey leapt up and stretched himself along the arm of the chair, gripping the end with his paws to stop himself falling off. He knew very well what stuff Carlos was referring to. It was the stuff that still formed the essence of the nightmares from which Carlos suffered on a regular basis, the nightmares that had him waking, his whole body sweating and aching with a dry throat from which the scream could not emerge. It was hardly surprising. It was bad enough to have your mother murdered, without then being held hostage by the psycho that had murdered her. It would be enough to give anyone the screaming abdabs. He watched as Carlos rested his forehead down on his knees, his long thin arms wrapped around his shins. Aubrey leaned in closer to hear him.

"I was worried when they first started talking about it and that, cos maybe they wouldn't be taking me with them." He raised his head again and stared at Aubrey, his expression slightly shame-faced. "I crept back downstairs and listened at the door when they thought I'd gone to bed. I knew something was up, I sort of sensed it. Mum said that we shouldn't never listen at doors," he added.

Maria had said a lot of things, thought Aubrey. Including God helps those who help themselves. A useful little phrase which she had taken quite literally, particularly when it came to helping herself to the possessions of others. Although, to be fair, nearly everything she had done had been for Carlos and the pursuit of the better life that she believed was always just around the corner. It was unfortunate that winning the lottery was one of the main planks of her scheme. He listened as Carlos continued.

"Because they don't have to take me, nobody could make them. Even tomorrow morning, they could just go and leave me; they could just say they didn't want me no more and that would be that. Then what would I do?" He sighed. "It's not like I could even go back and live with my Dad, nobody even knows where he is. I ain't heard from him since I was about five. He's probably dead anyway." He stared at the wall. "Most people drink orange juice for breakfast. He used to drink whisky. He used to stink of it the whole time, like in his hair and everything. Mum used to say it was a good way of saving money 'cos he wouldn't need embalming when he died." He squeezed his eyes shut. "The thing is Aubrey, I ain't got no family but I'm not old enough to live on my own, they wouldn't let me. So if Molly and Mr Goodman change their mind, I'd have to be sent back to that Alderman Wenlock place. But I couldn't go back there, honest, I couldn't. I'd have to run away, but I ain't got nothing to run away with." He turned to look at Aubrey, his expression suddenly tragic. "I ain't even got my own suitcase or nothing."

Suitcases or the lack of them would be the least of Carlos's problems if he was threatened with Alderman Wenlock House. The local home for children in care, it was where Carlos had been placed after his mother was murdered and prior to his fostering by Molly and Jeremy. Alderman Wenlock House sounded to Aubrey like the stuff of nightmares. Worse even than Sunny Banks Rescue Centre, and that was saying something. At least at Sunny Banks any cruelty was mostly the result of ignorance and indifference. At Alderman Wenlock it seemed to be a badge of honour. But in any event, it was irrelevant now. As far as Aubrey was aware, they were all going to the new place. All four of them. Together.

Carlos sighed and unfolded himself from the chair, stretching as he straightened up. Aubrey stared at him. He hadn't really noticed it before, but the lad must have grown about a foot in the last year. He looked like one of those tall spindly plants that stood in the reception area at the vets.

"I suppose I'd better get to bed. Mr Goodman says we've got a lot to do tomorrow." He turned his head and smiled suddenly at Aubrey, the brilliant unexpected smile that always lit his eyes and transformed his face. "It's weird, I don't have no problem calling Molly by her first name, but I still can't call Mr Goodman Jeremy. I try it sometimes but it sort of gets stuck in my mouth."

He went over to the little chest of drawers that stood under the window. Pulling open the bottom drawer, he carefully lifted a pile of T-shirts and drew out a battered brown handbag. Gently, he placed it on top of the chest. Aubrey watched as he muttered to himself, methodically going through his nightly ritual. The broken rosary, the pink plastic comb, the scuffed brown leather purse, each item laid out carefully across the surface while he stared at them, brushing his fingertips across each in turn before putting them back and placing the bag gently under his pillow.

CHAPTER FOUR

"DO YOU THINK it would be safe to let Aubrey out yet?"

At last. Aubrey jumped down from the window sill and wove himself in and out of Jeremy's legs, allowing a loud deep purr to come rumbling up from his chest. Sometimes they needed a bit of encouragement. Jeremy reached down and scratched him behind the ears.

"Come on then, old boy. Let's open that cat flap and get some fresh air in you."

Outside a faint autumnal tang hung in the air. Someone further down had lit a bonfire and a curl of smoke drifted across the gardens. Summer was fading. Jeremy and Carlos would be starting at Ferndale within the next week and he would be at home with Molly. He wondered what Vincent and Moses and the other lads were doing. Nothing, probably. Just hanging around and avoiding Rupert and Roger as usual. He sat down on the grass for a moment and stared around him. It was fine, it was a garden. Not as big as their own one, but a garden nonetheless and now that Jeremy had peeled the tape from the cat flap, he would presumably have open access to it. From his limited view via the downstairs kitchen window, he hadn't seen any other cats, but that didn't mean that there weren't any. In fact, he would be surprised if there weren't. As if on cue, a large, orange coloured animal leapt the fence and strolled purposefully towards him. For a moment they stared at one another.

"And you are?" The big orange cat spoke slowly, head to one side, as if considering.

"I am what?"

Aubrey held his gaze. The merest blink would indicate submission. His time living on the streets hadn't been wasted. This was child's play compared to some of the things he'd faced in the past. At least this cat hadn't leapt straight for his throat. He settled his paws more firmly in front of him and continued to make eye contact. The important thing was not to back down. What he said and did now would set the marker for the rest of their stay here. While he didn't want an all-out turf war, neither did he want to be afraid to step into his own back garden. The orange cat remained unblinking; his big amber eyes fixed on Aubrey.

Jethro," he said. "I live next door."

"Aubrey," said Aubrey, feeling his back muscles relax slightly. Clearly, this Jethro didn't want trouble any more than he did.

"Come far?"

"A fair way."

To be honest, he had no idea. Strapped securely in his cat basket and placed on Carlos's lap on the back seat of the car, he had managed to sleep most of the way. It was the only way to get through it.

Jethro nodded.

"Staying long?"

"Not sure."

Jethro nodded again and then turned instinctively at a movement behind him. A woman was leaning forward, peering over the fence, her face half-covered by the curtain of hair which swung down across her cheek. She slipped the stick that she was carrying on to her wrist and pushed the hair back with one hand, gripping the gate post with the other. For a moment she stood perfectly still, frowning slightly, her gaze fixed on the kitchen window.

"Who's that?" asked Aubrey. "Why is she looking over our fence?"

Jethro shrugged.

"I don't know," he said, turning back to Aubrey. "She doesn't live in the village. She just turns up and stares and then goes away again. It's always your house though. She doesn't look at ours."

Without a word the two of them leapt on to the fence and watched her walk away, head down and shoulders hunched as she made her way towards the bus stop. She stopped for a moment and switched the stick to the other hand.

BACK IN HER room Josie settled back into the armchair with a mug of tea and switched the television on, staring for a moment at the drama unfolding on the screen. Not like a real murder. Not like a real murder at all. It didn't matter. She'd seen enough reality to last several lifetimes. She kept the television on nearly all the time now, it was company of a sort. The low babble of voices gave her the comforting illusion that she wasn't on her own.

She pulled her tablet towards her and searched again for the pictures. Stretching her leg in front of her, she leaned back and grimaced. For the first time in years it was actually aching. Probably from all the walking she'd been doing.

CHAPTER FIVE

"SO, WHEN THEY got their homework diaries out, I thought at first that they were having a laugh."

"Their what?"

Molly put the coffee mugs she had been carrying onto the little table and sat down.

"Homework diaries. Honestly Moll, I'm not kidding. They've all got these little blue books and they write their homework down in it. A couple of them took their phones out and I thought, oh, here we go. I was just about to start the lecture about mobiles in class when I realised that not only were they not sending obscene messages, they were actually taking a picture of what I'd written on the white board."

Jeremy ran his hand through his hair and then leaned down to stroke Aubrey, who had draped himself across his feet, partly because he just felt like it but mostly so that he could be sure of following him if he went to the kitchen. Ever the optimist, there was always the chance of a little something, even though he'd been fed less than an hour ago. "And when they want to ask a question, they actually put their hands up. When the first one did it, I had a sort of adrenalin rush. I thought he was going to throw a punch. It's like an alternative universe. In a good way," he added.

Molly smiled. "A bit different to Sir Frank's then."

"Only totally." He paused and reached over for his coffee. "It's interesting, the school seems to have a positive philosophy of encouraging interest outside of your own curriculum area. So, they sometimes sit in on other teachers' lessons. Not as part of any formal peer observation or to criticise or anything, just to see how they do things in other subjects. At Sir Frank's, if another teacher came into your classroom unannounced, you'd assume they were hiding or running away from something. Like their own students," he added. "Do you remember that time I observed one of Peter's lessons, when the Head tried to introduce peer observation in preparation for Ofsted?"

Molly shook her head.

"I'm sure I told you. Anyway, Peter said, 'Have any of you got any questions?' and Karl Winton said, 'Yeah, why are you such a tit?'"

Molly laughed.

"Poor Peter. What are the staff like at Ferndale?"

"Very nice, as far as I can tell. Friendly, helpful, showed me where to make tea and coffee, that sort of thing." He held his mug against his chest for a moment.

"What do they think about the exchange?"

"They seem to think it's a good idea. Apparently, the whole scheme is the headmaster's project. He's keen to bring new ideas into the school on a regular basis and for his own teachers to widen their experience. The official name of the scheme is Fresh Blood." Jeremy grinned suddenly. "Slightly worrying when applied to Sir Frank's."

He paused. "But I kind of got the impression that our Quentin isn't particularly popular. Nothing specific, just a feeling. Nobody actually said anything. But I sort of had this sense that it was about what they weren't saying, if you know what I mean?"

Molly nodded.

"No doubt you'll find out soon enough." She took a sip of her coffee. "What about Carlos? Did he cope all right on his first day?"

"As far as I could tell, he seemed fine. When we got to the car park, I let him get out of the car and set off into school before me so that he wasn't seen turning up with the new teacher and then I deliberately made a point of not going looking for him. I didn't want to embarrass him. He's got my mobile number if he needs me and, as luck would have it, he's not in any of my classes. Or maybe it's not luck. Maybe it's deliberate." He took a sip of coffee and sat back again. "Where is he, by the way?"

"He's gone to check where the bus stop is, apparently he's decided to go by bus tomorrow with some of the other boys. Which reminds me, I'd better make sure that he's got the right money for the fare in the morning."

Jeremy nodded. "He said on the way home that he might get the bus rather than drive in with me. I saw him at break time talking to a group of lads and they seemed like they were all getting along."

"Well, that's a good sign." Molly hesitated for a second. "Did anybody say anything about… you know, Maria?"

Jeremy shook his head. "Well, the Head obviously knows that we foster Carlos, but whether he knows anything of the circumstances surrounding it, I don't know. Obviously, I didn't mention it. So, either there's a conspiracy of silence or everyone's forgotten about it, if they ever knew in the first place. It was over a year ago and it wasn't local to here."

"True." Molly nodded.

"Anyway," Jeremy continued, "So far so good. Unlike Sir Frank's, there were no traditional first day fights to sort out, no checking to see who was under the probation service or being held in custody. And that's just the teaching staff. Even the first day of term meeting seemed good-natured, in that everyone turned up and nobody started crying."

"Sounds great."

Jeremy nodded.

"So, what have you been up to today? Did you go out at all?"

"No, I meant to just have a stroll around the village and find my way around a bit but I started looking at some courses online and the day just sort of ran away with me. Oh, and this morning when I was making coffee, some woman was peering over our fence. It was weird, she was just standing there staring into the kitchen window."

"What did she want?"

Molly shrugged. "No idea. When she saw me looking back at her she went away. Probably just a nosey neighbour, come to check out the newcomers. I had a visitor this afternoon, as well."

"Who?"

"A woman called Lucinda. Apparently, she's Quentin's aunt by marriage. She promised him that she'd call round and see if we were all right and had settled in ok. She's very nice. A bit dippy, if you know what I mean, but very sweet. She was telling me all about the village. Apparently, a lot of the new development was built on the grounds of an old convent. These few cottages are the last of the remaining old buildings. Some of the locals think they're haunted. Strange sightings when the new building works were being done, that kind of thing. Anyway, I've invited them to dinner. I hope that's ok."

"Them?"

"Lucinda and her husband. She's married to a local headmaster. Not yours," she added hastily. "Some school called Arcadia Academy. It's a private school, just on the edge of the village. She left one of their leaflets. I thought you might find it interesting."

Molly reached behind her and pulled a sheet of pastel coloured paper from the magazine rack.

Jeremy took it from her and began reading aloud.

"Arcadia – from the Greek, referring to a vision of pastoralism and harmony with nature…" he paused and looked up at Molly. "What a load of shite."

Molly smiled.

"I must admit, it does sound a bit fanciful."

"I bet all the kids are called Rainbow." He glanced down at the leaflet again. "I notice it doesn't mention their fees."

CHAPTER SIX

"AND THEN I ask them to draw all the fairies that they've seen."

Jeremy spluttered, almost choking on his wine. He reached for his napkin and wiped his mouth.

"The what?"

Lucinda beamed, her big blue eyes sparkling.

"Fairies, Jeremy." She paused and looked doubtful for a moment. "Some of the drawings are quite odd, I must admit. And I would have thought that most fairies have clothes, but the important thing, the thing that really matters you see, is that they reach far into their own imaginations. They are given the opportunity to express themselves freely, without limitation, and that's absolutely the key to positive and healthy development. That's what Harold always says. And of course, he's right."

She looked adoringly across the table at Harold as she spoke. He frowned slightly, his expression serious, and nodded in agreement.

"That's why we started the nature walks," he said. "Rain or shine, three afternoons a week, Lucinda walks them all down past the river and out across the spinney and then when they come back, they draw what they've noticed."

Molly leaned across the table, curious.

"And they've noticed fairies?"

Lucinda laughed. "Not all of them. Obviously."

"Obviously," said Jeremy.

"Don't they write about what they've seen as well as draw it?" Molly asked

Lucinda shook her head firmly.

"Oh no, Molly. The written word can be very restrictive. I do feel that art is the way to explore the inner self, to express any negativity, to let it out so that all the lovely things can come in." She fluttered her hands towards them as she spoke, as though wafting some of the lovely things across the table. Molly and Jeremy both instinctively leaned back.

"We take the same approach with music. Harold says, and I agree, that our children must not be stifled by artificial boundaries. They must be free to develop naturally. Really, half the problems in the world are caused by repression. We must all be free, just as nature intended." She lowered her voice and shuddered slightly. "We must avoid sterile environments."

"I'm not really sure I follow you." Jeremy sounded curious. "What's sterile about music lessons?"

"Oh, we don't call them lessons Jeremy." Harold smiled, his expression benign.

"Oh, no," Lucinda nodded in agreement. "Lessons suggest a formalised structure, a setting of limits, a virtual fencing if you like, which can," she added with a slight frown, "be very damaging for young minds."

"Right." Jeremy looked thoughtful. "If you don't call them lessons, what do you call them?"

"Just music." Harold waved his plump, rather large, hand in the air. "The children are free to go into the music room whenever they like and pick whatever instruments they choose."

"And we feel that it encourages the children to know that hands other than theirs have played them." Lucinda smiled her big beaming smile again. "That they can feel the call of the ages and be inspired."

"So, all the instruments are second-hand, then?"

"Oh no, Jeremy." Lucinda sounded shocked. "Pre-loved. And all carefully chosen. They have to have the right warmth, the correct texture," she added. "So that they can speak to the children."

"But if you don't have lessons, how do the children learn how to play the instruments?" Molly looked puzzled.

"It's a journey of discovery, Molly. Everything that we offer is a journey of discovery, it is at the heart of all that we do. We don't restrict learning in the straightjacket of timetables and lessons. That would stifle their natural curiosity. The children come to the knowledge of their own volition rather than have it forced upon them. Unlike the anachronistic system offered by the state."

"Right." Jeremy thought for a moment. "So, what happens if, say, they don't discover quadratic equations?"

"Then they don't" said Harold simply.

Lucinda laughed, a merry little tinkle of a laugh that wasn't altogether unpleasant.

"And really, Jeremy. Be honest, when have you ever needed a quadratic equation?"

Jeremy nodded. Actually, she had a point there.

"So, if you don't have timetables and you don't have formal lessons, how do you prepare for what they might discover?"

Lucinda looked confused. "What do you mean, Jeremy?"

"Well, if say a child turned up and wanted to know about, oh I don't know, Tudor kings and queens, what do you do? I mean, you can't just make it up on the spot."

"We encourage self-reliance," said Harold, draining his glass. Jeremy reached across and re-filled it. "In all that we do," he added firmly. "It is absolutely key to positive development. Absolutely key," he repeated.

"We're very fortunate," added Lucinda. "We have a number of outbuildings which we have been able to convert into discovery centres." She sipped gently at her wine. "The house was left to me by my uncle. I nursed him for the last year of his life. I used to be a nurse, you know. The house was originally the village manor house and far too big for just two of us to live in, so that's what gave us the idea for the school. A lovely way to put all our ideas into practice. We take boarders," she added, reaching down into her large straw handbag for a small lace handkerchief with which she dabbed at her nose. "Parents are very pleased to place their children with us."

Molly sipped at her wine.

"It sounds delightful."

"And how are you finding the village, Molly?" asked Harold, turning to her with a kindly smile. "A little different to the urban environment that you're used to, I imagine."

"It's very pleasant," replied Molly. "Peaceful."

"Yes," said Harold. "It really is tranquil here. We're very lucky, we have very little trouble, if any."

"Although," Molly said, "There was that murder that happened here. I read about it. It was in the spinney, wasn't it? As I understand it, whoever did it was never discovered."

Harold frowned, cutting across her as Lucinda opened her mouth to speak.

"That was years ago. Everybody's forgotten about it. Nobody really talks about it now. In any event, I think that we can safely assume that it was a stranger, a visitor to the village."

He turned directly to Jeremy.

"Do tell us a little about Ferndale, Jeremy." He smiled, a small sad smile and laid a hand on Jeremy's sleeve. "Now, be truthful. Is it working? Are your young people really exploring their inner selves? Do they have every chance of becoming the person that they want to be?"

"Not in every case, no. Which is just as well, really."

"Whatever do you mean, Jeremy?" Lucinda looked alarmed. "Surely it is our duty to ensure that all young people reach their aspirations?"

"At my previous school," said Jeremy, "there was one lad whose stated intention on his careers form was to go into business with his uncle Greg."

"A fine ambition, I'm sure," said Harold gravely.

"Not really. At the time uncle Greg was half-way through a stretch in the Scrubs for armed robbery."

CHAPTER SEVEN

"SOUNDS TO ME, Moll, like they've got it sorted. What my Grandad used to call being on the pig's back. They don't do any proper teaching; they don't have any lessons. They don't even do any marking. I mean, what was all that conkers they were talking about peer assessment?"

"To be fair, you've said yourself that children nowadays are over-assessed."

"That's true, they are, but that doesn't mean that they shouldn't be assessed at all. They need some kind of feedback, some guidance. Preferably from someone who knows what he or she is talking about." He laughed suddenly. "Can you imagine if they employed those methods at Sir Frank's?" He sat back and waved his hands about. "And now children, you are all going to mark each other's work." He paused and pulled a mock frown, wagging his forefinger in the air. "Oh dear Oscar, that's not very positive, is it? I think we can do better than, 'you're shit and you know you are'."

Molly laughed. Jeremy continued.

"I mean the kids even grow their own food, for God's sake. What was it Harold called it? Agricultural awareness or something. Really, as far as I can see, Lucinda and Harold don't do anything other than take the money."

"Well, they must be doing something right. I mean, how would they get it past Ofsted otherwise?"

"Well, Sir Frank's did. Sort of. Mostly by running convenient school trips. Amazing how the Head could suddenly find the money to fund a trip to the seaside when the Ofsted inspectors were due. That and off-rolling," he added.

"Off what?"

"Off-rolling. It's where a number of kids, those from whom our expectations are not so much low as non-existent, conveniently disappear shortly before GCSE's. So, they're there at the start of the previous year and then they magically disappear before the start of Year 11 with the result that, lo, our performance data magically improves."

"Where do they go?"

"Pupil Referral Units sometimes. Sometimes they just disappear. It starts with truanting, then they just stop turning up at all. The official line is that the parents have probably moved or that they're being home-educated. Although," he added. "Given that most of the parents are graduates of Sir Frank's themselves, I've always thought that the latter is the least likely of the various options."

"So where are they then?"

"Probably dossing about at home watching the telly. Home schooling isn't really regulated, not in the way that schools are. I've got a feeling that the law only really says that it's the parent's responsibility to ensure that their child is educated and some do it brilliantly, I don't doubt, although I don't think that they get much support. But as far as I'm aware, you don't have to get approval or anything. As far as I know, nobody goes looking for kids once they're out of the system. Although I did try once."

"What happened?"

"I got threatened with an iron bar by an irate parent," he said shortly. "It says it all that the said parent just happened to have an iron bar about his person. But the point is, most schools find their own way around the system and I doubt that Harold and Lucinda's place is any different. Anyway, I'm not sure how it works with private schools. I don't know if they have the same sort of arrangements." He looked thoughtful. "Did you notice that they didn't mention any other staff? Apart from the general housekeeper. What was she called?"

"Zofia."

"Sophia?"

"No, Zofia with a Z." Molly thought for a moment. "Did you like them?"

"I didn't dislike them. Lucinda seems very nice, genuine if somewhat misguided." He paused and smiled suddenly. "Fairies. Honestly."

"What about Harold?"

"I'm not sure. There's something about him."

"What?"

"I don't know. His hands?"

"His what?"

"His hands. Didn't you notice? They seemed sort of large compared to the rest of him. And his teeth are very white."

Molly smiled. "You can't condemn a person because their teeth are white."

"No, I know," conceded Jeremy. "But the other thing, didn't you think it was a bit odd the way he seemed to deliberately change the subject when you mentioned the murder?"

Molly thought for a moment.

"No, not really. When you think that the school is their livelihood, it's really hardly any wonder that Harold doesn't want any talk about unsolved murders. Given that they market the place as some sort of rural idyll, it's not going to be good for business, especially as they take boarders."

Jeremy nodded. "I guess an outbreak of random killings on the doorstep is not exactly the unique selling point that most people in their situation would go for."

From underneath the table, Aubrey listened contentedly to the conversation. All in all, it had been a good day. Now he was allowed out, he'd managed to explore some of the new neighbourhood and Jethro had taken him round and introduced him to some of the others. He thought for a moment about his new friends. He was missing Vincent and Moses more than he cared to admit, but these didn't seem like such a bad lot. Dino had definitely seemed like a good lad, and Gnasher was ok, too, although perhaps a bit excitable. He still wasn't quite sure about Trevor though. Trevor was what you might call clever. He hadn't exactly been unfriendly, but he had definitely been less forthcoming than the others.

Strange that there were girl cats in the crew. He'd never really thought about it before, but there hadn't been any females in the gang at the other house. Not that they wouldn't have been welcomed, just that they seemed to keep themselves to themselves. But here they just joined in with the lads. Maybe things were different in a village. That Edyth… he grinned. She might be small but she'd give Rupert and Roger a run for their money any day. And Molly and Jeremy's new friends had seemed all right, too, although he would have preferred it if Lucinda hadn't called him a lovely ickle pussy and insisted on hauling him on to her lap. But at least they hadn't demanded that he be banished from the room because of their allergies. Unlike some of Molly and Jeremy's other friends. He brooded for a moment on the unlovely Rachel and Clive and their revolting children, Caleb and Corrina. Not everything about the move was bad, at least there was no danger of Rachel and Clive dropping in without notice.

"Is there a window open somewhere, Jeremy?" Molly shivered slightly and pulled her cardigan more tightly around her shoulders. "I felt a distinct draft just then."

Aubrey lifted his head from his paws as a small figure appeared and waved at him before drifting through the far wall, the folds of her long dress fluttering behind her. His new friend, Maudie. He slipped out from under the table and followed her, banging his nose against the hard surface. There must be a knack to it.

CHAPTER EIGHT

"SHE'S GOT GREEN HAIR. Well, sort of green." Carlos thought for a moment. "It's got some blue in it, too. And she kind of piles it all up on her head. Like this," he added, pulling a tangle of his own hair up from his face and scrunching it into a knot.

Aubrey lay across the bottom of Carlos's bed and listened to the comforting murmur of his voice. Once he had been allowed outside, it had only taken a matter of minutes to find a way up to Carlos's bedroom and give his usual signal scratch on the window pane to be let in. Downstairs, Molly and Jeremy had opened another bottle of wine and were still talking, their voices drifting quietly up the stairs. From his cross-legged sitting position on the bed, Carlos reached over and stroked his head.

"She was at the bus stop. But she wasn't waiting for a bus or anything. She said she just likes buses. She started talking to me and she showed me how to read the timetable." He paused and thought for a moment. "At Sir Frank's, I didn't really know any girls. I mean they were in my classes and that, and I knew their names, but I never really talked to any or anything. There weren't no point really. Even if one of them had liked me, I didn't have no money so I couldn't really go anywhere, and I couldn't take anyone back to the flat." He hesitated and then said, "I weren't ashamed of it or nothing like that, but…"

He wouldn't blame him if he had been, thought Aubrey. Maria had been eccentric by anybody's standards. He couldn't imagine what might have been worse: Maria liking somebody that Carlos brought home or Maria not liking somebody that Carlos brought home. The words moderate and Maria were strangers to each other. Either way it would have been an emotional bloodbath. And that was putting it mildly. Even without Maria in it, the flat itself had been far from welcoming, containing as it did only the barest of essentials. He had only seen it once, on that dreadful day when he and Jeremy had discovered Maria lying dead on her bed, but there had been very little by way of comfort in it.

Unlike Molly and Jeremy's house, which was always warm and contained books and rugs and comfortable furniture, the flat that Maria shared with Carlos was cold and cheerless. The first thing to draw the eye when entering was a great spatter of a stain splashed across the wall in the hall which looked as though somebody had tripped while carrying a mug of coffee, and the rest of the flat didn't improve on further inspection. The only thing of any cheer had been some paper flowers which stood in a jug on the windowsill. It was no wonder Carlos hadn't wanted to take anybody there.

"But this girl, she seems really nice. Friendly," continued Carlos. "She asked me my name and first off I was tempted to say Jack or something but then I thought, what's the point, might as well get it over with. She'll find out anyway. So I said Carlos and she didn't, like, try not to laugh or anything. She's called Teddy. It's a nice name, don't you think? Probably short for something but she didn't say what. Anyway, she goes to that private school in the village. Academy something. Her brother goes there too. He's called Casper. They live there." He uncrossed his legs and rolled on to his stomach, his face inches away from Aubrey, so that Aubrey could see the faint smattering of tiny golden freckles that the summer had brought with it.

"I didn't know you could live in a school. Well, Young Offenders and that. But not a proper school." He paused and tickled Aubrey's ear. "They don't do any real lessons, like in a classroom, it's all just sort of mucking about. They can choose what they want to do and then they go on computers and start searching for stuff. They're not allowed to print anything because Harold, he's the headmaster, says that they all have a responsibility to save the environment, but Teddy says it's because it costs money."

He stretched out a finger and drew it gently down Aubrey's nose.

"There's only two teachers there, Harold and Lucinda. That's what they call them. Not Miss or Sir or anything, just Harold and Lucinda. Teddy says that Lucinda does most of the teaching, Harold just does a sort of assembly sometimes. Most days they go outside and look at trees and things and then they go on nature walks and draw stuff. When it's raining, they go in the discovery centres or they do drama. Only they don't call it drama. They call it spontaneous something. In one of the bedrooms there's a big dressing-up box full of clothes, Teddy says some of them are really old, and they can wear anything that they like and just sort of make up plays and stuff. She said Lucinda's really good at it. She said that when Lucinda pretends to be someone else, you really believe it. Once, she dressed up as a witch and some of the younger kids started crying."

He fell silent and rested his chin on his hands.

"Mum was good at acting. Sometimes she used to pretend that she didn't understand English." He smiled suddenly. "When we first come to England, we used to go on train journeys. That was before she had so many cleaning jobs. We used to go on a Sunday because it was cheaper. She used to get this old map out and say, 'Carlos, where shall Lord and Lady go today?" and we used to look at it together and just sort of choose a place. We used to go and sit in First Class and pretend that we were rich. When the ticket man came round, she used to pretend that she didn't know what he was talking about. She used to sort of talk really quickly in Brazilian and put her hand on her heart. Like this," he added, placing his hand across his chest. He smiled. "She could just start crying when she wanted, too. Mostly the ticket man used to get fed up and go away."

Aubrey watched as Carlos turned on his side and rolled off the bed in one long graceful arc. Standing at the window with his back to the room, Carlos continued.

"Teddy said that they liked their school at first but now they're bored. She said that her and Casper would rather be at Ferndale, but their mum and dad say they need to be able to express themselves. So they can develop or something. Teddy says it's because the school takes boarders. She says that sometimes it's more like a prison than a school. Like, they're not allowed to go into the village without permission," he added, "but Teddy says that her and Casper just do what they like. They made a friend the other week when they bunked off tree drawing. Some woman. She was just sort of hanging around by the back gates and now she texts them and then brings them sweets and comics and stuff."

Aubrey yawned and stretched his paws out in front of him. Now the autumn was getting underway, he must work out how to switch the electric blankets on. It couldn't be that difficult, Vincent had told him that he did it all the time when his owners were out.

"Teddy's mum works in television. Like, not on it but technical stuff, producing programmes and that. Documentaries and things. And she said her dad does something in finance. I don't know what that means," he added. "A bank, I s'pose. She says they're always busy anyway. That's why her and Casper live at the school. They only go home in the holidays." He fell silent for a moment and dropped his head, staring down at the curtains, his long thin fingers picking at the fabric. "She asked me about my mum and dad so I told her about me living with Molly and Mr Goodman, like being fostered and that, and she asked me why. So then I told her about mum. I mean about her being dead. I didn't say what happened or anything in case she went off me, I just said that she died. I said my dad was dead, too. I mean, he probably is anyway."

Almost certainly, thought Aubrey. And even if he wasn't, he couldn't imagine him being much use to Carlos. From what Carlos had said about him, he seemed to be either permanently drunk or asleep and Carlos had never said anything about him having any kind of a job. For all her faults, at least Maria had managed to feed her son and keep a roof over his head. And nobody could ever accuse her of being idle. Stark raving mad, yes. But idle, no. And he didn't blame Carlos for not telling Teddy about how Maria had died. At Sir Frank's it had made him a minor celebrity. And not in a good way.

Aubrey turned his head as a flutter of muslin appeared through the wall and Maudie settled down on the bed next to him.

CHAPTER NINE

"OH, AUBREY, THERE you are. Well done, mate. You found us. I was just going to ask Jethro to go and look for you."

Aubrey emerged reluctantly from the side of the rose bush and took the place indicated to him in the circle of cats. Careful to keep his expression neutral, inside he felt a rising sense of dread coupled with a flicker of irritation. It had been such a good day so far. It was the first time since they'd moved to the village that he'd felt really relaxed. Not only had he been given his normal breakfast, Molly had given him some of his special biscuits as a treat. He'd had a short snooze in the early autumn sunshine to sleep it off and then set off for a snout round the garden before leaping the fence and strolling off down the road. Time to do some exploring.

The small community garden sat at the centre of the village, planted in honour of the village men who went to war and never came back, and still tended by volunteers. A bright, happy place with little shrubberies dotted about and pathways that a cat could roll about on and scratch his back to his heart's content, Aubrey liked it already. It was just the kind of place he could be on his own undisturbed if he wanted to think for a bit. There was even a little shelter with a seat in it, brilliant for rainy days. But if he'd known that it was where they held their meetings, he would have avoided it like the plague, shelter or no shelter. He didn't want to be unfriendly, but neither did he want to get caught up in any sort of gang fight, either. And this was looking horribly like a council of war.

At the centre of the circle was Dino, his back straight and his expression serious.

"First of all, thank you everyone for coming."

Well, that was a nice change thought Aubrey, mellowing slightly. He couldn't imagine Rupert or Roger thanking anybody for turning up to a meeting, on the basis that there had never been any choice. It was either turn up or take the consequences, the latter which didn't even bear thinking about. He felt his earlier resentment evaporate slightly.

"I thought it was important to call this meeting," Dino continued. "I think you know, we all know, about the goings on lately."

Gnasher leapt to his feet suddenly, his face grim and his green eyes ablaze. "We could hardly miss it. We've got to do something about it. We can't just sit back like nothing's happened."

Oh, here we go, thought Aubrey. He'd obviously relaxed too soon. This lot might be more polite but it was still the same old same old. Some cats from another neighbourhood invading their territory. Some master plan for domination. Rupert and Roger re-loaded. He could write the script. They'd all start working each other up with tales of ever worsening atrocities committed by the enemy until they were ready to storm the barricades and start ripping the fur. He had hoped that he'd left all that behind. For the first time he regretted Jeremy opening up the cat flap. At least when it was stuck down, he'd always have a ready excuse about not being able to get out. Although, on reflection, that wouldn't really wash. Every cat knew that there was nearly always a way out, if you put your mind to it.

"And now," continued Gnasher, his whiskers quivering, "for those of you that haven't already heard, it's Blue."

Blue? What was blue? Aubrey looked from one cat to another. What were they talking about?

Around him he felt the unease, the slight frill of panic rise up and ripple around the circle. Something was going on here that he didn't understand.

"No. Not Blue. It can't be. I only saw him yesterday." Edyth's voice was hushed, her little face pinched. "What happened?"

"It was Brewster who told us. Blue was found by the side of the road just after it started to get dark."

"Was it... the same as the others?"

Dino nodded and turned to the big cat sitting by his side. "You tell them, Brewster."

The large black and white cat sat up straighter, adjusted his collar, and addressed the gathering.

"He was carried into the bar last night, one of the early evening crowd saw him as he drove up. Blue was still breathing. Jo called the vet."

The cat next to Aubrey nudged him and whispered, "Brewster lives in the village pub."

Brewster continued. "The vet came out straight away." He paused and swallowed. "It was too late. No good," he said, shaking his head. "Nothing to be done."

"He wasn't just hit by a car or something?" asked Edyth, hopefully.

Brewster shook his head. "No. It was deliberate. The vet said that the knife wounds were the same as the others. Straight to the neck and chest. It's been reported to the police."

"Much good that's going to do." Trevor's tone was weary, his expression set. "Let's hope for Blue's sake that he didn't feel too much pain."

"We can't just carry on as though nothing's happened." Edyth's tone was anguished, her face turned beseechingly towards the group. "There must be something we can do."

"Like what?" said Trevor.

"Well, at least they're taking it seriously," said Dino. "They've started making posters to put up around the village."

"They were talking about a reward in the pub last night, too," added Brewster.

"That's because Blue was valuable," said Trevor. "I didn't see anyone offering a reward when it was Oscar. Or Max."

Several of the cats nodded in agreement.

"I've been thinking," said Jethro. "All the attacks seem to happen just before dark, and they're all along the same stretch of road." He turned to Aubrey. "Just at the back of the village hall, next to the pub. Near the bus stop," he added helpfully. "I think for now the best thing is that we all avoid that area and, if we must go there, make sure that it's in daylight and always travel in pairs."

"And keep an eye out. Suspect everyone," added Dino. "Look out for anyone with any injuries, like scratches. They all must have put up some kind of fight. Especially Oscar."

"Oscar preferred a fight to his dinner," agreed Gnasher.

Dino nodded. "He could start a fight in an empty room."

Trevor looked at him, head on one side. "Even if we do suspect someone, what do you propose that we do about it?"

Good point, thought Aubrey. Provided that there were enough of them, he supposed that they could always spring out mob-handed but then what? One human with a knife could still do an awful lot of damage, no matter how many cats were there.

"Call for back-up," said Gnasher.

Aubrey and Trevor exchanged glances. Yeah, right. Call for back-up. Like they were all going to whip their mobiles out. Gnasher had obviously been watching too many cop shows.

"We could have a signal. A cat signal…" Gnasher continued.

"Well, one thing we can be fairly sure of," said Dino, ignoring Gnasher.

"What?" said Jethro.

"Whoever it is going around doing this, it's almost certainly someone who hasn't got a cat."

Jethro nodded. "True. Stands to reason. Although that still leaves half the village," he added.

"Well, that's it for now." Dino stood up and stretched. "If anyone hears anything, make sure you tell me or Jethro."

Trevor turned to Aubrey.

"I'll walk back with you."

Slightly flattered, Aubrey nodded. Together, the two cats headed out of the shrubbery and padded towards the little gate.

"This used to be a nice place." Trevor stopped and looked around him. "Now it feels sort of different. Like you have to watch your back. When it was the first one, Jumble, everyone thought it was some sort of accident. Jumble was old and he didn't see too well. Half the time, he didn't know where he was. When he was found, we didn't know about the knife wounds, we all just assumed that he'd been hit by a car."

Aubrey nodded. It happened. All too often. Cars were the enemy. It wasn't so much that they were trying to kill you, more that they just didn't see you. Well, didn't see you until it was too late. Trevor continued.

"But then it was Delia and then Oscar. Last week it was Max. And now it's Blue. I liked old Blue," he added. "He was a bit posh, but he didn't shove it down your throat. He was a good mate. You could rely on him, if you know what I mean."

Aubrey nodded. He did know. He felt a sudden rush of longing for his old friend, Vincent. He wondered what he was doing now. Out somewhere with Moses tagging along behind him probably, both of them avoiding Rupert and Roger. On a fine day like this he'd be strolling around the gardens or draped across a wall soaking up the sunshine watching Moses chasing butterflies.

"All this only started a couple of months ago," continued Trevor. "Nobody seems to know who's responsible, but there's lots of people moving in here lately, so I reckon it must be someone new to the village. No offence, Aubrey," he added.

"None taken," said Aubrey.

CHAPTER TEN

ON THE BRANCH of the oak tree along which he was stretched, Aubrey yawned and flexed his claws. On the branch next to him lay Trevor, one paw hanging casually down. It was difficult to tell if he was asleep or not. Above him patches of clear blue sky showed through the tracery of branches, the white clouds drifting slowly past. Below him the villagers strolled around the stalls and peered into animal pens. He let out a small sigh. He still wasn't convinced that this was a great idea of Gnasher's. He couldn't see how simply watching people was going to take them any further in finding the cat killer. But he'd joined in anyway, it wasn't like he had anything else of any urgency on hand and it never did any harm to show willing. It gave them a sense of purpose, he supposed, a feeling that at least they were doing *something*. Better than sitting back on their paws wondering who was going to be next, at any rate. Although one thing was for sure, he'd made his mind up that it wasn't going to be him.

He glanced across at Trevor. As if sensing his scrutiny, Trevor raised his head and glanced back.

"All right, Aubrey?"

Aubrey nodded

Suddenly curious, he asked, "Have you always lived here? In the village, I mean."

Trevor shook his head.

"No. I've been here and there." He paused and thought for a moment. "There, mostly." He nodded into the distance "On the railway," he added.

"On the railway?" Aubrey felt confused. How could someone live on the railway?

Trevor laughed.

"Not on the tracks. On the station. I used to live in the waiting room. It's where I was born. There were five of us originally but the others left. I stayed. I liked it. Hardly anybody uses it and there's a gap up under the roof so it's easy to get in and out. It was good. There was always loads of stuff in the bins and the staff in the ticket office used to feed me as well. Sometimes the train managers used to take me with them on the train. Got to see a lot that way. I was called Beeching then. It's the new lot that call me Trevor."

Aubrey nodded. It wasn't unusual for new owners to rename their cat. Vincent had once confided that his first owner, an elderly lady who had died, had called him Mr Fluffpot. It was only his immense respect for Vincent that had stopped Aubrey collapsing and rolling on his back with laughter. But, as far as he knew, he'd never had another name himself. Raj used to just call him Cat and at the rescue centre they weren't called anything. Or if they were, he'd never heard it.

"So how did you end up here?"

Trevor sighed. "I cut my foot jumping off the waiting room roof, someone had left a load of broken glass lying around, and Reg in the ticket office took me to the vet. Then, usual thing, somebody decided I needed a better home. They put a poster up at the station. One of the commuters took me home with him."

Aubrey nodded in sympathy. It was just like the woman who'd decided he was lost when she'd seen him scavenging around the bins. She had bundled him off to the rescue centre before he'd had time to draw breath. Before he knew where he was, he'd found himself banged up with all the other rejects. It had been one of the worst days of his life. Trevor continued.

"Don't get me wrong, I'm not complaining. It's good here, I got lucky. Proper meals. Cat flap. The lot. I just miss the railway sometimes. It was sort of free, if you know what I mean."

"Couldn't you just go back there?"

Trevor sighed.

"No, not really. My new lot have got me micro-chipped. And the ticket office knows me, they'd just think I was lost and take me back. Anyway, as I said, I'm not complaining. There's a lot worse places."

Aubrey opened his mouth to answer and then jumped suddenly, almost losing his grip on the branch, as a great cacophony of noise burst out and filled the air. In the centre of the paddock a group of men and women wearing hats and jackets with gold braiding had set up and started to play instruments, their cheeks puffing with the effort. The villagers gravitated towards them and stood watching, clapping their hands together each time there was a break. Among them Aubrey spotted Jeremy, beer glass in hand and near to him the woman with the stick that he'd seen now almost every day since they'd moved here. As he watched, she moved away, slipping through the spectators and making her way to the outer edges of the little crowd.

At a short distance stood Molly and next to her Carlos, the pair of them leaning over a pen containing two sheep. Carlos's tall gangling body wavered above Molly's neat frame as he took a photograph on his mobile. Aubrey watched as he nudged Molly and turned sideways, grinning, as he took a picture of Jeremy lifting his beer glass.

He closed his eyes. He wished they'd stop making that Godawful noise. It was enough to give a cat a headache. He opened his eyes again and glanced down. At the foot of the tree sat Gnasher.

"Oi, Trevor. Aubrey."

Aubrey looked across at Trevor who nodded. Together the two cats slid down the trunk to the waiting Gnasher.

"Meeting. Behind the beer tent."

Without waiting for an answer, Gnasher set off, keeping to the edges of the paddock and glancing rapidly from side to side as he ran. Aubrey and Trevor followed him, keeping low to the ground.

Behind the beer tent sat Dino, Jethro, Edyth, and Brewster.

"We think we're going to wrap it up pretty soon," said Dino. "Anyone got anything to report?"

Edyth and Brewster shook their heads.

"Me neither," said Dino. "Not sure we're any the wiser. They all look like they normally do. What about you Trevor? You and Aubrey spot anything?"

"Only Morris, up to his usual tricks," said Trevor. "Weaving in and out of the beer tent. Barely able to put one foot in front of another. At least living so close to the paddock he won't have too much trouble staggering home. Even Morris can manage two or three yards without falling over. Probably."

The other cats laughed.

"I wonder they don't get fed up with him," said Brewster. "He had to be helped to find his way out of the pub last night, which wouldn't have been so bad if he hadn't been sitting next to the door. He was drunk before he even came in so Jo only served him with one drink. He could hardly see, every time he stood up he kept barging into walls. Jo was threatening to bar him. He won't though," he added.

The other cats nodded. The village pub was about Morris's only form of social contact and Jo was far too good-hearted to deprive him of it, even though he did stretch Jo's patience to the limit sometimes.

"He's harmless enough," said Edyth. "And he was always very good to Lulu." she added.

The others nodded. When Lulu had been old, ill and found wandering about the village, apparently without an owner, it was Morris who had taken her in and looked after her. He might not meet the exacting standards of some of the other villagers, but none of the cats doubted that he had a good, albeit usually drunken, heart. When she died, he had even made a little grave for her in the weed-strewn patch that passed for his garden.

Brewster opened his mouth to speak and then stopped as a blood-curdling scream echoed out across the paddock, slicing through the noise of the brass band and bringing the music to an abrupt halt. For a split second, each cat sat frozen in the absolute silence that followed. It was Dino who spoke first, his voice low and urgent.

"Right. Scatter. Go straight home. Make your way separately. Whatever's happened, we'll find out soon enough but in the meantime we don't want them seeing us all together."

CHAPTER ELEVEN

AUBREY SLIPPED THROUGH the cat flap and made his way reluctantly towards the corner of the kitchen and the fur-lined cat dome that Molly had bought for him. To help him settle in, she'd said. It was very nice of her and he knew that she meant well, but he didn't particularly like it. There was something just slightly uncomfortably lumpy about it and it had a strange sort of institutionalised smell that reminded him a bit of Sunny Banks. They had all had their own beds there too, like that somehow made the enforced incarceration all right. As if. All the cat beds in the world wouldn't make up for the loss of freedom. There wasn't a cat in Sunny Banks that wouldn't have rather slept on cold wet gravel on a winter night, as long as it was somewhere without locks and bars. But he must make more of an effort to use this one occasionally, he knew. If only to show willing. Trouble was, there were far more comfortable places in the house when he wanted to get his head down. Molly and Jeremy's bed when they were out, being just one example. He turned around as the back door opened and Jeremy came in, followed by Molly and Carlos. Molly began filling the kettle.

Jeremy pulled back one of the black leather high-backed kitchen chairs and stared down at the granite work surface of the breakfast bar, one hand gripping the surface and the other ruffling the back of his head.

"This feels unreal," he said. He raised his head again and looked at Molly and Carlos, his expression puzzled. "The whole thing was like watching something on the telly. In fact, the funny thing is, I thought at first it was part of the fete, some sort of play enactment or something. You know, like one of those murder mystery things. Something put together by the local drama group. I was waiting for a Hercule Poirot lookalike to enter stage left and start talking about his little grey cells." He sat down heavily and gave a great sigh.

Molly nodded.

"I know. I just kept staring. I felt like I ought to be doing something, but I didn't know what."

"Then all that hanging about in the beer tent while we waited for the police to question us." Jeremy exhaled loudly, as though to relieve the pressure. "Why was everyone so quiet? It was spooky. On the television, when all the suspects are put together, there's always at least one stroppy character. Like, demanding to be allowed to go home or see a solicitor or whatever but there we were, all herded together in one space and not one of us could think of anything to say. Not a word. It was as if the very fact of opening our mouths would somehow incriminate us. I mean, there were some of the blokes from the pub in there and we all looked as if we'd never seen each other before. Even Morris looked sober. Well, relatively speaking," he added.

"I know. I sort of wanted to say something, if only to break the tension, but I couldn't think of anything sensible. I mean, what is there to say when something like that has just happened?"

Jeremy nodded.

"I felt exactly the same. But we could hardly break into the 'good weather we're having for the time of year' or 'planted your spring bulbs yet' routine."

Molly passed him a mug of tea and handed another to Carlos who put it down untasted.

"Mr Goodman," Carlos spoke slowly and edged towards him sideways, leaning back against the work surface, his long fingers gripping the edge. Aubrey could see the whitening of his knuckles as he clenched harder before speaking. "Why did the police question me?"

Jeremy looked across at him, surprised.

"They questioned everyone, Carlos. Not just you. That's why they put us all in the beer tent."

"But I was with Molly. I didn't see anything that she didn't see."

"It's just procedure, that's all. It's what they have to do. It's nothing to worry about."

"Yes, but what with mum and all that…" His voice trailed off and he slid into the chair next to Jeremy, resting his elbows on the surface in front of him.

"I shouldn't think that they even know about your mother. Why would they? But anyway, that's got nothing to do with anything here."

"But they probably will start sort of investigating everyone, won't they? Like looking into their past and that. And then they'll find out. They're bound to."

Jeremy nodded. "Well, yes, I expect so. But it won't make any difference. Why should it?"

"Well, like it might make me more of a suspect."

"Carlos, everybody who was at the fete will be a suspect in the short term. But not you more than anybody else," he added hurriedly.

Carlos nodded; his expression uncertain.

"Can I go up to my room?" he asked, standing up suddenly.

"Of course you can," said Molly. "You don't need to ask. But Carlos, try not to dwell on things. It's a horrid thing that's happened, but it's nothing to do with us. We just happened to be there, along with most of the village."

All three of them watched as he trailed out of the room, his bony shoulders slumped and his hands stuffed down into his pockets. Within seconds the sound of his music began the customary low insistent throb through the ceiling.

Molly sat down on the chair he'd just vacated and sipped at her tea.

"This must bring it all back to him but I don't really know what to say to make it any better. He must be feeling terrible."

"I know," agreed Jeremy. "But there's nothing that we can do about it. Probably the best thing to do is just leave him alone. He'll come down when he's ready. To be honest, I'm not feeling too great myself. And at least Carlos didn't see the body. Thank God that you were both too far away."

From the comfort of Jeremy's lap, where he had parked himself as soon as he had sat down, Aubrey agreed. There were some mental images that it was entirely possible to live without and Carlos, especially, had faced enough in his short life. Aubrey had seen it though, all the cats had. Fleeing away from the paddock, they had all witnessed the figure of Harold staggering in small sideways trotting steps across the paddock, his big hands fluttering up and down, and then collapsing in front of the band, a great fountain of blood spouting from the gash in his chest and spattering the feet of the musicians. The little crowd in front of the band had drawn back in a moment of collective silent revulsion before somebody let out a great scream and someone else pulled out a phone and called for an ambulance. Not that there was much point. Even at a distance, nobody could fail to see the amount of blood pumping out of Harold's chest. Aubrey had seen enough animals dying on the street to know that the chances of Harold surviving were roughly nil.

"What I don't understand," continued Jeremy, "is how whoever did it managed to get away unnoticed. He, or she I suppose, must have been covered in blood."

"If they did." Aubrey glanced across the room. "Get away, that is," added Maudie, who was sitting on the window sill, swinging her legs. "They might have just stayed where they were."

She was right, he thought. Most of the village were there, including Maudie herself whom he'd noticed sitting in the driving seat of the St John's ambulance. And not everybody had been watching the band. Some of them were manning stalls or working in the beer tent. Whoever it was could have just stayed and carried on mingling with the crowd. But surely, they would still have been covered in blood?

"It depends on what they were wearing," said Molly, as if in answer to his unspoken question. "If whoever did it went prepared then there was nothing to stop them tearing off some kind of protective clothing. In which case," she added, "it must have been shoved somewhere immediately afterwards. And there's the weapon. What do you think he was killed with?"

Jeremy shrugged.

"A knife I should imagine. Although," he added, "nobody has actually said."

"Then that must surely mean that the murderer went prepared. I mean, who just happens to have a knife about their person?"

"Quite a lot of people, as it happens," said Jeremy, dryly. "Half the pupils at Sir Frank's to start with. And one or two of the staff, I shouldn't be surprised."

"I guess so, but it must have been quite a big knife. Surely, it's been found by now?"

"It might have been thrown away but I should imagine that the police will search the area pretty thoroughly," said Jeremy. "If they haven't found it yet, they soon will."

"It might be somewhere that they won't look," said Maudie, before melting through the closed door and following Carlos upstairs.

CHAPTER TWELVE

FROM THE TOP of the fence Aubrey watched as Jeremy let the door of the pub swing to behind him, his hands in his pockets and his face solemn, matching the mood in the village. Apart from the brief discussion when they had first returned from the fete, Molly and Jeremy had avoided speaking about what had happened. It had been as if merely to frame the words would somehow invite the horror into their home. Carlos had remained in his room, venturing out only when tempted by Molly with a toasted cheese sandwich and a can of Coke.

Outside, where people would normally have been mowing their lawns or walking their dogs, the streets were empty of villagers. In their place had been a litter of police cars and news vans dotted across the little roads and lanes. Only now had they started moving away, one by one, a slow procession trailing off as the late afternoon turned into evening, until at last there were only two police cars left, one solitary vehicle parked at the top of the lane where the road forked and the other at the gates of Arcadia Academy. The whole area was blanketed in a kind of soft expectant silence which stretched into the dusk. It was as though every inhabitant was holding their breath. Even the bus shelter, which normally attracted two or three bored teenagers on most evenings, stood empty and deserted.

Aubrey jumped down from the fence as Jeremy waved to him and joined him for the last few yards, tail erect to show he was pleased to see him. It had turned into a very satisfying little early evening routine, Jeremy having a pint in the pub and

Aubrey waiting for him. It gave a pleasing sense of predictability to the day. It also meant that, as Jeremy went in by the back door, there was every chance that he'd get something extra to eat as he passed through the kitchen.

"That was Lucinda," Molly said, placing the handset back on the shelf as Jeremy and Aubrey came into the sitting room, Aubrey rapidly swallowing the last few biscuits that Jeremy had palmed him. Lately Molly had become a bit over-interested in how much he was eating. She'd even put him on those scale things in the bathroom. Not that she'd been able to read the result. He'd jumped off straight away and stalked back downstairs. A cat had to keep some sort of dignity and there was a limit to what he was prepared to accept. Even to please Molly.

"I'm not sure why she rang me," Molly continued. "It's not like we're close friends or anything. Perhaps she couldn't think of anyone else."

Jeremy nodded and leaned back against the mantlepiece; his expression thoughtful.

"I expect so. I did kind of get the impression when they were here that she didn't have much by way of family, apart from that uncle she talked about and he's dead. And I don't think that she and Harold have mixed in the village much either. I expect that she just wanted someone to talk to, a friendly voice. How is she?"

"Well, not great, as you may imagine. She's still in the hospital, she's being treated for shock and they're keeping her in overnight, just to be on the safe side."

"Probably as well," said Jeremy. "What about the children at the Academy?"

"Zofia is still there." Molly paused for a moment. "Poor Lucinda. She looked absolutely dreadful when they took her away."

"It's hardly surprising," said Jeremy. "Of all the things that she thought might happen today, that almost certainly wasn't one of them."

Aubrey thought about the fleeting glimpse he'd had of Lucinda as he fled back through the paddock towards home. Sitting on the step of the St John's ambulance, her long floaty dress covering her feet, with her head down and her hair hanging over her face, she had looked exactly like Carlos did that time he'd come weaving up the garden path and spent the afternoon with his back parked up against the back of the shed wall, retching into the flower bed, and watched with interest, albeit sympathetically, by Aubrey, Vincent and Moses.

"Did she have any further news?"

Molly shook her head.

"No. If the police know anything, they're keeping it close to their chest. She said that they asked her lots of questions about Harold, including whether he had any enemies. She said that he didn't, obviously."

No enemies? Aubrey snorted. Clearly, there was at least one person who didn't have Harold on their Christmas card list. In Aubrey's experience, unpredictable as humans might be, they didn't usually go around killing people that they liked.

"Although," continued Molly, "she did say that she told the police that she had seen some woman hanging about by the Academy gates recently. She thought that she was a stranger to the village. The police are going to look into it."

"What's happening about the school?" Jeremy asked. "Did she say?"

"No. She didn't mention it other than to say that Zofia is looking after the children. I wonder if anybody has told them?"

"I think they'll work out that something is going on as soon as they spot the police car stationed up at the main gates," he said, dryly. "But in any event, they know, trust me. They won't need anyone to tell them. Kids of that age are like something from the Twilight Zone. I don't know why they need social media. They can just thought wave each other."

Molly nodded.

"You're probably right." She paused for a second before adding, "God, it only happened this afternoon and we're already talking about it like it was weeks ago."

She reached down and ruffled her hand across the thick fur on Aubrey's back. He twisted his neck slightly and gave her hand a tiny lick with his rough tongue.

"I expect that the police will be back to question everyone again," said Jeremy. "It was all a bit rushed this morning. They're bound to return."

Molly looked grave.

"Probably."

"What else do you think they asked Lucinda? Apart from whether Harold had any enemies, I mean."

"Like what?"

"You know."

"No," said Molly. "I don't. What?"

Yeah, what? Aubrey looked expectantly up at Jeremy.

"Well, about the state of their marriage. How they got on, that sort of thing."

"Why should the police ask Lucinda about their marriage? What's that got to do with anything?"

"Well, probably nothing, but in most murder cases, apart from random serial killings—and even they aren't as random as they sometimes seem—the spouse is usually the first suspect."

"You can't be serious." Molly half-smiled. "Lucinda and Harold?"

"Think about it, Moll. It's obvious. The spouse usually has the most to gain. Freedom. Money. Lots of people have life insurance," he added.

Molly looked thoughtful.

"I see what you mean. But I think that Lucinda had money of her own. I mean, the house was hers. What reason would she have to kill Harold?"

Jeremy shrugged.

"Don't know. But it has to be a possibility."

"No." Molly shook her head. "I can't believe that Lucinda could be a suspect, she adored Harold. Anyway, she was there watching the band along with everybody else."

"Was she?"

Molly paused.

"Yes, I think so. Wasn't she?"

Jeremy shrugged.

"I'm not sure. I thought that she was but it was all a bit of a blur." He thought for a moment. "To be honest, I couldn't really swear as to who was there and who wasn't. I said that to the police, too. It was surreal, like everything stopped for a split second, kind of frozen, and then it was chaos with everyone running in all directions and shouting."

Molly nodded.

"I know. I remember looking at some of the animals with Carlos and then there was that terrible scream and, really, I'm not sure what happened after that. I know that I turned around and it was all a bit of a blur. The next thing I remember clearly is that police woman ushering us all towards the beer tent."

"Where is Carlos now?"

"Still upstairs. He's been there most of the afternoon. He's been very quiet, although when I walked past his room about an hour ago, I did hear him talking on his mobile so maybe he's made a new friend."

"Let's hope so. He seems to be settling in well at school."

Jeremy slumped down on the sofa and leaned back. Aubrey slumped down with him and felt himself relax. As long as Molly, Jeremy and Carlos were in the house and the rest of the world was not in the house, all would be well.

"I still can't quite believe that this has happened," Jeremy continued. "I thought we were moving to a nice quiet village, a bit of an escape from it all. Part of the reason for coming here was to experience something more rural, a change from suburbia and Sir Frank's." He paused. "I can't help feeling guilty about Carlos, too."

"Why?" asked Molly.

"Well, one of the reasons for applying for the exchange was to try and get a fresh start for him too. Get him into a decent school and away from Sir Frank's and all the bad memories. And now look what's happened. We've barely been here six weeks and there's a murder practically on our doorstep."

He clasped his hands beneath Aubrey's stomach and lifted him, placing him carefully on the rug. Jumping immediately back on to the sofa, Aubrey watched as he moved to the small cabinet in the corner of the room and took out a whisky bottle and a glass. He stared at it for a moment.

"If this is village life, they can keep it. Right now, it feels like something out of a sixties horror movie. A bad one," he added.

For a moment they were both silent, and then Molly asked, "Who was in the pub tonight?"

Jeremy poured himself a drink and flopped back down on the sofa, scooping Aubrey towards him as he did so and tucking him into his side as if for comfort. Aubrey resisted the urge to wriggle free. This was supposed to be a two-way thing, after all. Sometimes even comforters needed comforting.

"The usual crowd of early evening drinkers. Everyone was a bit quiet, except for Malcolm Dryden who was parked in his usual place at the bar, gobbing off like he always does. I don't know how he manages it, he's not a particularly big bloke, but he always seems to take up about twice as much room as anyone else."

Aubrey agreed. Even walking along the little high street to Bradley's, the newsagents, Malcolm Dryden seemed to fill the pavement, as if his ego swelled up around him and billowed into every available space. Jethro had warned him early on about Malcolm, who referred to the cat population of the village collectively as filth, and had been known to aim a passing kick at one when he thought that nobody was watching. Malcolm kept a huge German Shepherd dog called Humphrey, whom Aubrey actually felt quite sorry for. From the safety of the gate post, he'd quite often seen Malcolm yanking on Humphrey's heavy leather collar and lead, pulling him up close and almost choking him, as though to emphasise the necessity to restrain the snarling beast within. The joke of it was that Humphrey, in spite of looking like he could tear a small bear limb from limb never mind a cat, couldn't knock the top off a pint of milk. Trevor said that he thought Humphrey was a bit soft in the head and Aubrey suspected that he was right. It was something to do with his habitual half-witted expression and the way his mouth seemed to be permanently hanging open.

"What did he have to say?" asked Molly.

"Well, everything and nothing, as usual. Talked a lot but didn't really add anything, other than criticising the police who, according to him, don't know their arses from their elbows. Of course, he could do it all better. I expect he knows who Jack the

Ripper was, too. Anyway, he's talking about starting a Neighbourhood Watch scheme. With him as chairman, obviously."

"Well, is that such a bad idea?"

"What, him being chairman? You must be kidding. He'll have us all out doing midnight patrols before we've even had time to say arses and elbows."

Molly laughed.

"No. Neighbourhood Watch."

CHAPTER THIRTEEN

AUBREY TUCKED HIS head under his paw and listened harder. There had been one of those neighbourhood watch things at their last house. It was run by a retired police officer, a small balding man with a ginger moustache who went round annoying everybody by pointing out how he could break into their houses. Jeremy had called him a little Hitler, whoever Hitler was.

"Anyway," Jeremy looked thoughtful. "This isn't some pathetic little twat writing 'bum' on the bus shelter wall. A case like this needs specialists with specialist equipment. What on earth can a group of amateurs achieve that the police can't? I mean, think about it. It's a joke. What does Malcolm think he's going to do? Dress up as Batman and protect the mean streets of Fallowfield? You can just see it, can't you? Him and Deputy Dawg prowling around wearing capes and masks and scaring old ladies. But anyway, it doesn't really matter what I think. Or what anybody else thinks for that matter. I get the feeling that stopping Malcolm would be a bit like trying to stop a runaway train. He was busy taking everyone's contact details when I left, tapping them into a little tablet that he whipped out of his pocket before anyone could draw breath."

Molly smiled.

"Oh, I'm sure he's not that bad. Anyway, who else was in there apart from Malcolm?"

"Morris, obviously."

"Was he …?"

"Need you ask?" said Jeremy. "I don't think I've yet seen the man sober. But," he added, "I do kind of like him." He let out a sudden snort of laughter. "He started making faces behind Malcolm's back until Jo gave him one of his looks."

"I like him too. I saw him talking to Aubrey the other day when he was sitting on the gate post."

"Why was Morris sitting on our gate post?"

"Aubrey, not..." she smiled and continued. "Anyway, apart from Malcolm, did any of the others have anything to say?"

"You mean when they could get a word in edgeways? Well, there's a lot of speculation, in a muted sort of way. Everyone seems to have their own theory, none of them particularly plausible, although most of them seem to think it was someone that Harold knew. An outsider, for preference. But I'm getting the impression that, like Quentin, Harold wasn't particularly popular. There was a lot of 'not talking ill of the dead' and all that but you could kind of get the underlying current. I don't think he went out of his way to ingratiate himself with the locals."

"Did they say anything in particular?"

"No, not really. As I said, it was just an impression. There was some talk of Harold objecting to an application for planning permission a year or so back but that's hardly a motive for murder. I don't think he succeeded anyway; it was only some sort of outbuilding."

Molly nodded.

"What do they think of Lucinda?"

"Difficult to tell. I think that, overall, there seems to be more tolerance of her than of Harold. But then, at this particular moment I would be surprised if the mood was any different. The poor woman has just been widowed in the most dreadful of circumstances." He paused and then continued. "I think that most of them in the pub think she's a bit strange but harmless enough. She's keen on ladybirds apparently."

"What?"

"Ladybirds," repeated Jeremy.

"What on earth for?

Jeremy shrugged.

"No idea. She's built a little house for them in the grounds. Like a sort of dog kennel, only for ladybirds. It's got a red roof with black spots on it. To make them feel at home, apparently."

Both Molly and Jeremy fell silent while they considered Lucinda's ladybird house and then Molly said, "Did they say anything else?"

"Well…" Jeremy paused.

"What?"

"As I said, the word in the pub generally is that it's someone that Harold knew. But an outsider, not an original village person. What with the housing developments, there's been a lot of new arrivals in the village in the last couple of years. Including us, I guess. Of course, they could be going with the outsider theory to comfort themselves. And you can hardly blame them for that. The alternative might be a bit too close to home. Literally," he added.

Aubrey thought for a moment. The word in the pub could well be right. Harold had come staggering across the grass with those strange little prancing steps from the right of the paddock where there stood a small clump of trees. What if he'd arranged to meet someone? And, as both Jeremy and Trevor had pointed out, there were a lot of newcomers to the village. Who was to say that one of them hadn't come here specifically to find Harold?

Jeremy continued.

"Interestingly, the one thing that nobody mentioned was the murder that took place before. It was like the old elephant in the room. Only bigger. I mean, when you think about it, to paraphrase Oscar Wilde, to have one murder may be regarded as misfortune. To have more than one starts to look like carelessness. And this is a small sleepy village. It's not exactly the great metropolis. Statistically, it must be completely against the odds."

"You don't think that they're linked?"

Jeremy shook his head.

"No, I shouldn't think so, not really. The other murder was years ago and, as far as I know, it was a one-off. That normally means that the killer is out of action."

"Out of action in what way?"

"Dead, usually. Or inside."

CHAPTER FOURTEEN

FROM THE TOP of the shed on which he was stretched out, Aubrey watched as Trevor inched round the gate post and strolled confidently across the grass, his rich tortoise shell fur lifting slightly in the warm September breeze. He shifted to make way for him. Maudie drifted down from the chimney pot to join them, the pale folds of her long dress floating behind her. The roof of the shed, Aubrey had discovered, was the perfect place from which to watch the village. Pitched on a slight incline, from here he could see right down to the communal garden and beyond the pub to the paddock where the fete had taken place.

Normally fairly quiet on a Sunday morning, and in contrast to the sombre blanket of silence that had enveloped it the previous evening, now the village was buzzing with activity. On the narrow high street, and surrounded by a little gaggle of interested bystanders, a news reporter was talking avidly to the newsagent, Bradley, who—being the fount of all local gossip—was standing outside his shop and obviously enjoying himself. From their vantage point all three of them could see his hands gesticulating wildly, pausing only occasionally to hold down the huge comb over that was lifting from his head and flapping upwards in the breeze.

Trevor turned towards Aubrey.

"Pity we can't hear what they're saying."

"I'll go," said Maudie, gliding across the gardens and down towards the newsagents.

"She's all right, is Maudie," said Trevor.

Aubrey turned enquiringly.

"Known her for ages. She used to come over to the railway sometimes."

"Do you…" began Aubrey and then stopped as Maudie rushed back towards them, her tangle of rich auburn curls flying around her head and her small hands fluttering in alarm.

"It's Morris. The police are at his cottage. They're questioning him."

Without speaking both cats jumped down from the shed roof in one graceful leap and made their way across the gardens and towards the newsagents where Bradley was still being interviewed. From beneath the news placard where they'd slipped unnoticed, they strained their ears. To their right Maudie hovered over the litter bin.

"Well, he never really fitted in, so I'm not exactly surprised. If you know what I mean." The thin spiteful tones crackled in the air. "I've never been one to gossip," Bradley paused, as if surprising even himself with this outrageous lie, and then continued. "But it's hardly a secret that he likes a drink." Bradley's long melancholic face pulled back in a sneer, his thin lips pressed together. "And that's putting it mildly. More than once he's been in my shop, upsetting other customers. Quite often he's barely able to stand. On several occasions I nearly had to ask him to leave."

But you didn't though, did you, thought Aubrey. Mainly on the basis that Morris was a paying customer. Although he might be a habitual drunk, even Morris had to buy food. Given that he was often too inebriated to find his way out of his own front door, let alone the village, he generally made do with the few cans and packets that Bradley stocked. His alcohol he had delivered from the off-licence in town, the joke in the village being that it would be easier to just have it delivered by tanker, like petrol.

The news reporter adjusted the small microphone in his hand and twiddled with something inside the bag which was slung over his shoulder. He leaned in a little closer, his eyes narrowed.

"When you say he never really fitted in…"

The question was left hanging on the air, but not for long.

"Well, have you seen the state of that cottage he lives in? I shouldn't think it's seen a duster from one year's end to the next. Certainly not since his mother died. Why he doesn't get a cleaner I do not know. It's not as if he can't afford it." Bradley pursed his lips and raised his eyebrows in a dramatic display of disapproval. He folded his arms across his narrow chest and continued. "And the garden is an absolute disgrace. It's a positive eyesore, bramble and weeds everywhere. It's no wonder we didn't win the best kept village last year."

"More likely due to the fact that they didn't enter it," muttered Trevor to Aubrey. "There was some big row about it all. Brewster told us. He heard about it in the pub. Apparently some of the older inhabitants didn't like being told what to do with their gardens. It was nothing to do with Morris."

Reaching up to stop his comb over escaping again, Bradley turned to the doorway of the shop where a tall, pale youth in a sweatshirt several sizes too large for him and skin-tight jeans that emphasised the bowed thinness of his legs peered out from behind the door.

"Tyrone, get back behind the counter. My nephew," he added to the reporter as the boy disappeared back inside the shop, taking with him the stench of cheap cologne. "He comes over to help on Sunday mornings and after school. Much use he is. If he spent as much time serving customers as he does preening in front of the mirror he might actually earn what I pay him." He assumed an air of pained martyrdom. "I only do it help his mother out."

"You were saying?" prompted the reporter. "Morris?"

"Yes, well," Bradley returned eagerly to the subject. "He came here some years ago with his mother; nobody seems quite sure where they were before that. The mother died about three years ago. And the village a better place for it, I can tell you." He gave a faintly theatrical sniff.

The reporter nodded and waited for him to continue. He didn't have to wait long.

"One shouldn't speak ill of the dead, of course." He paused and moved forward, lowering his voice slightly. "Absolute monster. Dreadful woman. Marched around the place as though she owned it, putting everyone in their place and telling them what to do. It's no wonder really that Morris took to the drink. Who wouldn't, with a mother like that? She was a liar, too," he added, viciously.

Maudie jumped off the litter bin and joined Aubrey and Trevor by the news placard.

"She got the local environmental health out to Bradley. She said there were mice in his shop."

Aubrey turned to look at her, interested.

"And were there?"

Maudie shook her head.

"No. Rats."

Aubrey turned back as Bradley's thin stream of invective continued unabated.

"And the local children from the primary school are afraid of him, I can tell you that for a fact." He nodded sharply as if to confirm the statement.

Trevor looked at Aubrey.

"No they aren't," he said. "They like him; all the children do. Everybody likes Morris really. Except Bradley. Bradley doesn't like anybody."

Aubrey nodded. He wasn't surprised that the children liked Morris. He was almost like a child himself. He hadn't had a chance to get to know him that well yet, their contact to date having been limited to Morris stopping by the fence to chat to him, but he had never got the impression that he would hurt anybody. And anybody who would take in an injured stray animal, as Morris had done with Lulu, must have something good about them.

Bradley continued, his breath coming faster, a small bead of spittle forming at the side of his mouth.

"Is it true that they've found the weapon in his garden?"

Aubrey and Trevor looked at each other. Wordlessly, they slipped out from beneath the news placard and made their way towards Morris's cottage. Floating gently above them on the breeze came Maudie.

CHAPTER FIFTEEN

SLIPPING THROUGH THE cat flap that Morris had installed for Lulu and wincing at the faint clacking sound it made as it swung shut behind them, Aubrey and Trevor padded their way silently across the kitchen towards the voices. Maudie drifted through the wall and joined them.

"And can you think of any reason, sir, any explanation, as to why this knife should have been found in your garden?"

The police officer leaned forward in his chair, his large hands clasped together and swinging between his knees, his gaze kindly but intent. His fellow officer, a young police woman with her hair tied neatly back, remained standing, her hands behind her back, her expression impassive.

Morris, sitting in the chair opposite, shook his head and locked his own hands, pressing them tightly together. From where they sat huddled behind the open door, Aubrey, Trevor and Maudie could see the faint trembling of his fingers which he was unable to suppress. The frayed cuffs of his plaid shirt were just visible beneath the grey wool of his hand-knitted jersey. On the small coffee table in front of him, among the rubbish of papers and glasses, lay a plastic bag containing what looked like a large kitchen knife.

"Does this knife belong to you, sir?"

Morris shook his head again and pressed his hands together even more tightly.

The police officer tilted his head to one side and studied Morris for a moment before continuing.

"Have you ever seen it before?"

Morris shook his head for a third time. The police officer looked across at his fellow officer. She raised an eyebrow and moved closer to them, stooping so that her gaze was on a level with Morris's.

"Are you quite sure?" Her voice was unexpectedly light and not unfriendly, a sonorous note in the stuffy little room. "You've never seen it, or one like it perhaps?"

Morris cleared his throat, a small grating sound like a key in a rusty lock, but failed to find any words. The police officer tried again; her voice gentle.

"Perhaps you could check? See if you have one like this missing?"

Trevor nudged Aubrey and nodded backwards over his shoulder towards the kitchen.

"Like he'd know. Look at the state of it. You could lose a rhinoceros in there."

Aubrey nodded and wondered what a rhinoceros was. He scuttled quickly towards the tall waste bin as Morris rose, followed by the two police officers. Trevor squeezed in to the space next to him while Maudie perched herself on the edge of the sink. All three watched anxiously as Morris began ineffectually pulling open drawers and rifling through them, running his hands through the contents—clearly anxious to please, but also clearly having no idea what was in each drawer that he pulled open. The two officers watched from the doorway. From outside the rustling and muted voices of the officers searching the garden continued, the incongruous noise of music from a radio playing next door giving a macabre air of jollity to the proceedings.

Morris straightened up, finding his voice at last. His complexion, usually ruddy, was now tinged with grey. He reached up and scratched at his neck, where a rash was starting to spread slowly up towards his face. He looked helplessly at the two officers.

"I don't really use kitchen knives."

"Not even for cooking, sir?"

Maudie raised her eyebrows and looked across at Aubrey and Trevor.

Morris looked at the police officer, his face bewildered.

"No," he said simply and paused as though searching for further explanation. Failing to find any, he continued. "That knife in there," he nodded towards the small sitting room, "it's not mine. I don't know how it got into my garden. I've never seen it before."

"Did you know Mr Harold Fairchild?"

Morris shook his head.

"No."

"Not at all?"

"No."

"Never spoken to him? Not even in the village?"

Morris shook his head again and swallowed hard.

"No," he said for the fourth time. Aubrey watched as he ran his tongue around the inside of his mouth as though trying to dislodge some words. "I've seen him, but I've never spoken to him. I don't go into the village much, only sometimes to Bradley's. And to the pub," he added.

The male police officer nodded thoughtfully. He tipped his head to one side and spoke slowly, staring intently into Morris's face as though to make sure that he understood.

"I think sir, that it would be better if we continued this down at the station. To be clear, we are not arresting you and you are under no obligation to accompany us. But," he paused and looked stern for a second, "it would probably be better for all concerned if you came with us voluntarily. The sooner we can clear this up the better." He hesitated and looked towards his colleague, raising one eyebrow slightly. She nodded back at him before speaking.

"We can call the duty solicitor if you would like that?"

Morris shook his head. The police officer continued. "Well, is there anybody else that you would like to be with you?"

Spotting the cats behind the bin, Morris smiled slightly, his shoulders relaxing, and then turned back to face the police officers.

"No."

The female officer looked concerned.

"Nobody at all? A friend, perhaps?"

Morris thought for a moment.

"Jo?"

"Who is Jo?" asked the female police officer. "Is that a relative?"

"The landlord at the pub."

She nodded and pulled open the back door.

"The pub's only along the road. I'll go and see if he's available, sir."

Morris and the police officer waited in silence. The sun, beating through the window, lit the dust motes making them dance and sparkle in the air. The radio from next door stopped playing and a strange soporific tranquillity descended, broken only by the sound of the gate scraping across the path and the Jo's voice as he walked towards the door.

"Now then, Morris. What's all this about?"

Jo sounded cheerful, but he was clearly anxious. His broad brow crinkled in a slight frown.

"Shall we go, sir?"

Aubrey and Trevor jumped onto the window sill and watched as Morris was led out to the waiting police car, the holes in his socks evident as he climbed in the back. Jo climbed in next to him.

Aubrey turned to Trevor.

"Now what?"

"Depends if Morris can hold his nerve. If they frighten him enough, he might say anything."

Maudie looked grave and nodded.

"At least he's got Jo with him. Anyway, they're only taking him in because they've got nothing else to go on. It makes them look as though they're at least doing something."

Trevor shrugged.

"In any event, there's not a lot we can do for now."

Aubrey stared after the departing police car. Trevor was right. The police station was in the town, over five miles away, and short of riding on the roof of the car there was nothing else that they could do but wait.

CHAPTER SIXTEEN

MOLLY AND JEREMY stood at the front room window and watched as Carlos walked down the little front path, his shoulders hunched and his hands thrust deep into his jeans pockets. Jeremy turned to Molly.

"Well, that's the first time I've known him to want a breath of fresh air. The last time I suggested that we go for a walk together he looked at me as though I'd invited him to go ballroom dancing." He paused and looked puzzled. "And he smells different."

Molly nodded and smiled.

"I'm surprised that you don't recognise it."

"Don't recognise what?"

"The smell. It's your after-shave."

Aubrey jumped down from the window sill and strolled back into the kitchen. He glanced towards his food bowl, more in hope than expectation. Too early for his night time biscuits, he might as well see where Carlos was going. There was nothing else happening. Slipping through the cat flap he padded his way down the garden path and out into the village. In contrast to earlier in the day, the village was quiet again now, the lingering smell of cooked Sunday roasts hanging lazily in the gathering dusk. Up ahead Carlos paused and looked about him and then lifted his hand to smooth his hair. Reaching into his back pocket he drew out a small plastic-backed mirror and peered into it. Aubrey recognised it as the one that Maria had carried in her handbag. As he watched, Carlos shoved the mirror back down into his pocket and veered suddenly left into the communal garden. Following ten paces behind, Aubrey veered with him.

"Carlos, over here."

From behind the bushes a small, pretty girl emerged, blue and green strands showing through the dark hair piled up on her head. Carlos made his way towards her.

"You got out ok, then?"

Carlos nodded. Aubrey could see the back of his neck flushing.

"Yeah, I just said that I fancied a walk. They did look a bit surprised though. Did you have any trouble?"

The girl smiled and shook her head.

"No, not really. We've still got the police parked up at the Academy, but they're only at the main gates now. They said that everyone's got to stay inside but it's a big house, I could be anywhere. Casper will cover for me. I got out of a back window and legged it across the kitchen garden. The back gates are supposed to be locked but they usually aren't. Anyway, the key is hanging on a hook in one of the sheds."

Aubrey saw the unmistakeable look of respect cross Carlos's face.

"How will you get back in?"

Teddy smiled.

"Same way I got out. I left the window on the latch. Even if someone's noticed and locked it again, I can always text Casper to let me in. There's only Zofia there anyway, Lucinda's still in hospital. Quite a lot of the other kids have gone," she added. "They went this afternoon. Their parents came to take them away."

"Are yours coming too?"

Aubrey saw the sudden look of consternation flash across Carlos's face. Teddy shook her head.

"No, they're abroad. I told Zofia I didn't know where they were. I do really," she added. "They're in Los Angeles. Their mobile numbers are in Harold's office but I didn't tell Zofia that. I don't want to go home. This is exciting."

"What about Casper?"

"He agrees with me, he doesn't want to go home either. Anyway, if we went home, we'd only be sent away again so we might as well stay here."

Carlos nodded and the two of them walked towards the small shelter and sat inside, close but not quite touching. From a safe distance Aubrey followed and parked himself under the nearest bush from where he could both see and hear them. Nearby a solitary barn owl marked its territory, the slow beat of its wings hanging on the air. For several moments both Carlos and Teddy stared at their feet. Carlos spoke first.

"What's happening at the school? Why are the police still there?"

Teddy shrugged.

"I'm not sure. This morning there were millions of them, swarming all over the place. They had cameras and stuff and everything and they asked tons of questions."

"What sort of questions?"

"Loads of stuff. Like what we were doing yesterday, what we knew about Harold, what he was like and that, whether he went out much, that sort of thing. They asked whether he'd been any different lately."

"What did you say?"

Teddy shrugged and picked at the hole in the knee of her jeans, her small finger wriggling its way through the threads and making the gap bigger.

"Nothing really. I mean, he was just Harold. It's not like any of us really knew him or anything. We didn't see that much of him. They asked whether there had been any strangers hanging around the school lately as well."

Carlos looked at her.

"And have there been?"

Teddy shook her head.

"No, I haven't noticed anybody." She hesitated. "Well, there is that woman, Josie, the one that gives us sweets, but I don't think she counts. We just meet her up with her sometimes, that's all." She glanced sideways at Carlos. "Do you think I should have mentioned her? I don't want to get her into any trouble. She's our friend."

Carlos thought for a moment and shook his head.

"No, not really. What else did they ask?"

"They asked whether there had been anything unusual going on, or if we'd noticed anything and then they started looking round. They went all over the place. Even our bedrooms. Casper stood behind the door and watched them. He said they looked under our mattresses and in the wardrobes and everything."

"Are they allowed to do that?"

"I suppose so. They did it, anyway. They probably had a search warrant or something. They spent ages in Harold's office."

They both fell silent again, and then Carlos said, "What do you think happened? Why do you think he got killed?"

Teddy shrugged.

"I honestly don't know. I mean," she paused and considered for a moment. "Like, to be honest, Harold was alright really. He was just like everyone else. We hardly ever saw him. Lucinda does all the activities and Zofia does everything in the house. Harold mostly just sits in his office. I don't know what he does in there. Office stuff, I suppose. He always says he's busy, anyway." She stared ahead for a moment, thinking. "You don't think it was an accident or something? Well," she paused and thought for a moment before continuing. "Not an accident exactly but like, maybe somebody thought that he was somebody else?"

"You mean, some sort of mistake?"

Teddy nodded.

"Could be." Carlos tipped his head slightly to one side and considered. "It's possible, I suppose. But if you were going to kill someone, you'd sort of check first, wouldn't you? Make sure you'd got the right person and all that."

"I guess so." She turned her head directly to face him. "Did you know that they had someone down at the police station today?"

Carlos nodded, suddenly feeling slightly dizzy as a faint floral scent wafted from her hair.

"A bloke called Morris. I heard Molly and Mr Goodman talking about it. How did you know?" he added.

"Casper said. He heard it from Zofia."

"Morris is the drunk bloke, isn't he?"

"He's not always drunk," protested Teddy and then paused. "Well, actually he is. But he's really nice, and he doesn't smell or anything. Not like some drunks," she added. "There used to be a drunk that lived outside the station at home. We used to have to go there every day when we went to our other school. This bloke, the drunk, he used to smell terrible and he had eyes like a dead fish, sort of flat and wet. He used to shout abuse at people. One day he wasn't there and Casper said he'd gone on holiday to another station."

Carlos laughed. He looked, thought Aubrey, relaxed. For the first time since Harold's death his face had lost that hunted look.

"How come you know Morris?"

"Me and Casper met him when we went out one afternoon on our own. We were supposed to be doing PE but we got bored."

"You do PE? What, like games and that?"

"No, not that sort of PE. We don't do anything like that, and especially not games because Harold says that being competitive stifles originality of thought and Lucinda says that it causes irreversible damage to the enquiring mind. Casper says it's because they can't be arsed to organise it. Our PE means Personal Expression."

"Personal what?"

"Personal Expression. It's where you have to get in touch with your inner self. It's meant to be good for you. Casper says he can't do it because he hasn't got an inner self, only an outer one. I'm not sure I've got one, either," she added. "Anyway, Lucinda says that you just have to let yourself go and do whatever your inner self tells you to and in that way you find complete understanding. Or something like that. So Casper and me, we just sort of flopped down and started rolling across the grass. Lucinda looked really pleased so we carried on rolling until we got near the gates and then we slipped out and went down to the village."

"I thought you weren't allowed down into the village?"

Teddy smiled.

"We're not really. We're only supposed to go outside the grounds when we're with Lucinda, but she got distracted with the fairy skipping game."

"The what?"

"The fairy skipping game. It's where… oh, never mind. I don't really understand it myself. You all go in a circle and hold hands and then you just sort of run about waving your arms and then whatever comes into your head you say it out loud and it's a poem and Lucinda writes it down in a little notebook and then pins it up on the noticeboard in the common room. Last time we played it Casper started shouting 'bollocks' and 'arse' and Lucinda went all red in the face but she still wrote it down." She thought for a moment. "She didn't pin it up, though. Anyway, after we slipped out of the gates, we went down to the village and we were just sort of wandering about, like looking at things, and then we went into the paddock and Casper climbed over the wall into Morris's garden. And he came out and started talking to us."

CHAPTER SEVENTEEN

THE BARN OWL swept down again, brushing across the tops of the trees that edged the paddock. Aubrey looked up into its beautiful heart-shaped face as it hovered momentarily, its unblinking gaze focused on the ground next to him. He tucked himself more tightly beneath the bush.

"Weren't you afraid of Morris? Like, with him being a bit weird and that?"

Teddy shook her head.

"He's not weird. Not really. He's just different, that's all. Anyway, he gave us some crisps. They were a bit stale, but we didn't say anything. And he gave us a drink of milk and told us about a cat he used to have called Lulu. He said he couldn't have a cat while his mother was alive because she was allergic or something. Anyway, Lulu died. He showed us her grave. It had some daisies on it in a jam jar." she added.

"Did you know, there's a cat killer in the village? They were talking about it at school this week." Carlos lowered his voice. "We've got a cat called Aubrey. I've told him to be careful, but I haven't told him why. I don't want him to be scared."

From his place beneath the bush, Aubrey smiled.

"There used to be a people killer here, too."

Carlos stared.

"Did there? How do you know?"

"Oh, it was years ago. Before we were even born. Me and Casper found out one day when we were doing IE.

"IE? What's that? Like RE or something?"

"No, it's Inventive Exploration. It just means that we look up stuff on the computers and that, and then make projects. Casper and me, we couldn't think of anything to be inventive about so we started looking up stuff about the village and we found a newspaper report."

"Who was it that got killed?"

"A girl. She was found over in the spinney by a dog walker." She jerked her head towards the small patch of trees and bushes beyond the paddock.

"What? And she was dead?"

Teddy nodded her head

"Yes. The report said that she'd been stabbed. Or strangled. I forget which."

"How old was she?"

"About the same age as us, I think. How old are you, by the way?"

Carlos opened his mouth to lie and then changed his mind. She knew he was still at school and, anyway, he didn't want there to be lies between them. Apart from Aubrey, she was about the only proper friend he had. Well, there were the lads at school he supposed but he didn't know them that well yet. Not well enough to meet them after school or anything. Besides which, Teddy was very pretty.

"Nearly fifteen."

"And me."

"Did they ever catch him, the killer I mean?"

"Or her." Teddy shook her head. "No. Never."

They both fell silent again. Aubrey stifled a yawn. This was getting boring. It must be nearly biscuit time at home. And if it wasn't, he could always make a nuisance of himself until one of them gave in. He turned his head and watched as a small field mouse scuttled into the next bush.

"Your mum got killed, didn't she?"

Aubrey's ears pricked and he turned back. How did Teddy know about Maria? He watched as Carlos's face whitened. Teddy moved closer to him and covered his hand with her small one.

Carlos swallowed hard and licked his lips which were suddenly unexpectedly dry. His adolescently prominent Adam's apple bobbed up and down with the movement.

"I Googled you," said Teddy. "It wasn't difficult because you've got quite an unusual name and I remembered you saying where you lived before. Do you mind?"

Carlos shook his head.

"No, not really. It's just, well, it's just… "

"It's ok. You don't have to talk about it. I just wanted to tell you that I knew. So we don't, sort of, have secrets."

With his free hand, Carlos reached down and wriggled his hand into his back pocket. Fishing out a small square of paper, he held it towards Teddy.

"That's her," he said. "That's mum."

Aubrey watched as Teddy studied the small photograph, battered and creased from the number of times it had been stuffed into various pockets. He'd seen it before, often. There was a copy in a frame on the chest of drawers in Carlos's bedroom. The picture showed a different Maria to the one that Aubrey had known. That Maria, the short, fat, careworn, cat-hating domestic cleaner was nowhere to be seen. This Maria was a young, slim, laughing girl, her thick hair swept back and her large dark eyes sparkling with laughter as she tried to shield them from the Brazilian sun.

"She looks really nice. I bet she was good fun."

Carlos nodded. For a moment neither of them spoke. Teddy glanced down at her phone.

"It's getting late. I'd better get back. I don't want to get Zofia into trouble."

She stood up and looked down at Carlos.

"Shall we do this again?"

Carlos smiled up at her in agreement.

"Ok, I'll text you."

She turned to move away and then stopped as the sound of shouting and laughter, followed by the noise of breaking glass crashed through the evening air. For a moment they stared at one another.

"It's coming from Morris's cottage."

Wordlessly they began to run towards the noise, followed by Aubrey.

CHAPTER EIGHTEEN

"WAS THAT the gate?"

Molly zapped the remote towards the television and turned to Jeremy.

"About bloody time. We're going to have to start introducing some rules. He can't just go wandering off for hours at a time without telling us where he is, and then not answering his mobile. Especially not now. Not with everything that's happened."

Jeremy strode through to the kitchen and pulled open the back door just as Aubrey jumped through the cat flap. On the threshold stood Carlos and Teddy. The blood from Carlos's nose dripped steadily down and soaked into his T-shirt, spreading fat red blossoms across his chest.

"What the…" began Jeremy.

Teddy sprang forward, one hand clutching protectively at Carlos's arm.

"It's not his fault, Mr Goodman. Honestly."

Molly emerged from behind Jeremy and pulled Carlos into the kitchen. Reaching across to the work surface she grabbed a handful of kitchen paper, holding it briefly under the cold tap before pressing it to Carlos's face.

"Carlos, what on earth has happened? And why haven't you been answering your mobile?"

From behind the wodge of kitchen paper came a glugging noise as Carlos struggled to get some words out.

"It was Morris's cottage, Mrs Goodman." Teddy rushed in, her words tumbling over one another. "We heard a load of shouting and there were these boys there, throwing stones and things."

"Who were they? Did you recognise any of them?"

Carlos shook his head and pulled away the kitchen paper.

"No, I've never…" he stopped and blew his nose, "…seen them before."

"I'm Teddy, by the way," said Teddy, advancing towards them and holding out her hand. "I'm very pleased to meet you."

A corner of Jeremy's mouth twitched slightly as he reached to take the proffered palm.

"And I'm very pleased to meet you, too. Now suppose we start at the beginning."

He gestured towards the high-backed kitchen chairs and waited until both Carlos and Teddy had sat down. After first inspecting his food bowl for an update, Aubrey parked himself under the table to listen, interested to hear what they had to say. His left ear throbbed from where he had been kicked by the boy wearing shorts, retaliation for the scratch he'd left down the back of his bare leg. He would have thrown himself back in to the fray but the kick had left him momentarily dazed and, by the time he had pulled himself together, it had all been over and the boys had fled.

"So, what happened?" said Jeremy.

Carlos clutched the kitchen paper in one hand, squeezing the sodden mass between his long fingers. A smear of dried blood crusted across his chin.

"Well, we were just talking…"

Molly interrupted.

"Where were you? We were worried. Jeremy was just about to come out and start looking for you."

"Only in the village." He turned to look at her, surprised.

"Carlos, surely you must realise that with everything that's happened recently…" She looked at his stricken face and sighed. "Yes, alright. Carry on."

She turned away and began spooning powdered chocolate into mugs. Carlos continued.

"And then we heard all this shouting and laughing."

"And it sounded like glass breaking," added Teddy. "And it sounded like it was coming from Morris's cottage and so we ran over there." She paused for breath. "And there were these boys there and they were all shouting and throwing things. Carlos told them to stop and they just laughed and told us to f…" she hesitated. "To go away."

"Then what happened?" Molly placed two mugs of hot chocolate down in front of them. Carlos dipped his head and took a long draught. Wiping his mouth with the back of his hand he spoke slowly, the tone of admiration in his voice unmistakeable.

"Teddy told them that her dad is a Chief Inspector and then she got her phone out."

Jeremy turned to Teddy.

"And is he? A Chief Inspector?"

"Sort of."

"What does that mean?"

"He's a financial analyst. But it worked," she protested. "Especially when I started pretending to ring him."

"So, how did this happen?" He gestured towards Carlos's nose.

"They all started running away and then the biggest one turned around and punched Carlos in the face."

"These boys," said Jeremy. "Do you think they were local?"

Carlos shrugged.

"I don't know."

"Would you recognise them again?"

"I'm not sure." He turned to Teddy.

"It all happened really quickly, Mr Goodman."

"And what about Morris?" said Molly. "Is he all right?"

"I think he was upstairs," said Teddy. "I thought I saw his face at a window, but it was dark inside the house, I couldn't really tell."

Molly glanced across at the clock on the wall.

"Teddy, does anyone know where you are? It's getting rather late; your parents must be worried."

"Oh, it's all right Mrs Goodman. My parents aren't here."

"What?"

"I mean, I don't live at home. I live at the school."

"Arcadia Academy?"

Teddy nodded.

Jeremy stood up suddenly.

"Come on, I'll walk you back. And then," he turned to Molly, "I think I'd better call in on Morris and see if he's all right."

CHAPTER NINETEEN

JEREMY STOOD AND watched the small figure dart up the gravel drive, dodging between the trees to avoid setting off the automatic security lights before disappearing from view. Clearly, she'd done this before. He debated with himself whether to go after her. As a responsible adult, he ought really to check that she had got in safely, but she had been very insistent that he remained where he was. Also, he was beginning to be uncomfortably aware that if anybody saw him he might have some trouble explaining why he was hanging around a boarding school after dark. Particularly one where the principal had just been murdered. He sighed. She was definitely what you might call an independent spirit, possibly a little too independent. Maybe not the best friend for Carlos to have at this stage.

He watched as a light showed briefly in an upper window and then went dark again. He hesitated for a moment longer and then turned back towards the road leading towards the village and Morris's cottage. He had been rather hoping that Carlos would get in with some of the lads in his year at Ferndale. They seemed a decent enough bunch and, by comparison to the likes of that little shit Jed Caparo who had been the main player in getting Carlos into trouble at Sir Franks, they were positively golden. But, to be fair, independent spirit or not, Teddy had stuck by Carlos throughout the events of this evening, and that was worth something. It was worth quite a lot actually, now he thought about it. She had even accompanied him home, ready to, literally, stand next to him and shoulder any blame. Some kids would have run away at the first hint of trouble, he knew. Anyway, at least he'd made her promise to text him as soon as she got in. Even as the thought formed, his phone buzzed in his pocket. He scanned the message. Safe indoors. Thank you.

Stuffing his phone back in his pocket, he glanced up at the night sky and caught his breath, transfixed by the scene spread out above him. The darkness had descended suddenly, dropping like a cloak across the village. The stars glistered in brilliant sparkling pin points of cold white light, clustered against the uncompromising blackness. He had never seen quite such a magnificent sight. In the town it was never completely dark. The nearest he'd got to anything like this was a school trip to the Planetarium when he was about twelve. He stood still for a moment, staring upwards and then jumped, his heart thudding, as something soft brushed against his legs.

"For God's sake, Aubrey. You nearly gave me a heart attack. What are you doing out here?"

Following you, mate, thought Aubrey. Checking that you're ok. Jeremy leaned over and stroked his head. In spite of being startled, he was actually quite pleased to see Aubrey. As well as the absolute blackness of the night, there was a real feeling of being totally alone. There were no houses on this stretch of road, only trees. Trees behind which anything could be hiding. Around him not a soul stirred. It was the kind of night where anything might happen. And anything nearly did, he thought soberly. He quickened his pace towards Morris's cottage.

"MORRIS, ARE YOU ok? Can you hear me? It's Jeremy Goodman. Jeremy Goodman," he repeated, raising his voice slightly.

He straightened up. His back was already starting to ache and he was beginning to feel rather foolish shouting through Morris's letterbox. Morris clearly didn't want to speak to anyone or he would answer the door. He turned away and then turned back at the rattling of the chain being lifted and the door slowly opening. Morris's face peered round the side, the perfumed smell of gin drifting out into the night air.

"Jeremy." Morris spoke quietly, his voice barely above a whisper.

"Are you ok?" repeated Jeremy.

Morris nodded and opened the door a crack wider. He hesitated for a second and then turned back into the house. Jeremy stepped across the threshold and followed him down the narrow hallway. Squeezing past Jeremy's legs, Aubrey followed.

Inside, the small room was lit by a single lamp, the fringed lampshade tilted to one side. As if suddenly aware of how stuffy the atmosphere was, Morris leaned over and pushed open the window, allowing the cool night air to rush in. Jeremy looked around him curiously. It was definitely untidy, and could possibly do with a bit of a clean but it was a far cry from Bradley's descriptions of dirt and decay. In fact, now he thought about it, how would Bradley know anyway? Morris wasn't the kind to invite people into his home and, even if he was, Jeremy doubted that Bradly would be on the guest list. This room wasn't unhomely at all. In fact, in a strange way, there was something distinctly friendly about it. It was the sort of room that you'd be glad to get back to after a trying day. Morris cleared a few newspapers away and indicated towards one of the chubby cracked leather armchairs.

"Would you like a drink?" he asked.

Jeremy was about to refuse but then changed his mind. Drink was Morris's thing and it wouldn't hurt to join him.

"Just a small one."

"What about your cat?"

"He's trying to cut down."

Morris smiled, the lines crinkling around his soft blue eyes, and turned towards the kitchen. Jeremy waited, listening to the sound of the kitchen tap running. Morris was obviously rinsing a glass. There was no doubt about it, Morris was distinctly odd. He'd not batted an eyelid at the sight of Aubrey, who had strolled in behind him and was now sitting upright on the windowsill as if he belonged there. But being a bit odd didn't make Morris a killer. Lots of people were odd, including his own great-uncle Rupert who regularly went off on walkabout, frequently wearing only a string vest. And anyway, what on earth reason would Morris have to kill Harold? He probably hardly knew him. It was well-known that Harold hadn't mixed in the village much. He doubted that their paths had ever crossed. He looked up as Morris came back into the room and handed him a glass.

"Cheers," he said, raising his drink and taking a sip.

For a moment there was silence and then Jeremy said, "I just wanted to check that you were ok. Carlos told me what happened here tonight."

Morris nodded slowly; his fingers wrapped around his glass.

"Carlos? Is that your boy?"

"Yes, well, sort of. He lives with us. His mother died."

Morris nodded.

"Mine too."

For a moment neither of them spoke. On the window sill, Aubrey tucked his paws under him and settled down. At this rate they were going to be there for some time.

"They broke a window." Morris spoke flatly, as though he were merely remarking on the weather. "At the front. Mother's parlour. Chucked a stone at it. There's glass all over the floor. I'll have to get it fixed tomorrow. Mother won't like it; she won't like it at all."

"I thought…" Jeremy began, and then hesitated, feeling suddenly tense. This was getting into slightly weird territory. He barely knew Morris. What if he was a pyscho? Norman Bates re-loaded? Perhaps it hadn't been such a good idea to come into the cottage. Perhaps he should have just checked that Morris was ok and gone straight home.

"Not that she'll know. Obviously."

Jeremy breathed a small sigh of relief and felt his shoulders relax. Morris continued.

"They had me down at the police station today."

"I heard."

"Of course, you did. This is a village. The surprise would have been if you hadn't heard. I expect it's half-way across the county by now." Morris paused and took a large mouthful of gin. "That's why those boys came here. They were shouting things. Calling me names."

"Do you know who they were? Were they village boys?"

Morris considered for a moment.

"I don't know. It was getting dark. I couldn't really see."

"Morris, you need to let the police know. These lads, whoever, they are, they can't just go around terrorising people and damaging property."

"I know. But suppose I ring the police? Then what? It won't change anything, will it? It won't stop people thinking the worst. Everybody will still think I did it, otherwise why would the police be questioning me? No smoke without fire and all that. Malcolm bloody Dryden will have a field day. I'm surprised he hasn't been down here already with a lynch mob and that half-witted mutt of his."

"Oh, who cares what Malcolm Dryden thinks. He'd have something to say, no matter what. But anyway, the police have let you go. They haven't charged you or anything. If they thought you'd done it you'd still be there. It's obvious."

Morris turned to stroke Aubrey, speaking with his back to Jeremy.

"They've let me go for now. That's what they said. For now." He turned back; his expression bitter. "They didn't quite tell me not to leave the country, but that's what they meant," he added.

Jeremy glanced down at his watch.

"Morris, I have to go in a minute. I've got school in the morning."

"Bit old for school, aren't you?"

"No, I..." Jeremy began and then smiled. Morris must be feeling a little better if he could crack a joke, no matter how feeble. "Maybe it would be a good idea if you had my mobile number. Just in case of... well, just in case."

He pulled his phone out of his pocket and jabbed at the screen. Looking up he said,

"What's your mobile number? If I call you now, you'll have my number saved."

"I haven't got one."

"What?"

"I haven't got a mobile," repeated Morris.

There was a moment's silence while Jeremy digested this information. Morris got up and pulled open a drawer in the small bureau that stood under the window. Aubrey watched as he scrabbled around among the old envelopes and receipts. Pulling out a small reporter's notebook he tore off two sheets and scribbled something on the top one.

"That's my number." He passed the sheets across. "Can you jot your mobile number down for me?"

Silently, Jeremy obeyed and passed the sheet back to him.

"Will you be all right here on your own? Is there anybody that might stay with you tonight?"

Morris shook his head.

"No, not really. Anyway, I think I'd prefer to be by myself." He thought for a moment. "There is one thing that you could do for me though."

"What's that?"

"Could you give me a hand covering the broken window? I put some cardboard across but it keeps falling off."

AUBREY LOOKED ABOUT him. Unlike the cosy atmosphere in the back room in which they had been sitting, this room felt cold and sterile with an underlying reek of stale perfume—an old-fashioned smell that prickled unpleasantly at his nostrils. The furniture looked of good quality but hard and uncompromising, not the sort that you'd want to sink down on after a hard day ratting along the canal bank. Even the tapestry cushions looked lumpy and uncomfortable. On the wooden mantlepiece stood a silver photograph frame divided into two, the silver tarnished to a dull black.

"That's mother," said Morris, nodding towards the picture. "And that was her husband. I never knew him. I was adopted," he added.

Aubrey looked up at the photographs. A broad-shouldered, grim-faced woman in a high-necked blouse looked back at him, her expression for all the world like one who had just had her stitches out. In her eyes there was an unpleasant suggestion of a challenge. Next to her was the photograph of a tall, thin, sour-faced man with a straight back and small dark eyes, dressed formally in a suit and tie. They looked, he thought, exactly like the sort of people who completely failed to understand the concept of keeping an animal as a pet. If they kept a cat it would be strictly to keep the mice down. No warm laps to sit on there. He supressed a shudder and turned away.

Morris raised his hand slightly, gesturing around him.

"This was always mother's favourite room. That was her chair by the window. She used to like seeing who went past. I used to sit with her most evenings, but I hardly come in here now. I prefer the back room, it's more private."

He propped one elbow on the mantlepiece, his expression thoughtful.

"She spent most of her time in here, particularly towards the end. Reading mostly, and listening to the wireless. She didn't really approve of television although she'd watch it with me sometimes. Documentaries and so on. She liked history programmes," he added.

"Where did you live before you came here?" asked Jeremy, suddenly curious.

"Essex. Then one day Mother decided that it would be good for us to live in the country so she bought this cottage. It's mine now. We still kept the house in Essex. It's got tenants in it."

He turned and indicated towards the window where a flattened cardboard box which had once contained a wine delivery lay across the window sill.

"I can't make it stay up."

Jeremy picked up one edge and inspected it.

"Morris, it won't stay up because you've used Sellotape. Have you got any drawing pins?"

They both jumped as a loud rat-tatting echoed down the hallway. For a moment neither of them moved and then Jeremy dropped the cardboard and strode towards the door.

"Stay there. I'll go and see who it is."

From the hall the murmur of voices drifted through and then the sitting room door opened. On the threshold stood a woman.

"Hello Morris."

She advanced further into the room and laid her stick down across the arm of the chair.

CHAPTER TWENTY

THE EARLY EVENING sun filtered gently through the window, tipping the beer pumps with a soft golden light. Dipping his head and sipping at his pint, Jeremy pocketed his change and wandered away from the bar towards one of the small tables. It was fairly empty tonight. Not even Morris was in, which was unlike him. Normally he would have been sitting in his usual place for at least an hour by now. He toyed momentarily with the idea of finishing up his pint and then calling in at his cottage, but decided against it. Probably better not to go round there. Morris was a grown man. It was up to him whether he wanted to come to the pub or not. Anyway, that woman, whoever she was, might still be there.

It was strange the way she had just turned up. From the look on his face, Morris hadn't been expecting her and after her initial greeting, neither of them had said a word but simply stared at each other. The atmosphere had become uncomfortably strained and they had obviously been waiting for him and Aubrey to go. Jeremy wondered suddenly how old Morris was. He had one of those sort of ageless faces that was difficult to assess. He wasn't young, but then he wasn't old either. He could have been anything from about forty to sixty. He didn't seem to work anywhere so perhaps he was retired. But from what? Maybe the civil service or something like that? Definitely an office worker of some kind. He couldn't imagine Morris in any sort of physical job. Maybe he hadn't worked at all. In any event, he didn't seem short of money if the amount of booze he bought was any indicator. Perhaps he was retired on a decent pension. Or maybe he had inherited money from his mother, along with the cottage and the house in Essex.

Jeremy took another long, appreciative sip of his pint. It had been a good day at school today, in spite of his apprehension. After a restless night's sleep, he had pulled into the car park this morning half-expecting the place to be abuzz with ghoulish chatter of Harold's murder, with all the pupils turning over every grisly detail and inventing a few of their own. Like the kids at Sir Frank's had been when Maria had been killed. He had prepared himself with a few anodyne responses but he needn't have worried. The head at Ferndale had very cleverly headed the whole thing off by raising the subject at the morning assembly. All the kids had listened in silence while he talked, his deep, sombre voice flowing across the big hall like a powerful but benevolent river. His words had been strangely moving and Jeremy had seen that one or two of the pupils had been on the verge of tears although he thought it unlikely that any of them had actually known Harold.

The Head had talked about the violent and tragic nature of Harold's death, how this wasn't some television show to be taken lightly and then forgotten about. It wasn't a computer game, a story in a book. This was something that had really happened, and, while Ferndale wasn't actually in the village, it was close by. They were all part of the same community and, as such, had a duty to support each other. They were, he said, neighbours in the true sense. He had finished by saying he was sure that all the pupils would join him in offering the deepest condolences to Harold's widow, which he intended to express in a gift of flowers and a card. After that, he hadn't heard it mentioned. Not a whisper. It was as if it would have been in poor taste. Which, actually, he supposed, it was.

Leaning back, he felt himself relax. Even the fact that Ferndale held daily assemblies was a novelty. They hardly ever had them at Sir Frank's. The risk of gathering all the kids together in one place with the potential for a riot that it carried was too great. But Ferndale was different. Unlike Sir Frank's, where nearly every day presented a new challenge, and not in a good way, the days at Ferndale were taking on a pleasing predictability. The pupils were open, friendly and polite. The majority managed to get out of bed in time for the first lesson. Most of them did their homework and even if they didn't, they usually had an excuse ready which bore at least a passing resemblance to plausibility. He even found himself enjoying the marking. At least at Ferndale the pupils made an effort to frame an answer to the question that was put to them. Although, he had to admit, some of the responses from the kids at Sir Frank's were nothing short of admirable in their brevity. The most memorable to date being the answer to the question, 'Why do you think that King Lear gave away his property to his daughters?' which had elicited the response from three pupils who had copied each other, 'becos he wos a twat.' Which, to be fair, did indicate at least a rudimentary understanding of one of the key issues of the play, and vindicated his decision to introduce them to some of Shakespeare's works, albeit in a limited fashion.

He took another sip of beer and let out a small sigh of contentment. All in all, and the dreadful murder of Harold aside, things were turning out very nicely. Better than he could have hoped, really. Carlos seemed to be settling in well, Aubrey hadn't run away, and Molly was enjoying her break from working at Donoghue's. A pity he'd have to go back to Sir Frank's at the end of the year but that was months away. He'd worry about that when the time came. Anything could happen between now and then. Maybe even a vacancy at Ferndale would arise. He sat back and closed his eyes for a second, relishing the peace and quiet.

As if on cue, the door flew open and one great hefty leg appeared followed by the rest of Malcolm Dryden. Behind him pattered Humphrey, his usual gormless expression pasted across his face.

"Evening, Jo." The voice boomed across the previously tranquil room. "No Morris tonight, I see. I suppose you've barred him at last. Not before time, in my opinion."

Jo turned and pulled a pint, placing it quietly in front of Malcolm who dipped his head and sipped across the top, leaving a moustache of foam across his top lip. Humphrey sat at his feet, staring around the room with an expression of amiable surprise, as though he'd never seen it before. Malcolm continued, seemingly oblivious to Jo's silence.

"Can't say I'm surprised. So, what happened down at the police station?"

Jo shook his head. "I'm afraid you'll have to ask Morris that."

Malcolm threw back his head and laughed, a great throaty roar that unsettled the very air around him and revealed the dark tufts of hair sprouting from the neck of his shirt.

"Come on, Jo. Everyone knows that you went down there with him."

Jo shook his head again. "Sorry, Malcolm."

Disappointed, Malcolm turned to survey the room. Spotting Jeremy, Malcolm strolled purposefully towards him.

"Sorry, Malcolm. Got to go." Tipping his head back, Jeremy gulped down the rest of his pint and made for the door.

CHAPTER TWENTY-ONE

"YOU TWO ARE back early. It's not even in the oven yet."

Molly turned to face them, the cheese she had been grating still in her hand. Aubrey eyed it with interest and sidled up a bit closer. Might be a chance she'd drop a bit. Ok, true, he wasn't exactly hungry, but there was always room for a bit more. Also, life on the streets had taught him that only a fool turned down a food opportunity. There might not be another one.

Jeremy sank down on one of the kitchen chairs.

"Malcolm Dryden," he said shortly.

"What about Malcolm Dryden?" asked Molly.

"Nothing. Just Malcolm Dryden." He watched for a moment as she started grating the cheese again. "Molly," he spoke slowly. "That woman. The one I told you about last night. The one who turned up at Morris's place…"

"What about her?"

"I've been thinking about it again today. It was odd. I mean, his reaction was odd. It was like he was sort of shocked, but also like he wasn't really surprised." He paused. "It's difficult to explain."

Aubrey agreed. Morris's reaction had been odd. He had clearly known the woman and obviously she had known him or she wouldn't have been there. But also, clearly, he hadn't been expecting her. What, he wondered, was her connection with Morris? To him and Trevor she was a familiar figure, but they'd never actually seen her talk to anyone. She just sort of walked around with that stick. She didn't live in the village though; he was fairly sure of that. The bus stop was visible from the shed roof and several times he had seen her get off the bus from the nearby town and then get back on the bus later in the day.

He watched as Jeremy pulled back the ring from a can of beer which Molly had placed in front of him. He lifted the can to his mouth and then set it down again without drinking.

"You know, I had a feeling," said Jeremy, "that they were sort of waiting for me to leave. Everything suddenly got really tense. It was like I was in the way or something."

"In the way of what?"

Jeremy shrugged.

"I don't know."

"What does she look like?"

"Well, I'm not sure really." He shrugged. "Ordinary."

Molly smiled.

"Ok, Sherlock. Hair colour? Age?"

Jeremy thought for a moment.

"Sort of brownish, I suppose. Aged about, oh, I don't know, difficult to tell. Oh, and she walks with a stick. At least," he hesitated and then continued, "she had a stick with her. I'm not sure that she was actually using it."

"Jeremy," Molly stopped what she was doing and stared at him. "It's her. I'm sure of it. That woman. The one I told you about."

"What woman?"

"You remember, the one that was looking over our fence when we first moved in."

"Have you seen her since?"

"A couple of times. Three, maybe."

"Does she still look over the fence?"

Molly nodded.

"Does she ever do anything else?"

"Like what?"

"I don't know. Open the gate or anything."

Molly thought for a moment and shook her head.

"No, never. Not when I've been looking, anyway. She just sort of peers over, hesitates for a bit as though she's going to come in, and then she goes away again. Sometimes she puts her hand on the catch as though she's going to open it, but then she doesn't."

Jeremy tipped his head back and drained the can.

"How odd. Why do you think she does it?"

"No idea. The last time she did it I went out to ask her what she wanted, but by the time I got there she'd gone."

"Perhaps she's looking for Quentin."

"Then why doesn't she just knock on the door?"

"It's probably a perfectly simple explanation, like she used to live here when she was a child or something." He hesitated for a moment and then said, "Although it does seem a bit odd that she knows Morris because he definitely wasn't here when he was a child. He told me last night that he grew up in Essex. Maybe they worked together or something."

"Was Morris in the pub tonight?"

Jeremy shook his head.

"No. It's the first time I've ever known him not to be there." He hesitated for a moment and then shook the can. He often did that, thought Aubrey, as though he was hoping that there was some left. There never was. "Do you think I should go round and see if he is all right?"

"No. Leave him. He probably just wants to be on his own for a bit. I wouldn't be surprised after what's happened."

"I expect you're right. He's got my mobile number if he wants to talk." He stood up and stretched. "Where's Carlos?"

"He's in the garden." She jerked her head over her shoulder. "With his new friend, Teddy. Apparently, she's got an app on her phone which identifies plants and flowers, and she's going to show them to him."

Jeremy stared at her.

"He's never been interested in plants and flowers before."

"He's never had a pretty girl offering to teach him before."

CHAPTER TWENTY-TWO

"AND THESE, CARLOS, are chrysanthemums." Teddy held up her phone as she spoke and the two of them leaned over and stared at the small screen.

"My mum liked flowers," said Carlos. "Big flowers," he added. "You know, like those big, really brightly coloured ones. We used to get them a lot in Brazil."

Aubrey stopped and lowered his paw. He had been just about to sharpen his claws on the fence post. He had hardly ever heard Carlos willingly mention his mother or their life together in Brazil before, not even to Molly and Jeremy. As far as he knew, the only person to whom Carlos spoke freely about Maria was him.

"My mum likes flowers too," said Teddy. "But she never does any gardening or anything. My dad doesn't, either," she added. "They always say that they haven't got time, so we have a gardener."

"We didn't have a gardener," said Carlos. "Well, we didn't have a garden. That was one of the things that mum always wanted." He looked down at the ground. "I used to think, when I grow up, if I get a job and that, I'll buy her a garden. I'll buy her a house with a garden, with a shed and everything."

Both Teddy and Aubrey moved slightly closer to him. He continued.

"We used to go to the park on Sunday mornings and look at all the flowers, especially in the summer, and she used to know the names of lots of them." He smiled suddenly. "Sometimes, after she'd checked that nobody was looking, she used to pick a flower and when we got home, she used to press it between pieces of tissue paper. I found them, after, in her chest of drawers. I've still got them." He turned away and stared ahead of him, his narrow shoulders slightly hunched. "Where we used to live, at the Meadows, there was a bit of space round the back, like a bit of land that never got built on, and she used to plant little bulbs there sometimes, but they always got dug up by dogs and that. She planted some vegetables too but they got nicked as soon as they came through."

"How come you lived in a house without a garden?"

He hesitated. "We lived in an apart... flat," he amended. "A council flat." Might as well tell her the truth. "I found out later, after she..." he hesitated and swallowed, running his tongue around his mouth, finding the words and pushing them forward. "After she... you know, died and that, we weren't even supposed to be there."

"Why not?" Teddy looked puzzled.

"We were renting it from a bloke who was, like, nothing to do with the council. It's called sub-letting. I looked it up. You're not supposed to do it without permission."

"Well, it's a beautiful garden here. I bet your mum would have loved it." Teddy smiled and waved her arms around, her little silver bracelets tinkling as they slid across her wrists. She wandered across to where some late roses bloomed and stooped to smell them. Carlos followed her, conscious of a slow tide of happiness seeping through him.

He leaned over the roses and then jumped back in alarm as an outburst of frenzied barking ripped through the air and shattered the peace of the early evening.

"Humphrey! Humphrey, heel sir!"

On the other side of the fence, Malcolm Dryden yanked on Humphrey's collar, pulling him up hard against his thigh. His face was scarlet with rage.

"Heel, sir, I said."

The barking continued, spiralling up to a new crescendo. Flinging open the back door, Jeremy strode across the garden towards the noise. "Carlos? Teddy? What's going on out here? I can't hear myself think."

He pulled open the gate, followed by Carlos, Teddy and Aubrey. Outside, Humphrey turned and twisted, spiralling up and down as though chasing his own tail, and pulling away from Malcolm's grip. His barking grew louder.

"What the…" began Jeremy and stopped.

"Oh no!" Teddy's cry rang out across the evening air as she sprang back and looked wildly around for Aubrey. "It's not your one, is it? It's not Aubrey?"

Aubrey stared down at the bundle of fur that lay huddled just the other side of the gate. Trevor. With his eyes closed and the blood oozing from the gash in his neck.

CHAPTER TWENTY-THREE

ON THE WORK surface, wrapped in the big fluffy bath towel that Carlos had raced to fetch, Trevor lay perfectly still, the sound of his breath coming in loud rasping gasps. Jeremy entered the room, his face grey.

"The vet is on her way." He leaned over and stared down at Trevor. "At least he's still breathing. Come on, good lad, hold on. Soon have you sorted."

He stroked one finger gently across Trevor's head. At Jeremy's feet sat Aubrey, staring mutely upwards. Next to him stood Maudie, her arms wrapped around her chest and her face anxious.

"Who do you think he belongs to?" asked Molly.

"I'm guessing that it must be someone in the village. I've seen him in the garden with Aubrey before now."

Molly nodded.

"With a bit of luck, he'll be micro-chipped."

"Mr Goodman, we could go and ask in the pub," said Teddy. "Somebody in there might know."

"Good idea. But Teddy," Jeremy turned to face her. "Why aren't you up at the Academy? I thought that none of you were allowed out."

"Oh, Lucinda said that it was ok if I was coming here. As long as I had my phone with me. Which I have," she added, patting her pocket. "She knows that you're a teacher and everything."

Jeremy looked at her doubtfully. Now wasn't the time to argue, but he'd check it out later.

"So, Lucinda's back then?"

Teddy nodded.

"She came back this morning. She's still not feeling very well so she's not doing any lessons or anything. Not that it matters really. There's only me and Casper left."

"And where's Casper?"

"Oh, he's searching Harold's office in case the police missed anything."

"He's doing what?"

"Bye, see you later."

Aubrey watched as Carlos and Teddy pulled the back door open and ran over to the pub. Suddenly conscious of an absence of sound, he turned and leapt on to the work surface next to Trevor. Jeremy moved to scoop him off again and then paused as Molly laid a hand on his arm.

"Leave him. He's upset. It won't hurt this once."

Too right he was upset. Thank God for Humphrey. He may just have saved Trevor's life. They would never have known that Trevor was there if Humphrey hadn't made such a fuss. Malcolm Dryden wouldn't have bothered, that was for sure, even if he'd noticed. He was usually talking on his phone in that great booming voice of his. Trevor said that Malcolm Dryden didn't need a phone and he wasn't far wrong. He stared down at his friend, watching the laboured rise and fall of his chest and willing him to survive. He would never laugh at Humphrey again, and none of the other cats would either, not when he told them what Humphrey had done. He leaned closer, listening for any sound. Trevor was still breathing, he could just about hear it, a faint but rough rattling as though every breath was elbowing its way through a tunnel of broken glass in an effort to escape.

"Do you think it's the cat killer?" asked Maudie, stretching full length on her stomach along the work surface so that her head was level with Trevor's.

Aubrey nodded.

"Has to be. Look at his injuries."

It was the cat killer, there was no doubt. All the hallmarks were there. But not, for some reason, at the usual bus stop location. But surely, the killer wouldn't have attacked Trevor right outside the house? It would be far too risky. He thought for a moment. The killer hadn't finished Trevor off. Perhaps he, or she, had been disturbed by a passer-by or something and Trevor had managed to crawl to Molly and Jeremy's gate. It was nearer than his own house.

"The door was open so I let myself in. I hope that's ok."

Aubrey and Maudie turned and looked at the large, pleasantly competent looking woman. A more different specimen to their vet at home, Jonathon Grimshaw, was hard to imagine. Apart from the fact that she didn't smell of stale whisky, she didn't have a face full of broken veins and a shaking hand.

"Is this the patient?"

She strode across the kitchen and looked down at the injured cat.

"I know this one. Trevor. He's one of my patients. His owners live up near the memorial garden."

She reached into her bag and pulled out a syringe.

"Come on old boy, let's get you stable and then we'll get you stitched up."

"DO YOU FEEL a bit cold?"

Teddy rubbed her arms and shivered slightly. From the branch of the tree on which she was perched, Maudie watched them while she slowly twirled a lock of hair through her fingers. Aubrey stretched out on the branch next to her, tail hanging down like a bell pull.

Carlos nodded. The little garden bench on which they were sitting was just wide enough to accommodate them both. He sat rigidly, careful not to touch her. He didn't want her thinking he was some sort of perv or something, that he was one of those boys, like at Sir Franks, who were always touching girls and then pretending it was an accident. Some of them didn't even bother pretending it was an accident.

Teddy continued.

"I'd better get back soon, I told Lucinda that I wouldn't be late."

"Will you tell her what happened to Trevor?"

Teddy shook her head.

"No. I'll tell Casper but not Lucinda or Zofia. It wouldn't be right. You know, not with Harold and everything."

"Yeah, I suppose so." He looked across to the kitchen window where he could see Molly and Jeremy talking, and then looked down at his feet. "I feel a bit sort of guilty."

"Why?"

He turned his head sideways and looked up at her.

"To be honest, my first reaction, when I saw Trevor and that, I was glad it wasn't Aubrey. I felt just, like, relief."

Aubrey lifted his head. He was glad it hadn't been him as well but he sure as hell wouldn't have wanted it to be Trevor, either. Or any of the other cats. Would it, he wondered, be possible to somehow see him later? He was fairly sure that Trevor's house had a cat flap, so maybe he could slip round there after dark and see how he was doing. If he was doing at all, that is. He pushed the thought away. If Trevor was strong enough to crawl away from where he had been attacked, then he was strong enough to survive this. But he had to admit, he hadn't looked too clever when the vet had carried him away in a cat basket.

"I don't think that you should feel guilty. I mean, it's not like you wanted it to be Trevor." Teddy paused and then continued, lowering her voice slightly. "Casper found something out today. He texted me when the vet was here. I was going to tell you earlier but I didn't want to say in front of Mr and Mrs Goodman."

"What did he find out?" said Carlos.

"Harold's got another name."

"Another name? He's called Harold, isn't he?" Carlos sounded confused.

"Casper says that he doesn't think that Harold is, was I mean, his real name."

"What is it then?"

"Aaron."

"Aaron?"

Teddy nodded.

"When Casper was in Harold's office, he found some letters and documents and things in the bottom of one of the desk drawers. Well, in a sort of drawer."

"What do you mean, a sort of drawer?"

"Casper's got a friend called Tarquin. His dad is an antique dealer. He showed Casper and Tarquin about secret drawers and stuff."

"And Harold's got a desk with a secret drawer in it?"

"Yes. Casper opened it and he found all these papers. And they had a different name on."

"But that doesn't mean anything. They could be anybody's. Harold might have just kept them there."

"Why, if they're not his? I mean, why would you have someone else's papers? And why would you keep them in a secret drawer?"

Carlos thought for a moment.

"I don't know. Looking after them, maybe? Keeping them safe?"

"One of the documents was a passport. With a picture in it."

CHAPTER TWENTY-FOUR

AUBREY NUDGED THE cat flap open very gently with his head and slipped through. In the glass pane of the back door, Maudie's small pale face appeared, glimmering faintly in the moonlight, and then she too slipped into the kitchen. Around them, the house was quiet and dark, the only sounds the faint creaking and knocking noises that every house makes as it settles down for the night. The aromatic smell of that evening's dinner hung lightly on the air, momentarily distracting Aubrey as he crept across the floor. He stopped and hesitated for a moment while he adjusted his eyes to the light and thought about what to do next. He hadn't really made a plan, other than to find out if Trevor was back at home. If he wasn't in the kitchen, would he then have the nerve to go upstairs and look for him? If Trevor was really in a bad way, his owners might have him in their bedroom with them. He thought for a moment. He could see that the kitchen door was open slightly but it was a gamble. Trevor's owners were very fond of cats, he knew that from the way Trevor talked about them, but that didn't mean that they'd welcome any old cat strolling around their house in the middle of the night.

"You stay here, I'll go."

He nodded gratefully. Maudie didn't have to worry about closed doors. More to the point, she didn't have to worry about being seen. He watched as she drifted through the wall. It was a great trick, if only he knew how to do it. Creeping under the shadow of the table just in case anyone came in, he wondered if any of the other cats had heard the news about Trevor yet. They probably had. Carlos and Teddy had gone over to the pub to see if they could find out who Trevor's owner was. If Brewster had been there he would have heard and told the others. He leaned his forehead against the table leg and tried to quell his anxiety. If Trevor wasn't here then it didn't necessarily mean that the worst had happened. Maybe he was still at the vets. Maybe they were keeping him there, while he recovered. It didn't mean that he was dead.

He glanced towards the empty food bowl in the corner and looked away again. Clenching his jaw, he tried to supress the tidal wave of panic that suddenly threatened to overwhelm him. The fact that Trevor wasn't here did not mean that Trevor was dead. In fact, he thought, suddenly cheered, the fact that the food bowl was still here was evidence, surely, that Trevor was still alive. Grieving owners would have got rid of it, he was certain. He'd once seen one of their old neighbours throwing away a dog lead and bowl after his dog had died, and then start crying and kicking the dustbin.

"He's not here."

Maudie's voice was flat, her tone expressionless.

"Are you sure?"

She nodded.

"I checked every room. Even the bathroom. He's definitely not here." She leaned back; one small satin-slippered foot propped up behind her against the wall. "What shall we do now?"

"THIS IS WHERE his cat Lulu's buried," said Aubrey, indicating a small bare patch on which stood a jam jar containing wilted flowers. "Trevor told me."

"I know, I came to the funeral."

Aubrey nodded and followed her as she drifted up the garden towards the back door. Overgrown and chaotic in the daytime, Morris's garden held a romantic silvery drama when lit by moonlight. He paused and looked around him with approval. This garden had been one of the first of the village gardens that he had explored and he liked it. Unlike some of the gardens in the village which had every blade of grass standing to attention and each flower staked to within an inch of its life, here there were lots of places for a cat to play or hide. He looked up as the back door opened and two figures came out, each holding a glass and a fat candle in a saucer. One of them had a bottle tucked under an arm. The other held a stick in the crook of her elbow.

"There's definitely a table and chairs out here somewhere."

It was Morris's voice. Aubrey and Maudie watched as he bumbled about and pushed away some of the undergrowth, finally locating a small scarred wooden table and some battered chairs.

"Josie, here," he called. "Over here."

The two figures sat down and faced each other, each placing their candle on the table top. After a moment's hesitation, Aubrey crept up and settled himself on one of the remaining two chairs. Maudie sank onto the chair next to him and leaned back, letting her arms flop behind her. He wasn't quite sure what they were doing here but at least they were doing something. It was too far to get to the vet's and the only alternative was just to go back home and spend the rest of the night worrying about Trevor. Morris glanced down and ran a hand across the top of Aubrey's head. That was what he liked about Morris, he thought. He never made a fuss.

"I'm sorry that I gave you such a start last night."

The woman's voice was soft, a gentle note in the night air. In the light of the candles, Aubrey could see the faint tremble of Morris's hand as he placed the bottle on the table and raised his glass to his mouth.

"I always hoped that you would come some day. I'm sorry," he paused and took another mouthful of his drink. "I'm sorry that I didn't really talk much last night. It was the shock. But I knew that you would come again tonight."

"That's ok. I had to get the last bus anyway or I would have missed my train."

"How will you get back tonight? The last bus has already gone and I haven't got a car."

Josie shrugged.

"I don't know. Taxi, I suppose."

"I could make up a bed in the spare room." A small frown crinkled his forehead. "I'm sure there's some clean sheets in the airing cupboard."

Josie smiled and for several minutes neither of them spoke, but the silence wasn't an uncomfortable one thought Aubrey. Not like the kind of silence when two people argue and neither one wants to be the first to say sorry, like that pair of screws at Sunny Banks rescue centre who were forever huffing and puffing about the place and generally adding to the already despairing atmosphere. One of them had once clunked the other over the back of the head with a metal feeding bowl, much to the delight of the resident cats.

He settled his chin down on his paws and listened to the sounds of the night. There was something very restful about the noise of small creatures rustling through the long grass. The faint jingle of next door's wind chimes drifted across the fence, carried along by the cool breeze, and added to his feeling of tranquillity. For the first time since they'd discovered Trevor laying injured by the gate, he was starting to feel a bit more relaxed. Next to him Maudie stretched out her legs and began plaiting her hair. Morris spoke first, his tone hesitant.

"Did they treat you well?"

Josie laughed suddenly, a surprisingly joyful chortle that broke through the night air and rippled the length of the garden.

"No, Morris. They did not treat me well. But then, they didn't treat me badly either. You don't live in a prison. You exist. Each day. One after another. It's how it is. Do you know the definition of a good day in prison?"

Morris shook his head.

"A good day in prison is simply one where nothing bad happens."

The silence fell again, a soft blanket that lay gently between them.

"How long have you been out? They sent my last letter back to me but they wouldn't tell me when you were released or where you were."

Morris's voice was low, as though shielding them from listening ears, although there was nobody there to overhear them other than Aubrey and Maudie.

"I've been out since February. February the third, to be exact."

"Where have you been living?"

"In a bed-sit. Just outside Watford. The authorities found it for me."

"What's it like?"

"It's ok. I've got everything I need. The best thing about it is the front door, which locks. From the inside." She paused and then said, "I've seen you before. In the village, I mean," she added.

Morris stared at her.

"What? When?"

"I've been here a few times. When I found out that Aaron was living here." Josie smiled slightly. "There seemed a brilliant sort of irony that of all the places that he could have been, he turned up where you are. And running a school of all things. Somebody less suited to educate the young is hard to imagine."

Morris smiled slightly. "From what I've heard, there's not a lot of educating going on. The kids seem to spend most of their time running around being fairies or something."

"Knowing Aaron, I bet the parents pay handsomely for the privilege. He ran the school with his wife, didn't he? What's she like?"

"I don't know really, I've never spoken to her. She comes into the village sometimes, and I've seen her over in the spinney, running about with the pupils. Lots of floaty scarves and hand-waving. Drippy, I suppose. She'd have to be, wouldn't she? Who else would marry a bloke like Aaron?"

"Me, once." She paused, crinkling her brow slightly. "I was absolutely besotted with him. Hard to believe now. He used to tie ribbons in my hair. I thought it was the most romantic thing that anybody had ever done. Not that I'd had much experience. I'd been out of the home for less than a year when I went to work for him and the only boys that were interested in me before then were the sort that expected someone partly disabled like me to be grateful. When Aaron started to notice me it was like something out of a romantic novel. Master in unhappy marriage. Falls in love with servant. Classic rags to riches story. He used to tell me how he and his wife argued. Always about money. He said he wanted to expand the business but she accused him of being extravagant, wasting money. It was only much later that I saw the reality." Aubrey watched as her jaw set and her eyes hardened. She suddenly looked years older. "God, he saw me coming, didn't he?"

CHAPTER TWENTY-FIVE

"DON'T BE HARD on yourself, Josie. For kids like us, well…" Morris tilted his head slightly and then said, "Why didn't you write and tell me where you were when you came out?"

Josie looked out across the garden.

"I guess it's because I wanted to confront Aaron before I did anything else." She looked thoughtful and took a sip from her glass. "It's like I had to clear the way first, before moving on to the next thing. Prison makes you like that. Everything in order. One foot before the other. In a way, I was fortunate. I coped with being locked up better than most of them in there. Some of them totally freaked out but, for me, I suppose it was a bit like when we were children. The routine, the rules, being told what to do and when to do it. It didn't seem that unusual. In an odd way, it was almost a relief. After everything that had happened, it was like being brought back to normal. As if being inside was reality and the time outside had been some kind of, I don't know, dream time or something."

She pulled her cardigan more tightly around her, as if for comfort, and played for a moment with a small gold bracelet on her wrist. "It's strange, I had it all worked out in my head. Every single word. I thought it would be so easy. Once I found him, I'd just march up to him and let him have it. I must have rehearsed it a thousand times. And let's face it, time was the one thing I had plenty of when I was inside. The strange thing was, I never thought about what he might say in reply. I guess I'll never know now."

"He might not have said anything," said Morris. "He might just have refused to see you."

"I know, I realise that now. But at the time, that never really occurred to me either. I didn't think past that initial meeting." She raised her glass and then set it down again without drinking, her face sombre. "The first time I went up to the school, I was really fired up. I'd been running it in my head all the way on the train so that when I finally got there, I thought that it would all just come bursting out. But when I arrived, I don't know, I just couldn't go through with it. I lost my nerve. I never even got further than the outside gate."

"What did you do then?"

Josie shrugged.

"Nothing. I just walked back down to the village and got the bus back to the station."

"But you came back?"

"Well, I didn't have a plan B." She fell silent for a moment. "In a strange way, when I was inside, thinking about it, planning it helped me to fill the days. It gave an odd sort of structure. It was comforting. Something to hold on to." The hard, bitter, look shadowed across her face again. "But it looks like I wasn't the only one out to settle scores with Aaron."

"You know that they had me in for questioning?" Morris's voice was soft, his expression pained. "I had to go down to the police station. They found what they think is the murder weapon in my garden."

Josie nodded.

"I heard about it in the newsagents. That rat-faced bloke was talking about it. That's really what made my mind up to come over last night. What did you say to them?"

Morris shrugged.

"The truth. That I had no idea it was there and that I had no idea how it got there. What else could I say?"

"How do you think that it did get there?"

"Chucked over the hedge I suppose. It wouldn't be difficult. I'm right next to the paddock. And," he turned slightly and waved his arm around. "It's not like it would be noticeable."

"I don't suppose the police told you anything else?"

Morris shook his head.

"No. Not really. They asked me a bit about Harold, as he was known here, but I said that I didn't know the bloke, which was true. I'd seen him in the village a couple of times but I never spoke to him."

Josie looked at him curiously.

"Did you tell them that you knew he wasn't really Harold?"

Morris shook his head.

"No. I thought that they'd find out anyway. I mean, it's unlikely this was just a random killing. The police are bound to start digging around in his past. But I didn't want to be the one responsible for all that being dragged up again. And," he smiled suddenly. "Early training tells."

Josie smiled back.

"Say nowt, you'll not regret it."

"Michael. He was really good fun. I wonder sometimes what happened to him."

Josie shrugged.

"He left the home before I did. He went back up north. The last I heard he was doing time for burglary or something. It was good advice though, especially when it came to Mrs Thorpe. It used to drive her mad when we all clammed up. Do you remember that day when Michael shouted and called her a bloody old bitch behind her back and we all pretended that we hadn't heard anything? What was it she called us?"

"The children of the damned. I found out later it was the title of a film. I saw it one Sunday afternoon when mother was laying down with one of her headaches. I think maybe Mrs Thorpe had a point. But she was still a bloody old bitch," he added.

Josie continued.

"When did you recognise Aaron?" she asked.

"One day, not that long ago, when I was in Bradley's. He was in the queue in front of me. I kept thinking that he looked familiar somehow, something about the set of his shoulders and the way he spoke. I just knew that I'd seen him before but I couldn't think where. I couldn't get it out of my head. And then, when I got home something made me start looking through the press cuttings. I kept them all, you know."

"Do you think that anybody else recognised him?"

"I shouldn't think so. It was a long time ago. I don't suppose that anybody else would have been particularly interested in the case. Some of the younger couples round here would only have been children at the time."

Josie nodded.

"Probably." She looked down at the table, tracing the grain of the scarred wood with her forefinger. "I was there you know, at the fete. I wasn't looking for him. Well, I was, but I'd lost my nerve again. I was in the village and heading towards the bus stop when I saw the posters for the fete, so I just went along for something to do. Days spent in a bed-sit on your own can be very long. There's a limit to how many quiz shows you can watch and shopping centres just get depressing when you're short of money."

"Were you there, when it... you know, when it happened? Did you see him?"

Josie shook her head.

"No. I must have left about ten minutes before. The first I knew that something had happened was when I was waiting for the bus to the station and I heard the sirens going."

"How did you find out it was Aaron?"

"It was on the news. That's why I came over again. I had to find out what was going on. Probably a stupid thing to do," she added. "When they find out who he really is, which they will, they'll put me on the list without a doubt. Especially if they discover that I've been here in the village."

"How would they know that it's you? Nobody here knows who you are."

"The children might tell them."

"What children?"

"I met some children by the school gates. They just started talking to me and I told them my real name. I suppose I was sort of hoping that they might mention it and it would upset him. The problem is," she added, "I'm only out on licence."

"What do you mean?"

"Once a lifer, always a lifer. It's like an invisible thread. The slightest thing and they can pull you back inside."

Morris shuddered and leaned towards her, the light from the candles casting long, flickering shadows across the table.

"Josie, please be careful. The last thing you want is to get caught up in all of this. Don't come to the village again, at least not until the murderer is caught. Aaron is gone. None of this is anything to do with you. There's nothing that you can say to him now. It's bad enough that he ruined the first half of your life. Don't let him ruin the second half."

"I know. But there's still that creepy nephew of his."

Morris nodded.

"It was ages before I recognised him, I must have seen him a dozen times before the penny dropped."

"I was going to have it out with him, too, find out why he lied." Josie's eyes narrowed. "There was no need for it. It just made the jury hate me even more. Even if I'd wanted to change my story, by that point it was too late. But every time I approached his house, I never got further than the front gate. Then I found out that he's gone, too."

"How did you know that he lived here?"

"Electoral register. Once I found Aaron, I started tracking down other people that were involved in the trial. It's strange, once you start, it's all much easier than you might think."

CHAPTER TWENTY-SIX

AUBREY AND MORRIS stood on the path and watched the lights of the taxi as it pulled away, the tiny pinpoints of red disappearing into the night. A lingering scent of Josie's perfume hung on the evening air. Morris stared straight ahead of him, his shoulders stiff and set, before walking slowly back into the house. Aubrey turned to speak to Maudie. Too late, she'd gone. She did that sometimes. She'd be back. He followed Morris into the house.

Inside, the cottage was lit by a small low-wattage lamp, the bulb showing dimly through the old-fashioned fringed shade. Following a primeval instinct, Aubrey headed for the fireside rug and lay down, even though the grate was empty. He watched as Morris picked up the glass that he'd left on the side table when Josie had arrived, standing for a moment with it clutched to his chest, gripping it with both hands, before dipping his head and taking a huge swallow. He ran his tongue across his lips as though to catch any last remaining drops.

"After I left, after mother took me home with her, I did want to write to Josie you know, but mother said that it wasn't allowed." Morris's voice sounded flat and defeated, as though surrendering an argument that he'd never wanted in the first place, although there was nobody but him and Aubrey in the room. "She said that the children weren't allowed to receive letters and that it would get Josie into trouble. I asked if I could go back and visit her but she said that wasn't allowed either. It wasn't that I didn't want to, Aubrey."

Aubrey lifted his head. That was interesting. He didn't know that Morris knew his name. He was beginning to think that there was a lot more to Morris than the village gave him credit for. Perhaps it suited him to play the slightly scruffy amiable drunk, the village idiot who barely seemed to know what day of the week it was. At least it meant that people generally left him alone. For which there was a lot to be said, he knew from experience. When he'd been forced to live on the streets there had been rather too many people over-interested in what he was doing, which was how he'd found himself banged up in Sunny Banks Rescue centre.

"I wanted to explain. I wanted to tell her. I didn't want her to think that I'd just forgotten her. She was my best friend," he added.

Morris moved across the room and sat down on the edge of the scarred leather armchair. Leaning over, he carefully untied his shoelaces and slipped off his shoes before reaching for a pair of plaid slippers that stood by the side of the chair. For a moment he stared at his feet.

"I hate these slippers. Mother bought them. Every year she bought a new pair. All exactly the same." He sighed. "God knows why."

Aubrey looked at the slippers. Morris was right. They were rather unpleasant. Jeremy had nice soft leather slippers, a sort of soft butter colour with fake fur on the inside, that were good for sleeping on or pushing your paws into when it was cold. Morris's slippers looked the colour and texture of a half-eaten piece of toast. His ears pricked suddenly and he sat up straight. From outside the sound of voices was growing steadily louder as it drew closer to the cottage. Gripping the arms of the chair, Morris half-rose. For a moment they stared at one another and then Morris sank down again as the voices passed and drifted back up the lane. He exhaled slowly, the relief on his face evident.

He settled back down again as Morris continued.

"That day when mother came, it was a Tuesday. I couldn't tell you the date, but I know it was a Tuesday. We were supposed to be doing games but it was cancelled." He spoke quietly, the words measured as he searched for the memory. "We were disappointed. We all liked games. It was the only time we got to run around and be noisy. Properly noisy. We were just going off to get changed when we were all told to go back to the dormitories. Mrs Thorpe came in and started herding us off to the bathrooms and scrubbing at our faces and dragging that horrible big comb that she kept in her pocket through our hair. She used that damned thing like a weapon. We knew why we were being tidied up, of course." He smiled. "We all knew why. We saw the cars rolling up the drive."

Suddenly, a vivid memory of Sunny Banks rescue centre flashed across Aubrey's mind. He'd forgotten about it until now. Like most of the memories of Sunny Banks, he preferred to blank them out. But when visitors had come to the rescue centre, they had all been brushed and air freshener frantically sprayed around, even though there was no need for it. Some of the screws smelled worse than they did. But the horrible scent, rich with the smell of chemically induced flowers had always made him sneeze and feel slightly sick. It sounded like Morris had been somewhere like that, too.

"I wanted to be picked. We all did. Even Michael, although he always said that he didn't. We were sent to the games room and Mrs Thorpe got all the board games out of the cupboard and we were told to start playing games. Nicely. That's what Mrs Thorpe said. Play nicely. When mother and the other visitors came in, we all sort of tried to pretend that we hadn't noticed.

They all stood there talking to Mrs Thorpe and we were trying to hear what they were saying. I remember Josie started giggling and that set Michael off and our table got one of Mrs Thorpe's looks. Then mother came over and started talking to me. When she left, she gave me a bag of sweets that she had in her handbag. I remember Mrs Thorpe smiling and nodding which was weird because we'd always been told not to take sweets from strangers. Not that anybody ever offered us any, stranger or otherwise." he added.

Aubrey rose and jumped up on to Morris's lap. For a moment Morris stared down at him and then lifted a hand and began to stroke the thick rich fur on Aubrey's back. He let out a small rumble of a purr in appreciation. He didn't always purr when he was stroked, it didn't do to be too predictable, but tonight was different. Tonight, Morris needed it.

"When Mrs Thorpe told me, honestly Aubrey, I couldn't believe it," he continued. "She called me into her office and said that a number of us had been under discussion for some time, and that mother had chosen me. She said the paperwork was complete and that I would be going with mother to my new home the next day. She said that it was for a trial period and I had to be on my best behaviour. I couldn't wait. I didn't know what a trial period was but I didn't care. I didn't realise then that I wouldn't see Josie or Michael or any of them again. I didn't know that it would be forever."

Morris fell silent and stared across the room, his expression morose. Aubrey looked at him more closely. He could see, in this light, that Morris had once been, if not exactly handsome, certainly attractive. The lamp light hid the harsh alcohol-induced redness of his cheeks and the thinning of his fair hair. It showed only the softness of his eyes and the gentleness of his mouth. Any cat would be lucky to have a home with him. Poor, sick

Lulu must have thought that she was in heaven that day Morris picked her up and brought her back here.

"When Josie's picture was in the newspaper," he continued, "it was mother who saw it first. It was an ordinary day, nothing special. It was raining and I remember thinking that she wouldn't be able to get out into the garden. Gardens and gardening were something that mother really loved. She tried to get me interested but, I don't know, I just wasn't." He gave a wry smile. "It's a good job she can't see the garden now. Anyway, we'd just sat down for breakfast and when she opened the paper, there it was." Aubrey felt Morris suddenly tense beneath him, his breath quicken. "I knew something was up straight away. Her shoulders went sort of rigid as though she was trying to hold herself in and she looked pleased. Like she did that time she caught Bradley short-changing her in the newsagents. She couldn't wait to show me. Couldn't wait to point out what a lucky escape I'd had, how different my life would have been if it hadn't been for her. And the hardest thing, of course, is that she was probably right. If I'd stayed where I was, I expect I would have ended up like Michael. Young Offenders and prisons were finishing schools for the likes of us."

The tone of Morris's voice was bitter and hard, the lines around his mouth suddenly much more pronounced.

"Don't get me wrong, Aubrey, I didn't really blame mother and I did grow to love her. In a way." He shifted slightly in the chair and Aubrey shifted with him. "And I was grateful to her. I didn't really know anything about my own parents, other than that they didn't want me. But mother did want me. She specifically chose me. Out of all the kids in there, she picked me. It was like winning the best prize ever. I can't tell you how good that felt."

Tell me about it, thought Aubrey. When Molly and Jeremy had turned up at Sunny Banks and chosen him, he had scarcely been able to believe it. In fact, for weeks he had been scared to put a paw wrong, convinced that they'd suddenly somehow realise that they'd made a mistake, that they'd look at him with an 'oh, no, we didn't mean you,' and bundle him into his cat basket, straight back to the rescue centre.

CHAPTER TWENTY-SEVEN

MORRIS CONTINUED TALKING, his voice softer now.

"And mother was rich. Her husband had died and left her well-off. She needed something to fill her days and that something was me." He paused and stared ahead of him, gathering together the words. "We had a comfortable life together; I can't deny that. I never had to do anything that I didn't really want to. We travelled. I saw and experienced things that I would never have had in my old life. The furthest I ever went before mother took me home with her was a day trip to the seaside and even that was a disaster. The coach broke down on the way," he explained. "By the time they got it going and we got there, it was practically time to turn around and come back again. We just about had time to run down to the sea and stare at it and that was it, bye bye Clacton. We never even got our feet wet."

He fell silent again and closed his eyes, as if he were dreaming.

"She sent me to a small private school in the town. We had to wear these stupid little jackets and caps. And short trousers. Can you imagine? Short trousers. I used to cringe every time I put them on. Michael and Josie would have died laughing. Well, Michael would have kicked my head in first and then died laughing. Mother used to encourage me to write and to paint and draw. She even set me up a little studio in the garden of our house in Essex. When I was a teenager, I had some pictures in exhibitions occasionally, just locally, nothing grand, but she couldn't have been prouder. Especially when they were bought." He snorted suddenly, halfway between a grunt and a laugh. "I found out after she died that she was the one who bought them. They were all stacked, carefully wrapped, at the back of her big old wardrobe. They're still there," he added.

Aubrey lifted his head and watched as Maudie glided gently down the chimney breast on her back and came to rest on the other armchair.

"Just wanted to make sure she got her train all right."

"And did she?"

Maudie nodded, lifting one of the satin ribbons from her long hair and threading it through her fingers.

"What would you have done if she hadn't?" Aubrey asked, suddenly curious.

"Spooked the driver and stopped the train." The small dimples around her mouth twinkled.

Aubrey opened his mouth to speak and then closed it again. He never really knew when Maudie was serious. He wriggled slightly as Morris lifted him gently and placed him back down on the rug. Standing up and moving over to the fireplace, Morris looked directly at Maudie, speaking softly, his voice barely above a whisper. Maudie dropped the ribbon and sat up straighter. Aubrey looked from one to the other. Surely Morris couldn't see her?

"Everything about me, I mean the real stuff like who I was and where I'd come from, mother tried to sort of erase until I could hardly remember myself." Morris raised his hand and scratched his head slightly, as though puzzled by what he had just said. "The only thing that she didn't change was my name, and that was probably the one thing that I wouldn't have minded losing. But everything else about me had to be altered and re-assembled in the boy blue-print that she wanted. Like one of those build-a-bear toys. Except that I was build-a-boy. She even chose my friends, always little snot-faced kids called Walter who played chess and didn't like rough games." He smiled suddenly. "I only knew rough games."

For several minutes there was silence as Morris stared down into the grate, one hand resting on the mantlepiece, clearly deep in thought. Maudie got up and began to fiddle with the curtains, twitching them one way and then the other creating a slight breeze. Aubrey watched curiously. She was obviously getting bored. Would Morris notice the curtains moving? Apparently not, or if he did he wasn't bothered. Strolling over to the door, Morris left the room. From overhead, Aubrey and Maudie could hear the sound of the floorboards creaking. He returned carrying a shoe box. Kneeling down and with hands that trembled slightly, he lifted the lid and pulled out some yellowing wads of paper. Leaning over he spread them out on the floor. Aubrey padded over and stared down at them. Morris turned his head sideways and looked at him.

"I went every day, you know. Right through the trial. Rain or shine." He ran his fingers across the pages of newspaper as though feeling the words. "I always got there really early to make sure I'd get in. I was never sure if Josie knew if I was there or not but I always tried to sit in the same place. I used to will her to look over and see me but she never turned her head. She just used to stare straight ahead. She looked in a sort of daze, like it was all happening to someone else. The strange thing was that, even though I hadn't seen her for years, she looked exactly like I remembered her. Even her hair, the way the curls used to sort of brush against her shoulders." He grinned suddenly, a splitting of the face that lit his features and showed the boy he had once been. "She asked me to cut it once. Right up to her ears, like some pop star that she liked, I think. We sneaked a pair of scissors out of the craft room and I just hacked at it until it was really short. Mrs Thorpe went bananas."

This Mrs Thorpe, thought Aubrey, was clearly some sort of screw. Although, now he thought about it, he wasn't sure what going bananas meant. He'd ask Trevor. He'd be bound to know. He settled his paws under him as Morris continued.

"I watched every moment of the trial. I didn't miss a single second. Even when there was a break, I didn't leave the court room in case I couldn't get back in for some reason. Mother didn't know where I was going, obviously. I told her that I was visiting the British Museum. I said that I was thinking of writing a book about early Egypt." He sighed. "She was delighted."

Morris fell silent again as he stared down at the newspaper cuttings, leaning over further and spreading them out until they filled half the floor. He shuffled several pages, rearranging them and then pointed towards a cutting on the edge of the others. A teenaged boy with a sharp nose and what seemed to Aubrey to be rather a lot of teeth grinned back at them.

"Look at him. That's Quentin. The little shit gave interviews to the tabloids after the trial, like he hadn't already done enough damage. Do you know, Aubrey," he paused and swallowed, as though the words were causing him pain. "When he was giving evidence, he turned up in his school uniform. Tie, blazer, the lot. He was seventeen years old, for God's sake. How many seventeen-year-olds go around wearing their school uniform? The jury loved it of course. Believed every word. I can see his face now, all earnest and shiny. And he played it just right. Not too confident, not too assured, looking across at the jury with that pathetic little half-smile. It was masterly. It was only when he turned up here and bought that cottage that I worked out why he did it. There's no way a school teacher could have afforded a house like that, not at his age anyway. When he bought it, he was barely out of college."

Morris picked up the cutting and held it closer to his face, his mild blue eyes hardening as he scrutinised the picture.

"I wrote to her after the trial, regularly. It wasn't difficult to find out which prison she was in. There are only about a dozen women's prisons in total. She didn't write back at first and then, suddenly, she did. It was about five years later. That's when she told me. When she told me what really happened."

CHAPTER TWENTY-EIGHT

AUBREY RAN SWIFTLY across the springy turf, his paws rustling through the fallen leaves from the apple tree, towards Trevor who was laying on a large faded velvet cushion, eyes closed and tail tucked tightly around him.

"Trev, all right mate?"

He spoke softly. If Trevor was asleep, he didn't want to wake him. Trevor opened one eye.

"Aubrey. Good to see you."

Aubrey settled down next to him and looked him over. He didn't look too bad considering that he'd been at death's door a few days ago. The vet had done a good job. Once Trevor's fur grew back from where she'd shaved it to stitch him up, he'd look as good as new.

"How you feeling today?"

"Not too bad, all things considered."

"They treating you all right?" Aubrey nodded towards the house. Through the open back door, he could hear people speaking, the voices talking in soft tones that chimed with the melancholy of the autumn day.

Trevor nodded.

"No complaints. They put this big cushion out here for me and they've been grilling me fish fingers. Nice. Ever tried one?"

Aubrey shook his head. He didn't even know that fish had fingers. Well, you learned something new every day.

"Did you go to the meeting last night?" asked Trevor.

Aubrey nodded.

"What happened?"

"Same as usual. Lots of talking about the cat killer. It's not looking like the posters that Jo put up are doing any good. They were asking me again if you'd said anything about what happened. I told them that you couldn't remember."

Trevor sighed.

"I wish I could. I'm the only one who's survived an attack but I can barely remember a thing about it. I've thought and thought but the only thing that comes back to me is what I've already said. I was walking along and then I suddenly had that feeling of my tail being tugged from behind and jumping round and then it all goes blank. The next thing I can remember is waking up at the vets." He hesitated and looked thoughtful. "I can't even remember now why I was near the bus stop, there must have been a reason but I can't think what it was. Although, there was a smell, now I come to think about it. Definitely something that I've smelled before, but I can't quite think where."

For a moment they sat in silence and then Aubrey said, "Gnasher wants to get the cats from the tip involved."

Trevor sat up straighter and winced from the effort.

"What on earth for? What does he think that they're going to do that we couldn't do ourselves?"

Aubrey shrugged.

"I don't know. You know Gnasher, he's not great on detail. Who are they anyway?"

"There's a gang of them that live at the local tip and sort of stick together. They're mostly feral or abandoned. I got to know a few of them when I was living on the railway. At one point I even thought about joining them, a sort of insurance for my old age."

"So, they're ok then?"

Trevor nodded.

"They're a good lot for the most part. The village cats don't like them much, but they just live a different life, that's all. There's been one or two run-ins over the years but nothing major really. Not what I'd call a real bust-up. They pretty much leave us alone and we leave them alone. So, what's Gnasher's great plan then?"

"Well, Gnasher said they could help us watch the bus stop, kind of round the clock type thing."

"And then what?"

Aubrey shrugged.

"I don't know. Gnasher didn't get that far."

Trevor looked thoughtful.

"I don't see them co-operating, not with Gnasher anyway. He seems to have forgotten that his last encounter with them didn't end well."

"What happened?"

"Some little misunderstanding about a cat flap and a bowl of missing food. Of course, being Gnasher, he went completely over the top just because he'd seen one of the tip cats in the village earlier in the day. Turns out that Beryl, whose food it was, had forgotten that she'd eaten it. Thick as two short planks," he added.

"Anyway, Dino suggested that someone should go and ask them if they'll help." Aubrey paused. "Someone who hasn't got a history with them."

"Who?"

Aubrey slumped.

"Me, apparently."

AUBREY WALKED SLOWLY along the weed-strewn pathway towards the great open gates of the re-cycling centre. Situated on the edge of the village, he had strolled along to investigate it when they'd first moved here and had gone no further than the main entrance. He had very quickly decided that he didn't like it. It was too easy to get hit by one of the cars rushing in and out, to say nothing of the great cavernous bins that people hurled things into. Jethro had told him that a dead and decomposing cat had been found in one once and the thought had haunted him ever since. Not just that the cat had been found there, but the possibilities of how it had got there. Either it had been walking round the edge looking down, then somehow slipped and been knocked unconscious by somebody throwing something in, or it had been dead already and somebody had chucked it away along with the rest of their rubbish. Neither was a pleasant thought. Most people had the decency to bury their animals when they died, or at least take them to the vet for disposal.

The noise got louder as he approached, a great clashing and thumping that reverberated around and made his head ache, not helped by the putrid stench that hung over the place. He stopped and watched as a fair-haired woman delved into the back of her car and heaved out a black plastic sack, humping it onto her back and climbing the steps to the nearest bin. A man, dressed in ripped jeans and checked shirt, rushed over.

"Not that one, love. General rubbish over there." The man pointed to one of the further bins. What was in that black plastic sack, he wondered. Could be anything. Did anyone ever check the contents? He moved further forward, treading slowly. Although he couldn't see them, he knew that he was being watched. Fifty pairs of eyes were observing him, waiting to see what he was going to do next. Trevor had told him; the tip cats were numerous but masters of disguise. You never spotted one until it was standing right next to you.

"What do you want?"

Aubrey turned and stared into the cold amber eyes of a thin grey cat.

"Gnash... er, I mean Dino, sent me."

Better not to use Gnasher's name. This cat wasn't exactly exuding the warmth of feline kindness and the mention of Gnasher was hardly likely to improve matters.

"You're the new one."

It was said as a statement of fact. Aubrey supressed the wriggle of discomfort that this cat knew who he was. He looked around as he became aware of more cats silently watching him, each somehow managing to blend in among the background of old electrical equipment and discarded oil cans stacked around the perimeters. He was surrounded.

"It's about the cat murderer."

The thin grey cat remained silent. Clearly not the talkative type then. Aubrey took a deep breath and continued.

"We, that is, Dino and the rest, we wondered if you might, sort of, be able to help?"

The grey cat tipped his head to one side.

"Doing what?"

"Help us with surveillance, that sort of thing."

The grey cat remained silent for a moment as though thinking and then said, "How's Beeching doing?"

"Beech... oh, Trevor. He's ok. Definitely on the mend."

"Good lad, Beeching."

Aubrey nodded. Around him he was aware of the other cats slowly creeping towards him. He watched as an aggressive looking tabby with rust-coloured ears emerged ahead of the others.

"What is it exactly that you want us to do?"

Aubrey cleared his throat. He was finding the collective unblinking gaze of so many cats disconcerting.

"We know that the attacks happen near the bus stop but nobody ever seems to see anything. I mean," he added, "if we even knew who was doing these killings it might help."

The grey cat nodded slowly and then turned to look at the other cats.

"What do you think?"

"Why should we? Why should we owe you lot anything?" The speaker, a large black and white animal with several teeth missing, thrust its head forward as it spoke. "Don't think we've forgotten all those things Gnasher said about us."

"I agree," said the grey cat. "But it's Beeching who's been injured this time. Don't forget when he lived on the railway. If it hadn't been for him, we would never have found Tubby."

Several of the cats nodded in agreement. One of them moved forward from the back and faced the others.

"It's true. Tubby would have been a goner if Beeching hadn't found him that day. It was only Beeching carrying him in his mouth into the station that saved him."

"What do you think, Tubby?" asked the black and white cat.

Tubby, a small ginger cat, almost completely spherical in shape, gazed back in simple bemusement as the other cats turned to look at him. Tubby, thought Aubrey, was almost certainly short of a full set.

"Ok, we'll do it," said the grey cat decisively, clearly recognising that asking Tubby a question that required anything approaching a coherent response was a completely pointless exercise. "On condition that Gnasher keeps out of it."

Aubrey nodded enthusiastically. Whether or not he had the authority to exclude Gnasher, he had no idea, but he'd worry about that another time. What he did know was that he wanted out of here and sooner rather than later.

The grey cat turned to him.

"Come on, I'll walk you out."

The two cats strolled towards the exit, Aubrey trying hard not to break into a run.

"Don't mind her." The grey cat nodded back towards where the black and white cat was staring after them. "Brenda had a bit of a bad start in life. She's been a lot better since she's been with us. Same as Tubby. In here, we look after our own."

Aubrey felt slightly more cheerful. They couldn't be all bad then. He searched around for something to say.

"Do you see much of the village?" he asked, feeling slightly foolish even as the words left his mouth. He'd be asking if they were going anywhere nice on their holidays next.

"A fair bit. We have a scout round now and then. We know pretty much who everyone is. Most of the village use the tip. For instance, that woman you were watching when you came in. She's the one that works up at the school. That academy place."

CHAPTER TWENTY-NINE

"HOW LONG WAS she here for?"

"Not long. About half an hour. She said that she just needed to get out of the house for a while."

Jeremy nodded.

"Can't say I blame her. It's a big old place to be rattling around in on your own, even without everything else that's happened. What did you talk about?

"Nothing much, really. We had a coffee. She said she had a lot to do but didn't specify what. I did ask if there was anything that we could do to help but she said no, not really. Apparently, Harold's nephew is coming down at the weekend to lend a hand."

"Quentin?"

"The very same. He's going to go through Harold's papers and stuff with her. She looked a bit anxious when she said it, so I'm guessing that admin isn't her forte."

"Did she say anything about the police? The talk in the pub is that they're on to something. Apparently, Jo's cousin Terry does some civilian job with them and according to him, things are livening up."

"Did Terry say what it was that they're on to?"

"No. Nothing concrete, anyway. Just the usual. They've got a suspect, only a matter of time and so on. My guess is that they're no further forward." Jeremy stretched his legs and leaned back slightly. "I hate these kitchen chairs. No matter which way I sit, they make my back ache."

Molly smiled.

"I think that they're designed for looking at, rather than sitting on."

She looked across to where Carlos was stirring something on the hob. She half-rose and then sat down again. There was always stuff in the freezer if he messed it up. Which he almost certainly wouldn't, she reflected. The last meal that he had cooked them, a seafood risotto, had been delicious. He definitely had talent as a chef. Anyway, this was his practice run and she ought to just let him get on with it. He'd asked if Teddy and Casper could have dinner with them one night so that he could cook them something and she and Jeremy had agreed, provided that it was all right with Lucinda. Something with meat in, he'd said, as a change from boiled whole wheat pasta and spinach which, according to Casper, was all they ate at the Academy.

Carlos turned his head and glanced back.

"Teddy says that Lucinda's not doing any lessons at all now," he said.

"I'm not surprised," said Jeremy. "She can hardly be in the right frame of mind for any teaching. There's only Teddy and Casper left now anyway, and I shouldn't think that they will be there for much longer. I expect their parents will be coming for them any day now."

"Probably," said Carlos, turning back to the hob.

Jeremy eyed his back thoughtfully. Carlos sounded very laid back for somebody who had practically gone into meltdown at the mere suggestion the other day that Teddy and Casper would have to return home. Molly rose and collected a handful of cutlery from the drawer. From the top of the cat dome across which he was laying, paws hanging down, rather than curling up inside in the cosy fake-fur interior, Aubrey half-dozed while he thought about his day. It hadn't gone too badly, all things considered. The trip to the tip had been ok. At least he'd got back in one piece. The tip cats weren't over-friendly but they hadn't attacked him and they had at least listened. Dino, Jethro and Edyth had seemed pleased, anyway. Even Gnasher had been all right, once he stopped sulking. As Edyth said, it was just possible that the vigilante group would get some results. In any event, somebody had to do something. The way things were going, soon there wouldn't be a cat left in the village.

Carlos turned the heat down on the hob and joined Jeremy at the table.

"Teddy says that the police have been back up at the Academy asking questions."

"What sort of questions?"

"More or less the same as they asked last time. Teddy says that they think if they keep asking the same questions then they'll get different answers. But, like Teddy says, how will they know which are the right ones?"

"True," said Jeremy. "But sometimes, when people lie, they forget what they said the first time and start contradicting themselves and that's when the police start catching them out."

"Well, there's only Teddy, Casper, Lucinda and Zofia there. What have any of them got to lie about?" He hesitated and then continued. "Mr Goodman, do you, like, have to tell the police everything? I don't mean, like, tell lies, but just not say something that they haven't asked about. I mean, like, even if it's got nothing to do with anything."

"Well, it depends on what you mean by having nothing to do with anything. If it's about Harold's murder then I think it ought to be for the police to decide if it's relevant or not. Why?" he asked, suddenly suspicious. "What is that you haven't told them?"

"Nothing, Mr Goodman. Honestly."

Jeremy watched for a moment as Carlos gazed back at him with an innocent smile. Too innocent, thought Jeremy. Years of working with adolescents had taught him any number of things. Not least of which was that when a teenager ended a statement with 'honestly', it was usually anything but. He felt a sudden pang of anxiety. Carlos was settling in so well. It had been at least two months since he had woken in the night shouting. He was making friends at school as well as being friends with Teddy and Casper. Recently he had even started to talk about what he might do after leaving school. In fact, Jeremy reflected, for the first time Carlos was talking about the future as if he actually believed that he might have one. The very last thing he needed right now was to get embroiled in something that was actually nothing to do with him.

"Carlos, this isn't a game. Somebody has been killed. Murdered," he added brutally. "Stabbed to death. This isn't a game," he repeated. "If you know anything, no matter how trivial, you must tell the police. It's not up to you to decide how important it is."

He frowned as Carlos looked away, unable to meet his eye. Suddenly, instinctively, he asked, "Is it Teddy? Does Teddy know something?"

It wouldn't be beyond the bounds of possibility, he thought. She was still up at the Academy. If anybody had seen or heard anything, it was most likely to be her. Or Casper. More likely Casper, he reflected. He hadn't met the boy but he had the distinct feeling that if there was anything to be found out, it would be Casper who found it. And hadn't Teddy said something about him looking in Harold's office?

Carlos shook his head.

"No, Mr Goodman. Honestly," he added.

There it was again, thought Jeremy. Honestly. It was only a matter of time before Carlos stated that he 'wasn't going to tell a lie' which would almost certainly be followed by a pack of lies. Had he been the same when he was a teenager? Probably. And he and his friends hadn't had half the opportunities that today's lot had for getting themselves into trouble. Not that they hadn't tried.

AUBREY WATCHED AS Carlos crept across the room and quietly closed his bedroom door before turning back to his phone. From the top of the wardrobe, Maudie gently floated down and joined them, pausing for a moment to stare at the posters on the wall, before settling the long folds of her dress around her as she draped herself across the chest of drawers.

"Teddy? It's me." There was a pause and Aubrey and Maudie could just hear the faint sound of Teddy's voice. "No, I didn't tell them," continued Carlos. "But I think that Mr Goodman suspects. He kept, like, asking me if I knew something." He paused and then said, "No, I won't. I promised that I wouldn't. But it doesn't seem right. I think that we should say something."

Aubrey and Maudie watched as Carlos pulled his phone away from his ear in response to the buzzing noise of Teddy's response.

"No, all right. Yes, I know. Anyway, about dinner, Molly says it's all right as long as Lucinda agrees. I practiced tonight. Bolognese."

Aubrey could hear the note of pride in Carlos's voice.

"Lucky, aren't they?" Maudie's voice sounded mournful.

"What?" Aubrey turned to look at her.

"Lucky. Them," she added, nodding towards Carlos. "All we ever got was stuff like mutton. Grim," she added.

"What did you…" he started and then turned back as Carlos continued.

"Yes, I can get most of the stuff on the list. What about you?" He nodded to himself as Teddy talked. "I thought of something else," said Carlos. "Matches. You're going to need matches. And we need to think of somewhere to keep things."

CHAPTER THIRTY

"MRS GOODMAN? Or may I call you Molly? Quentin Fairchild," he added, proffering a large damp hand. "We meet at last."

"Who is it, Moll?"

Without waiting for an answer, Jeremy ambled through to the hall. On the doorstep stood a tall young man, dressed in what were clearly designer jeans. A pale lemon-coloured cashmere sweater was draped elegantly around his shoulders. Jeremy tugged slightly at his own bobbled sweater and glanced down at his faded and unfashionably baggy denims, from which any structure had long since collapsed. They, too, were designer jeans. But only in the sense that somebody had once designed them. Probably.

"Quentin." He paused, trying to supress his irritation. He had just been looking forward to settling down with some crap telly and a bottle of wine. "How nice to meet you. Do come in."

Ushering the way through to the sitting room, Jeremy reached for the remote and flicked the television off.

"Would you like a drink?" said Molly. "Tea or coffee? Or wine, perhaps?"

"A glass of red would be perfect," said Quentin, sitting down without waiting to be asked. Although, thought Jeremy, fair enough, it is his house. He sat down opposite him.

"So, how's it going at Sir Frank's? Settling in all right?"

"It's going very well," said Quentin. "Very well indeed."

"Really?" Jeremy's tone of astonishment was evident, as well it might be, Aubrey reflected. Only yesterday he had heard Jeremy speculating on whether Quentin was actually still alive. He had concluded that he probably was on the basis that they hadn't heard anything to the contrary although whether all his limbs were still in place and attached in the right order was another matter. He jumped down from the windowsill from where he had been watching poor old Humphrey being yanked along again by Malcom Dryden, and sat on Jeremy's foot. He had been going to jump on to the arm of the sofa but he had a sudden aversion to being so close to Quentin.

"Oh, yes," continued Quentin. "Enormous fun. Such a refreshing change from Ferndale. Sir Frank Wainwright's is so, well, so real."

Aubrey stared at him. Real? As opposed to what? Quentin continued.

"And the staff are so friendly. Really chummy, if you know what I mean."

"Are they?" Jeremy's tone now was not so much astonished as frankly incredulous.

"Absolutely," nodded Quentin. "A really welcoming bunch. I don't think I'd been there a week before the head invited me to join her bridge club. Great fun," he added.

"I'll just go and give Molly a hand with the drinks. Shift yourself, Aubrey."

In the kitchen, Jeremy quietly closed the door and leaned with his back against it. Aubrey sat down on his foot again.

"He's gone straight into arse-licking mode with the head." Jeremy's tone was flat. "I can't say I blame him, not really. It's dog eat dog at Sir Frank's. Sorry Aubrey." He reached down and tickled Aubrey's head. "He's probably on a reduced timetable already. I wonder what excuse she used this time."

"What do you mean?" Molly turned from where she had been pouring drinks.

"It's what she does for her coven. Gives them special jobs so that she can cut their teaching hours."

"What sort of special jobs?"

"Oh, anything. Counting the board markers, tidying up the notice boards, that kind of thing. All key educational activities and vital for the smooth running of the school, obviously. I mean, where would education be without somebody to update the notice boards once a week?" He sighed and ran a hand across the back of his head. "It's all very well, but somebody else still has to pick up the hours. Mind you," he added, "it's the first time that I've known a man to be in on it."

"Well, never mind that now. Give me a hand with these drinks." She glanced back at the work top. "Might as well bring the bottles as well. If he's anything like Harold, we could be in for a long evening."

"SO, QUENTIN," SAID Molly, holding a glass of red wine towards him. "It's lovely to meet you."

Quentin took a large gulp from his glass, half-emptying it before sitting back with his legs splayed and his arms stretched out across the back of the sofa.

"Well, obviously, what with the terrible news about uncle Harold, I had to come down and I thought I'd call in while I was here to see how you're getting on. Obviously I needed to check if Lucinda is managing all right." He sighed. "She's a bit of an air head, you know. I really don't know how she's going to cope without uncle Harold. He was the one that looked after the business end of things. Lucinda is more of what I think you'd call the creative type."

"Well, she certainly has some creative ideas regarding education," agreed Jeremy.

"Oh, the children love her." Quentin sat forward slightly and took another gulp of wine, draining the glass. "Absolutely adore her."

Of course they do, thought Aubrey. They spend most of the time running around and doing what they like. Mind you, to be fair, from what he'd heard, they did that at Sir Frank's too.

"So," Quentin continued. "How are you finding the cottage? Everything ok? Have you got everything that you need?"

"Yes, thank you," said Molly. "It's very charming. Really lovely."

Aubrey glanced up to the curtain rail where Maudie was swinging hand over fist across the room, showing the frill of her cotton petticoat. She dropped down and sat next to Quentin on the sofa. Extending her forefinger, she tickled the back of his neck. He shivered slightly and pulled his sweater more tightly around his shoulders.

"Yes, these cottages are rather charming aren't they?" said Quentin. "Actually, I found out about this village from uncle Harold. He lived here for a while after his first wife died. He was taking some time out while he thought about what to do next. It's where he met Lucinda, she was living with her uncle at the time. She was looking after him. She used to be a nurse."

"Oh," Molly looked surprised. "I didn't realise that Harold had been married before."

"Poor uncle Harold." Quentin pulled the corners of his mouth down very slightly and dipped his head towards his now empty glass. "He didn't really have a very happy life, you know."

"Really?" said Jeremy. "Why was that? I thought that he was very settled here. He and Lucinda seemed so content."

"Well, yes. Now, of course. But I meant before that. Actually," Quentin lowered his voice. "It's a rather dreadful coincidence. His first wife was murdered as well."

"How terrible." Molly sounded truly shocked.

Jeremy put his glass down and leaned forward, interested.

"What happened?" he asked.

"It must have been, oh, about twenty years ago now. She was stabbed, too."

"Did they ever catch who did it?"

Quentin nodded.

"Oh yes. It was a woman who worked in their factory. She was called Josie. She worked for uncle Harold and auntie Charlotte. They had a small business, manufacturing high quality toys and games. Well, not that small really. They started it with some money that auntie Charlotte had inherited. The factory actually did rather well, although auntie Charlotte did sometimes accuse uncle Harold of being too extravagant. He always wanted to expand the business, you see. Really build it up, and of course that costs money."

Molly and Jeremy exchanged a glance. Quentin continued.

"Uncle Harold sold the business later, after auntie Charlotte was killed." Quentin sighed and tilted his head slightly to one side. "You can understand it. He kept it going for a while but then said that he just didn't have the heart for it anymore. He lived in a few places but didn't really settle anywhere. Finally he came here, to the village. The murder was in all the papers when it happened. I don't think a day went by when there wasn't some mention of it."

Yeah, and we know why, thought Aubrey looking across at him sourly.

"What happened to the woman?" asked Molly.

"She went to prison."

162

"Why did she do it? I mean, presumably she had a reason?" asked Jeremy.

"She was fixated with uncle Harold. As simple as that." Quentin lifted his shoulders slightly and gave a small, slightly sorrowful, smile. "Apparently, she honestly thought that if auntie Charlotte was out of the way, then she and uncle Harold would be together. Deluded, of course."

CHAPTER THIRTY-ONE

QUENTIN STARED INTO space as though thinking, his brow furrowed slightly. Almost, thought Aubrey, as if he was trying to remember the right words, to fit them together in the right order. He continued.

"She was absolutely besotted with him. There was no doubt about that. You know, sort of following him around and turning up at their house and that sort of thing. What we'd call stalking nowadays. And uncle Harold, being an innocent," Quentin paused for a moment, watching them through slightly narrowed eyes before continuing. "Well, he just didn't see it. He thought that, by taking an interest, he was helping her. He was very much like that, you know. He had strong views about assisting those less fortunate than ourselves. He did an awful lot for local charities, money raising and so on. He probably took on rather too much in that direction, which was why things got in such a muddle."

"A muddle in what way?" asked Jeremy.

"Oh, you know. With accounting and so on."

Molly and Jeremy both nodded sympathetically, although not before Aubrey caught a slight raising of Jeremy's left eyebrow. Molly leaned over and re-filled Quentin's glass.

"So what happened about your aunt?" asked Jeremy.

"Well, from what came out at the trial, it seemed that Josie was from a troubled background so, in a way, you had to have some sympathy with her." Quentin's face assumed a suitably tragic look before grasping his wine glass and half-emptying it again. "She was in care from the age of about two. Both her parents were some sort of drug addicts. They're probably dead by now."

"Dreadful," murmured Molly. "It's hard to imagine the kind of homes that some children are born into."

And cats, thought Aubrey. Don't forget cats. And dogs too, come to that. In a way it was even worse for dogs, they had those horrible farm puppies or puppy farms, whatever they were called, to worry about. Vincent had told him about those. He was lucky, he knew. While life had been more than tough on one or two occasions, he had never suffered any deliberate abuse.

Quentin nodded in agreement.

"So true. After she left the children's home, she had some part-time jobs in shops and so on, but the job at the factory was her first real one." He paused, again thought Aubrey, as though he was trying to remember the script. "I suspect that uncle Harold took her on because he just felt terribly sorry for her. She was slightly disabled as well, you know. Walked with a limp. Some sort of childhood injury. But that's the sort of man uncle Harold was. Always thinking of others. Honestly, I think half his staff had a hard luck story of one sort or another."

Quentin dipped his head and gave a small, almost tragic, smile that didn't quite reach his eyes. Suddenly Aubrey could see the family likeness. There was something about the turn of the head and the shape of the hand as he ran it across his brow and up into his receding hairline. Harold had made a very similar gesture when he had been talking to Jeremy about the state education system.

"I was only a school boy at the time, but I was called to give evidence at the trial," Quentin added, looking up again.

"Were you? What sort of evidence? Blimey, you weren't a witness were you?" asked Jeremy.

"Jeremy," said Molly, a faint note of reproval in her voice. "I'm sure that Quentin doesn't want to go over it all again."

"No, it's fine. Really. This dreadful thing happening to uncle Harold has, well, I suppose it's brought it all back. In a way, it's quite a relief to talk about it." He glanced down at his polished loafers, his expression wan. "I heard it all you see. Everything. And then, when the police asked me about things, well, obviously, I had to tell them. I really had no choice."

"You weren't there when it happened, were you?" asked Jeremy.

Quentin shook his head.

"No. But I heard her making threats that same afternoon."

"Isn't that hearsay, or something?" asked Jeremy.

"No, that's when someone tells you something that someone else has said. I actually heard her. I was in the room at the time. I was in the sixth form and I used to do some part-time shifts on the factory floor to earn some pocket money. One of my jobs was poking the eyes into the teddies."

Aubrey shuddered. What a horrible thought.

"The woman, Josie," Quentin continued, "she often worked on the bench next to me and I used to talk to her sometimes. You know, just pass the time of day, that sort of thing. She was always quite friendly. Not like some of them, they could barely bring themselves to speak to me. You know, being related to the boss."

An unmistakeable smirk crossed Quentin's face.

"Pass the sick bucket," said Maudie, flicking a small finger across the back of Quentin's earlobe. Quentin twitched in response and clapped his hand to his neck. Maudie smiled and did it again.

"Anyway," said Quentin, "she was in uncle Harold's office that afternoon, the afternoon of the day it happened, and she was threatening him. He was sitting at his desk and she was standing over him. He kept trying to get up but she kept just pushing him back down, shoving at his shoulder with the flat of her hand. She wasn't shouting but she was talking in this sort of strange way, like hissing really, and leaning right into his face. She kept saying that she loved him and that he belonged to her. Some nonsense about them being meant to be together and she knew that he felt the same. She said that if he didn't leave his wife, she was going to take matters into her own hands. For the good of them all, she said."

"Did they see you?" asked Jeremy.

"No." Quentin shook his head. "I'd gone to uncle Harold's office to ask if I could leave early because I had a dentist appointment that I'd forgotten to tell him about, and I walked in on them. I did knock but I thought he hadn't heard me so I opened the door. The woman was beside herself, honestly, positively deranged. Her hair was all over the place and she looked really wild-eyed. Poor uncle Harold looked ghastly, totally white-faced. He kept trying to calm her down but the more he tried to comfort her, the more hysterical she became."

"And you were actually in the office when all this was happening?" asked Molly.

"Well, standing just inside the doorway. I'll never forget the look on her face. Or uncle Harold's." He gave a small theatrical shudder. "At the trial she admitted that she'd been in his office but she denied that she had been threatening him."

"What was her version?" Jeremy asked, curiously.

"She said that she was in his office because they were talking about uncle Harold's divorce and that what happened with auntie Charlotte was an accident. I know," he said, as Jeremy raised his eyebrows. "Incredible, but that's what she said. She didn't deny doing it, but she said that she hadn't intended to hurt

Charlotte at all. According to her, she and uncle Harold had been having an affair for over six months and that auntie Charlotte knew all about her. The whole story was ridiculous, of course." he added. "As if uncle Harold would have an affair with a woman like that. Or any woman," he added hastily.

"Of course," said Molly. Jeremy, Aubrey noticed, remained silent.

"Her story was that she had gone to uncle Harold's house because he had asked her to, and auntie Charlotte attacked her and started hitting her. According to her, they were standing in the kitchen when auntie Charlotte just started going mad and so she grabbed a knife to protect herself. She said that she just meant to threaten her with it and it somehow slipped. I mean, how likely is that?"

He laughed, a small joyless sound.

Jeremy nodded.

"I must admit, it does sound pretty unlikely," he said. "Presumably the jury didn't believe her?"

Quentin snorted.

"Not for a second. You only had to look at their faces to see what the verdict would be."

Anyway," continued Quentin. "Uncle Harold got hold of the knife and managed to get it away from her, but it was too late. She'd gone straight for the heart. The autopsy report said that auntie Charlotte had died more or less instantly."

"Why did Harold let her in to the house in the first place?" asked Jeremy. "I mean, if she was being a nuisance? Why didn't he just tell her to go away or call the police or something?"

"They asked him that at the trial. He said that it was auntie Charlotte's idea. When Josie turned up and started banging on the door and shouting through the letter box, auntie felt sorry for her. Uncle Harold said that Charlotte wanted to explain to

Josie that she and uncle Harold were happily married and that anything else that Josie imagined was, well, exactly that. Her imagination."

"Bit risky, wasn't it?" said Jeremy. "Letting her in?"

"They didn't know then that she was dangerous. As far as they knew, she was just deluded. Anyway," he continued, "At the trial, Josie stuck to her guns and insisted that it was an accident. Even the judge commented on her apparent lack of ability to recognise her guilt. But do you know, uncle Harold always felt that he was partly responsible. He insisted that he should have seen what was happening. After it was all over and she had been sentenced, he he was a broken man."

"Not that broken," said Maudie. "He hadn't been here five minutes before he started getting friendly with Lucinda. They used to go for soppy walks together up to the spinney." She got up and drifted over to the bookcase. "I don't like him," she said, nodding towards Quentin.

Aubrey padded over to join her at the bookshelf.

"But he has got a cat, though. He can't be all bad."

"I don't like his cat, either. He's called Walpole and he's so fat that he," she glanced back over her shoulder at Quentin, "had to get a special cat flap from abroad because Walpole got stuck in the first one he put in. He had to unscrew it all to get him out. I haven't laughed so much for eighty years."

They both turned back as Quentin started speaking again.

"Poor uncle Harold. He really thought that he was helping Josie by taking an interest in her and being encouraging but, of course, she was interpreting it in an entirely different way. Well, Jeremy, you and I being teachers," he paused and raised one eyebrow, "I'm sure that we both know how easy it is to get drawn into that kind of thing."

"What kind of thing?" asked Jeremy. A bit too innocently, thought Aubrey. He'd seen that look on Jeremy's face before. It was the look he wore when he was about to start winding somebody up.

"Well, you know. You start by being nice, feeling sorry for a pupil and trying to help, taking an interest and so on." Quentin paused and brushed an imaginary speck of dust from his shoulder. "And before you know where you are, there's all sorts of silly accusations flying."

CHAPTER THIRTY-TWO

MOLLY SLID INTO bed and watched as Jeremy put his phone on charge. Sidling round the door, Aubrey crossed the room and jumped onto the duvet. Molly reached down to tickle his ears.

"Five minutes," she warned him. "And then back downstairs."

Jeremy sat down on the small bedroom chair and turned to face her.

"Where's Carlos?"

"In bed, I hope. He went up as soon as he came in and saw Quentin here."

"Where had he been?"

"Out somewhere with Teddy, I think. He was a bit vague."

"I'll have another word with him in the morning. I don't want him to think that he's got to report to us every five minutes, but he needs to get it into his head that for now he must tell us where he's going, at least until this murder business is sorted out."

Aubrey tucked his head under his paw and inhaled the lovely comforting smell of Molly and Jeremy's bed. Carlos had indeed been out with Teddy. He had seen them down at the memorial garden, heads together and making notes in a little blue notebook. At least, Teddy had been making notes. Carlos had spent a lot of the time simply staring at her.

"I'm so pleased that he's making friends here," said Molly. "Nice friends," she added. "Not like Caparo and those other boys he got in with at Sir Frank's."

"I know. I'm really pleased, too. They're a good lot at Ferndale." Jeremy took off his watch and laid it next to his mobile. He stared at it for a moment. "I wonder if watches will become obsolete eventually? Someone told me the other day that some kids can't tell the time on a traditional clock."

He started emptying his pockets of loose change and laying it next to the phone and watch.

"Carlos told me the other day that some of the kids in his year don't like Quentin. They were really pleased when he transferred to Sir Frank's. According to Carlos, there's graffiti in the boys' toilets that says, 'Who does Fairchild fancy? Himself.'" Not the wittiest of observations, but you kind of get the point. Carlos says that they were dreading him teaching them this year. Apparently, he was always making his classes read difficult poems. Out loud."

Molly smiled.

"Not the best way to endear yourself to a teenage boy, I shouldn't imagine."

"Hardly. Or a teenage girl, for that matter." He paused for a moment. "I can't see that approach going down well at Sir Frank's. The only thing he'll get them reading out loud there is the local paper's weekly round-up at the magistrates' court. And that's only so they can name-check."

"Well, he seems to have settled in alright. He seemed happy enough. He didn't mention any problems."

"No, he didn't, which I must admit surprised me somewhat. But I guess if the Head's taken him under her wing, he's getting an easy ride. Well, as easy as it gets at Sir Frank's, which isn't saying a great deal." Jeremy looked thoughtful. "Talking of teenage boys and girls, what did you think of that stuff he was saying about being nice to pupils and what he called silly accusations?"

Molly thought for a moment.

"I'm not sure." She hesitated. "Probably the same as you?"

Jeremy nodded.

"If asked to put money on it, I'd say that there's been accusations or, at the least, rumours. Nobody at school has actually said anything but that would explain why he doesn't seem very popular among the staff. I bet the Head couldn't wait to get rid of him. If I was cynical, I could even suspect that the whole teacher exchange thing was just a ruse to get rid of him."

"Not seriously?"

"No, probably not," admitted Jeremy. "But I bet his name was first on the list when it was up for discussion."

"Why didn't the Head just ask him to leave?"

"You can't just force somebody out on the strength of the rumour mill. He could have been suspended I suppose, but only if he was actually accused of anything. But my guess is that he wasn't. I suspect that our Quentin was a bit over-enthusiastic on the extra-curricular activities with one of the kids, or maybe more than one, and that there was talk going round but nothing was actually officially reported."

"Didn't that happen once at Sir Frank's? I mean, an inappropriate relationship or whatever it's called. I seem to remember you talking about it."

"Yes, not long after I started there. There was a huge row about it. Both the parents up at the school shouting the odds. Not that I blame them. Apparently, the mother discovered her daughter's diary and read it."

"What happened?"

"I can't remember the teacher's name now, although I can see his face. Fair-haired, quite young, but old enough to know better. A bit trendy, if you know what I mean. Anyway, he denied it all. Said it was just teenaged fantasy. The girl herself didn't admit anything and he left soon after."

"Did he get another teaching job?"

Jeremy shrugged.

"I don't know. Nobody ever mentioned him again. But, you know, mostly in those situations it's just one person's word against another's, and if the pupil or pupils involved won't say anything then there's nowhere to go with it. I suspect that Ferndale's teacher exchange scheme suited all concerned. It conveniently shelved the problem and allowed Quentin to go somewhere else until the fuss died down."

"Surely, the Head at Ferndale would have had a duty to tell Sir Frank's, even if nothing had been proved?"

"Molly, you know as well as I do that Sir Frank's has gone right down since the new Head took over. She'd employ anybody with a pulse. And let's face it, on occasion, even a pulse wouldn't be essential. Once the Head knew that I was determined to get out one way or another, it was simply a case of damage limitation. They knew they would need someone and the last time they advertised they didn't get a single application. They struggle to even get supply teachers to work there. In any event, I think that the way the school has gone in recent years, pupils at Sir Frank's are pretty safe from Quentin's clammy clutches. Can you imagine Quentin trying it on with someone like Sonia Crayle? I know who my money would be on."

Aubrey agreed. He'd heard all about Sonia Crayle when Jeremy had returned home ashen-faced from school late one afternoon and made straight for the whisky bottle, having spent the previous half-an-hour trying to break up a fight in the playground to which eventually the police had been called. Apparently, one of the boys in his class had made the fatal error of calling Sonia fat, which, while nothing less than the truth, would have been far better left unsaid. Not just because it was unkind, but because it was also an open invitation for having your face re-arranged. Sonia had simply waited for the bell to go before following her opponent through the main doors and then flinging him against the wall. Allowing him approximately two seconds to regain his breath, she had dragged him to his feet and followed it up with a drop kick to the groin. It had been less than half a minute before what looked like the whole of the rest of the school had piled in.

Molly smiled.

"I guess so. Although perhaps we're being a bit unfair. We don't actually know any of this. We're just guessing. We could be completely wrong." She reached down and stroked Aubrey's head. "Did you like him?"

Jeremy thought for a moment.

"If I'm honest, not really, no. I mean, I didn't actively dislike him or anything but, I don't know, there's just something about him. When he was talking, I kept trying to think who he reminded me of. And then I realised that it was Clive. A younger version."

From his place on the bed where he was surreptitiously kneading the duvet cover, Aubrey agreed. Clive, Jeremy's erstwhile colleague at Sir Frank's and now currently headmaster of a prestigious private school, was a very similar type. He and Quentin could have been related. They both had the same superior air that seeped out of every pore.

Molly and Jeremy fell silent and then Jeremy said, "Dreadful about Harold's first wife, wasn't it? And then for the same thing to happen to Harold. Incredible."

Molly nodded.

"I know, I didn't really know what to say."

Jeremy continued.

"There's not a lot we could say. But that stuff about it all being an accident was pretty weak though, don't you think? You'd have thought that her brief would have given her a better story than that. I mean, it is a bit far-fetched. Like, 'oh sorry guv, the knife just sort of slipped'. Straight in the direction of the heart," he added.

"It could have been true," Molly pointed out.

"Maybe." Jeremy looked doubtful. "But unlikely. Anyway, according to Quentin, she never said that she didn't do it, so wouldn't that still make her guilty?"

"I'm not sure. I guess that she might have claimed self-defence." Molly thought for a moment. "At Donoghue's we didn't do much criminal work. It's mostly probate and family. But," she added, "in any event, the jury clearly didn't believe her story."

Aubrey let out a contented sigh. Just lately they had established a nice little bedtime routine where he was allowed on their bed for a while. Molly always said five minutes but it was often much longer. If he played his cards right he might even get to stay all night. Or at least part of the night. He mustn't neglect Carlos. He wondered where Maudie had gone. After Quentin had left, she had slid up the chimney and hadn't reappeared. Where she went, he had no idea. He jumped as the sound of Jeremy's phone suddenly burst across the room. Unlike Molly's mobile, which had a soft melodic tune as its ringtone, Jeremy's had the strident note of an old-fashioned telephone bell. Jeremy raised his eyebrows.

"If it's somebody asking me if I've been involved in an accident that wasn't my fault, I might kill them."

"Not at this time of night."

"It's not this time of night everywhere."

Aubrey listened, head on one side, watching with Molly as Jeremy pulled the phone towards him. He looked up to face them, one hand covering the screen.

"It's Morris," he said.

CHAPTER THIRTY-THREE

JEREMY GRIPPED HIS torch harder and swept the beam across the faces of the small group of people. In the wavering light he could just about make out Morris, his expression anxious and his face even paler than usual. Edging towards the centre, Jeremy came up behind him and touched him on the elbow.

"What happened?"

Morris turned to face him. Even in this light Jeremy could hardly fail to see the fear stamped across his features.

"I went out for a short walk, like I usually do, just to get a breath of fresh air before going to bed." He paused and took a deep breath before continuing. "It helps me to sleep, especially since Mother died. I started to walk up the lane when I stumbled over something. It was laying right across the path. When I looked down…" his voice faltered and he cleared his throat. "When I looked down, I couldn't really see in the dark, and at first I thought it was just some rubbish or something that somebody had dumped. They do sometimes, along here. It used to make Mother furious. She wrote to the local council about it, several times. But then this thing, it started making a noise, sort of groaning, and I realised that it was a person."

"What did you do?"

"I leaned over, but he was lying on his front so I couldn't see who it was. I thought at first that it was a drunk person but then I realised that he didn't smell of drink or anything so I just went in and called an ambulance. And then I called you. I couldn't think what else to do."

"Have they said what happened?"

He nodded towards the paramedics leaning over the prone figure, who was now struggling to sit up. As Jeremy watched, the figure slumped back down into unconsciousness, one arm hanging limply by his side, the other splayed out at an awkward angle. He stared for a moment at the blanched face caught in the cold blue light of the ambulance.

"No. They just turned up and started working on him. Nobody's said anything to me." Morris turned as a large uniformed figure strode towards them.

"Do you know who he is, sir?"

Morris moved away slightly, stepping backwards into the shadow as though to distance himself from the paramedic.

"No."

"Actually, I might be able to help you there."

The paramedic turned to Jeremy.

"His name is Quentin Fairchild. He's staying up at the Academy with his aunt. He was walking back there. He spent the evening with me and my wife." He looked over towards the ambulance where the other paramedics were handling Quentin gently into the back of the vehicle. "Is he going to be all right?"

"He'll survive I should think, although there seems to be quite a bit of blood loss." The paramedic's tone was grim. "He was lucky to be found when he was. I wouldn't have given much for his chances if he'd been left out here all night."

Jeremy moved closer towards Morris.

"Do you need Morris for anything else?"

The paramedic shook his head.

"No, although from the wound on the back of his head, it looks like he's been hit with something heavy so I expect the police will want to ask a few questions at some point."

JEREMY GLANCED AROUND the kitchen while he waited for the kettle to boil. Stifling a huge yawn with one hand, he lifted a small china mug from the draining board with the other. It had been a long evening and he was beginning to feel the strain. He stared for a moment at the delicate flower pattern etched on the mug. Was he being foolish? Was he in danger of being too trusting with regard to Morris? Could it be that he was letting the fact that he felt sorry for him guide his emotions? It wouldn't be the first time it had happened, he knew, although he wasn't particularly gullible. He could spot a scam as well as the next man. It was just that, very occasionally, he stumbled across someone who tugged at his heart strings and try as he might, he couldn't just walk away. Which was how both Carlos and Aubrey came to be living with him and Molly. He'd been exactly the same as a child and was forever bringing in wounded birds and, once, a fox with a broken leg. His father had said that he hoped to God that Jeremy never stumbled across a wounded elephant because they just didn't have the room.

From upstairs he could hear the faint splash of water running. It sounded like Morris was having a wash. A slight wriggle of unease fluttered through him. Why was Morris having a wash? It seemed an odd thing to do, they'd only just got in the house. He leaned against the sink, pushing back the wave of tiredness that threatened to engulf him, and tried to order his thoughts. Was it really a coincidence that Morris seemed to be looming large in some of the goings on? For someone who rarely socialised and appeared to be half cut for most of the time, he seemed to be at the centre of some pretty key events recently. First the knife being found in his garden and now this. He thought about it for a moment. But, surely, if Morris was responsible for the attack on Quentin, he wouldn't have called an ambulance. Or would he? He had long suspected that there was more to Morris than met the eye. It would be a good way to deflect suspicion, especially on the remote chance that anyone had seen him out on the lane. Or perhaps he had seen that Quentin was still alive and had simply lost his nerve. But that didn't explain why he was washing now. If he'd needed to wash some kind of evidence away then surely he would have had ample time to do it when he went back in to call the ambulance. Perhaps it was just a kind of belated nervous reaction to the events of the evening.

In his weary mind the thoughts danced together, forming and re-forming with the same question spinning at the centre. Why on earth would Morris attack Quentin? What reason could he possibly have? As far as he was aware, Morris barely knew the man. He turned to peer out into the darkness of the garden and jumped as a whiskered, hairy face loomed up at him through the window. Jumping down from the sill, Aubrey slipped through the cat flap.

"Aubrey, you've got to stop following me. You'll get yourself into trouble one of these days, it's dark out there."

They both turned as Morris appeared in the doorway. It suddenly struck Aubrey how very large Morris was. His shape seemed to fill the whole of the door frame and block the light.

"Ok?" Jeremy fished the tea bag out of the mug and threw it in the bin.

Morris nodded.

"Just a bit shaken."

"I'm not surprised. Here, drink this." Jeremy thrust the mug of hot tea towards him. "Morris," he hesitated for a moment, not sure that he really wanted to hear the answer. "Why did you say that you didn't know who Quentin is? He lived in the village; we're staying in his house. You must have seen him around."

Morris frowned.

"I don't know. I just did. Anyway, they're not the police. I don't have to answer their questions."

He turned and went back to the sitting room. Jeremy and Aubrey looked at each other and then followed him. For a moment Jeremy and Morris regarded each other in silence and then Morris said, "I don't want to make any trouble for Josie."

He sat down and leaned his head back against the leather of the armchair. Floating through the wall, the ribbon from her hair loose and trailing behind her, Maudie joined him. Aubrey nodded to her as she perched on the arm of the chair. Morris, Aubrey suddenly noticed, seemed to be the only person who didn't shiver when Maudie turned up. Jeremy sat down opposite and hauled Aubrey on to his lap.

"Josie? Is she a friend of yours?"

Morris nodded.

"Josie and I were children together."

Jeremy clutched Aubrey slightly harder. This was the second time tonight that Jeremy had heard the name Josie. She was cropping up right left and centre, and not in a good way. Aubrey looked at Morris more closely. What if Morris told Jeremy something that he didn't want to hear? It was beginning to look increasingly likely and if that was the case then Jeremy would be obliged to report it. His words to Carlos must be ringing uncomfortably in his ears. As he'd said at the time, it wasn't for any of them to decide what was relevant and what wasn't, that was up to the police. He watched as Morris placed his mug on the small side table and stared down at his hands, turning them palm upwards as though inspecting them.

"When I say we were children together," Morris paused and licked his bottom lip, still staring down at his hands. "We were in the same children's home. She was my friend. My best friend."

"Right."

Jeremy nodded.

"I left the home before she did, when I was adopted by Mother. The next time I heard anything about Josie was when she was on trial. For murder," he added.

Aubrey turned his head and watched as Jeremy scratched his right eyebrow, something he nearly always did when he was worried. This was tricky. Was Jeremy going to say that he already knew about the murder, that in fact Quentin had filled both him and Molly in on the whole story that very evening? For the moment Jeremy remained silent. Good thinking, thought Aubrey. Let Morris do the talking. Morris reached across and unscrewed the top from the bottle of whisky that was standing next to his mug of tea. Carefully, he poured a large measure into the tea and waved the bottle in Jeremy's direction.

Jeremy hesitated and then nodded. It was looking like this was going to be a long night and he needed all the help he could get.

"So Morris, how is that connected to you telling the paramedics that you don't know who Quentin is?"

Morris continued as though Jeremy hadn't spoken, his gaze fixed on a point in the distance. The light from the dim bulb in the lamp barely lit the room, casting his face into shadow.

"Josie had a job in a factory that made toys. She got involved with her boss." He hesitated and then rushed on, as though caught on a rip tide of words. "Her boss, he owned the factory and he was married and she had an affair with him. It was Harold," he added, slowing down again. "Only his name wasn't Harold then. It was Aaron."

CHAPTER THIRTY-FOUR

JEREMY TURNED BACK the duvet and slipped quietly into bed, aware of the house sleeping around him. The light on the digital clock showed two-fifteen. He'd been with Morris for longer than he'd realised. Beside him Molly stirred and let out a gentle sigh before settling back down again, one hand tucked under her cheek. He leaned over and looked at her small blonde head, her hair spread against the pillow. He lifted a lock and let it run through his fingers, and then let it fall again. They had been together for over twenty years now and, while they didn't always see eye to eye on everything, she was still his number one person and he couldn't ever envisage that changing.

How fortunate he was, compared to Morris. He thought again about the sad figure that he had just left, the image of Morris staring out from the front room window printed on the forefront of his mind. As he had walked down the front path he had turned and waved. Morris had waved back and given a little half-smile. He had found himself suddenly choked and had to force himself to move forward more quickly. The urge to turn back and invite Morris home with him was almost irresistible. Poor Morris. Alone, drunk most of the time with very few, if any, friends. Who did Morris have to talk to? While the general consensus seemed to be that Morris's mother was a bit of a dragon, she had at least been another human presence around the place and there seemed no doubt that she had genuinely cared for him. Now, he had nobody. Apart from Josie, of course, and Jeremy was beginning to get the feeling that friendships with Josie had a tendency to end badly.

He lay back again, arms by his side, and stared at the small lop-sided spider of a crack in the ceiling. His thoughts raced on, each one leap-frogging off the next and almost colliding with the one before. So much for a quiet village life. First the murder of Harold, and now this vicious attack on Quentin. Both crimes were almost certainly committed by the same person, he was certain. Logic said that they had to be, the odds of two violent attackers living in the same village were roughly nil. And surely they weren't random attacks? Harold and Quentin were connected. They were uncle and nephew. More to the point, they were both involved in the trial following the murder of Harold's first wife, which, whatever way you looked at it, brought Josie neatly in to complete the triangle. Which meant that he should go to the police with the bizarre story that Morris had just told him. Swinging his legs silently out of the bed, he made his way back downstairs.

In the kitchen, the huge antique station clock above the cooker ticked loudly into the silence, a great clonking sound that jarred on his nerves. It was like dropping coins into a metal bucket. He didn't usually notice it when Molly and Carlos were around, but now it seemed to fill the whole room. Jeremy stared at it for a moment. Like everything else in the cottage, it had almost certainly cost a lot of money. Not usually sensitive to designer brands and expensive kit, Jeremy generally operated on the principle that if a thing worked, if it did the job that it was supposed to do, then that was good enough. It was a simple principle that he applied to anything with a plug or a motor. Now he looked around him as though really seeing it for the first time. The expensive coffee machine that he couldn't be bothered to work out how to use, the exquisite finish on the worktops that Molly told him had probably been shipped over from Italy, and the handblown pair of vases placed artistically on a high shelf, it all looked like something you'd see in a glossy magazine. Nothing was cheap, not a hint of the High Street or chain store about anything. Quentin must have spent a fortune. Restoring the antique clock alone must have cost a week's wages. But if what Morris had said was true, he was beginning to have grave suspicions as to where that money had come from, and it definitely wasn't from a teacher's salary.

Unable to bear the ticking any longer, he wandered into the sitting room and sat down on the sofa. It still smelled faintly of Quentin, an expensive woody cologne with an aggressively masculine undertone which was only just the right side of locker room. He glanced up at the painting on the wall above the fireplace. An original, by the look of it. Original of what, he couldn't exactly make out. There seemed to be some arms and legs in there somewhere. Presumably the artist could explain it. No doubt, like everything else, it had been expensive.

The room held a stiff coldness in the way that rooms do in the small hours with no human warmth to take the chill off the air. He toyed with the idea of putting the heating on but he knew what Molly and Carlos would say if he did. He was forever lecturing them about global warming and telling them off for turning the heating controls up behind his back. Huddling further into himself, he sighed. If he'd realised how chilly it would be down here he would have put his dressing gown on but he couldn't be bothered to go back up and get it now, besides which he didn't want to disturb Molly or Carlos by traipsing up and down the stairs. In common with many old properties, the cottage had a couple of treads that creaked and in the stillness of the night the sharp cracking noise ricocheted off the walls like gun shots.

At the back of his head a small headache started, a faint knocking that tapped irritatingly against his skull. Normally amiable and cheerful, he felt strangely sulky, almost resentful. He wished to God that Morris hadn't confided in him. It was the kind of information that he really could have lived without and certainly not anything that he had been expecting to hear. Now he was left with the problem of deciding what to do with it. In the light of what had just happened to Quentin, he should go to the local police, he knew. It was what he would tell someone else to do. But what if he was wrong? What if Harold's murder and the attack on Quentin weren't connected to the death of Charlotte at all? What if they really were just random attacks? Once he told Morris's story, it couldn't be untold. He might be guilty of stirring up one mighty hornets' nest. A hornets' nest with the capacity to really hurt people, not least of whom was Lucinda. Things were going to be tough enough for her as it was. Why make matters worse? Although, he reflected, it wouldn't be the first time that the story had been revealed.

Not quite trusting the police, when Josie had written to Morris from prison, he had been to see a solicitor. She had, he said, listened carefully but had offered the opinion that, really, there was little to be done. She had researched the case prior to his appointment and, as far as she was aware, there had been no problem with the police investigation at the time and the kind of letter that Josie had later written to Morris wasn't uncommon. There was also the inescapable fact that she had taken the blame at the trial.

Morris's words rang in his ears. "The thing is, Jeremy, she was sort of implying that convicted criminals often change their story later. They try to persuade people that they're innocent. This solicitor, she said that it was because they had time on their hands, time to concoct a different story and that often they even believe it themselves. And she said that even if there was some truth in the story, an appeal isn't automatic. You can't just do it. You have to get permission. And to get permission there either has to be something wrong with the trial, which there wasn't, or fresh evidence. Which there isn't. Although," he added. "I didn't know about the will business then. Josie told me that later, when she came to see me."

Jeremy reached behind him and pummelled the stiff cushion, shifting himself into a more comfortable position. The fact of the matter was, no matter how he looked at it, all roads seemed to lead back towards Josie. If the death of Harold and the attack on Quentin were connected to the murder of Harold's first wife then the common denominator had to be Josie. The motives were clear. She'd had ample time in prison to think about things. She could have planned the whole thing, including getting Morris on board. But also, he had to admit, it was possible that what she claimed was nothing less than the truth. The problem was that, as far as he could see, there was nothing to support it. Even if what she claimed about Quentin was true, he was never going to confess. Perjury was a crime and carried a prison sentence. Although Quentin had been only a teenager when he gave his evidence, he was old enough to know what he was doing and the law would judge him as such.

The knocking in his head moved up a notch. If it got any worse he would have to go in search of some aspirin. He looked up as Aubrey sidled round the door and jumped on his lap. He smiled, his earlier cloud of sulkiness evaporating. If ever a cat had the knack of turning up just when a bloke needed him, it was Aubrey. He leaned over and sank his hands into Aubrey's rich fur, breathing in the cold, fresh outdoors smell of him. He had obviously been out on the tiles after they had left Morris. Probably literally.

"What do you think, Aubrey? What should we do? I'm sure that the police will uncover all this stuff for themselves. It's their job. Should we just stay out of it? Let sleeping dogs lie?" Aubrey looked up at him. What was all this stuff about sleeping dogs? It wasn't the first time he'd heard it. Sleeping was a cat thing, everybody knew that. Dogs had their own stuff. Like barking. But sleeping, well that was for cats. Maudie floated through the wall and joined them on the sofa, drawing up her knees and tucking herself close against Jeremy as though for comfort. He shivered slightly and continued, oblivious to her presence. "I mean, the odds are that Josie was making the whole thing up. She had enough time while she was in prison to get her story straight."

"I don't think so," said Maudie, leaning over and lowering her voice conspiratorially, although clearly Jeremy couldn't even see her, let alone hear her. "It didn't sound like it. Especially the stuff about the will. I know about wills," she added.

Aubrey turned to her, interested. It was at that point in Morris's story that he had been completely lost. He'd never heard of these will things before. He doubted if even Vincent or Trevor had.

"It's like a list," Maudie explained. "It says what happens to all your things when you die. And your money. Especially your money."

Aubrey nodded. He knew how important money was. Raj had been worried about it all the time. He had spent many a long evening watching Raj drinking whisky and going through the things he called his books, only to watch him repeat the same process the following evening. Aubrey had wondered why he kept doing it. It never seemed to make him any happier.

"And Molly's going to ask what happened," said Jeremy. "She's bound to. And I know what she's going to say." He paused and hugged Aubrey more closely to him. "She's going to say that we should go to the police. And she'll be right."

CHAPTER THIRTY-FIVE

JEREMY YAWNED. OVERHEAD the sound of the shower thrummed through the ceiling. He pulled the cereal box from the cupboard and stared at it before pushing it back. He had barely slept last night and he didn't feel like breakfast this morning. When he had gone back to bed he had mostly just stared into the darkness. Even his favourite method of nodding off, finding names and makes of car that began with every letter of the alphabet starting with Alpha and ending with Zephyr, had failed to work. He had finally drifted into a fitful doze just as a motor bike roared through the village and woke him up again.

He turned around as Molly came in, towelling her hair dry.

"What happened last night? Is Morris all right?"

"Well, yes," he hesitated. "And no."

Molly leaned back against the work surface and looked at him.

"What does that mean? Is he all right, or isn't he?"

"He's not hurt or anything like that."

"Well, something's happened. Why did he ring you?"

"It's Quentin."

"Quentin? What about Quentin?"

"Somebody attacked him when he was on his way back from here and Morris found him."

"Oh, my God." Molly gripped the edge of the sink, the knuckles on her small fingers showing white. "What happened? Is he ok? How bad is it? He's not…"

"No, he's not dead. But I think that he's been pretty badly hurt. The ambulance took him off to hospital. But Molly, that's not all."

"What do you mean, that's not all? Isn't that bad enough?"

"Sit down." Jeremy pulled a chair out and gestured towards it. "You remember Quentin telling us about Harold's first wife? And the woman Josie?"

Molly nodded and sat down; her expression wary.

"I'm hardly likely to forget."

Jeremy continued.

"No, I know. Me neither. Anyway, when I got to Morris's cottage an ambulance was there and Quentin was just lying on the ground. After the ambulance took Quentin away, I went back to the cottage with Morris. Just to make sure that he was all right, he looked really shaken. And then he started telling me things."

Molly looked worried.

"What sort of things? Why am I already thinking that I don't want to hear this?"

Jeremy took a deep breath.

"Morris knows Josie, the woman that Quentin was talking about last night. She's the woman that visited him that time when I was at his cottage, the same one that keeps looking over our fence. They were children together. Apparently they were in the same children's home."

"So Morris was adopted?"

"Yes. But that's not really the point. According to Morris, that story Quentin told us wasn't true. For a start, Harold's real name is Aaron. He changed his name when he came here."

They both turned as Carlos came into the room, his hair sticking up and the old blue woollen dressing gown of Jeremy's that he had worn when he first stayed with them after his mother was killed and to which he had taken a liking, wrapped loosely around his thin frame. His bare feet looked cold and strangely vulnerable against the polished tiles.

"Carlos, you're up early. And where are your slippers?"

Molly stood up and moved towards him as though to usher him back upstairs to fetch them. Carlos stepped sideways.

"I heard you talking. What's happening?"

"Nothing for you to worry about."

She cast a warning glance at Jeremy.

Ignoring them, Carlos remained where he was, looking from one to the other.

"We might as well tell him." Jeremy sighed. "It'll be all over the village by this evening. It's Quentin. The bloke that was round here last night, the one that I swapped jobs with at Sir Frank's."

"What about him?" Carlos tipped his head to one side, his expression wary.

"He's been attacked," said Jeremy flatly. "Morris found him."

"Why was he attacked? Was he mugged or something?"

Jeremy shrugged.

"I don't know. I expect that the police are looking into it."

"Isn't Quentin Aaron's... I mean Harold's... nephew?"

Jeremy turned back from where he had been filling the kettle.

"What did you just say?"

"Nothing."

Carlos wheeled towards the door but Jeremy was quicker and blocked the way.

"I knew it. Carlos, you know something don't you? You must tell, don't you see that? Things are even more serious than we thought."

Carlos looked towards Molly.

"Jeremy is right, Carlos. If you know something you must say what it is."

"Can I have a hot chocolate?"

Jeremy looked at him. It never ceased to amaze him, that facility that teenagers had for veering off in a completely different direction when the conversation took a turn that didn't suit them. He had first really noticed it at Sir Frank's when a pupil, on being asked why he had just stamped on the foot of the boy next to him, asked, "Sir, do you think that Elvis is really dead?" He didn't know which was more surprising, the fact that the lad had heard of Elvis or the sheer audacity of the diversionary tactic.

"I'll make it." Molly stood up. "In fact, I think I'll make us all one. And Jeremy, you can tell us whatever it is that Morris told you last night."

"Carlos," said Jeremy, determined not to be deflected again. "How did you know that Harold was called Aaron?" Carlos fidgeted with the cord of his dressing gown, wrapping and unwrapping it around his thin fingers. He kept his eyes fixed firmly on the floor. "Carlos, how did you know..."

Carlos interrupted, the dressing gown cord tightening against his palm.

"Teddy told me. Casper found it out."

"I see." Jeremy's voice was grave. "And how exactly did Casper find it out?"

Carlos dropped the dressing gown cord and looked up, his voice pleading.

"He wasn't doing anything wrong, Jeremy. Not really."

Jeremy's heart gave a sudden jolt. That was the first time that Carlos had ever called him anything other than Mr Goodman.

"I think that we'd better all go into the sitting room and sit down comfortably. You too, Aubrey," he added, as Aubrey slipped through the cat flap and joined them. "And Carlos, get some slippers on."

CHAPTER THIRTY-SIX

FROM OUTSIDE, THE sounds of the village stirring into life filtered through. For several moments the three of them listened without speaking to the noise of bottles from the pub crashing into recycling bins, accompanied by doors banging and Jo's cheerful whistling. Aubrey looked from one to the other. He couldn't sit on all their laps, but they all looked as though they could use a bit of comfort. Maudie drifted in through the closed window and settled herself on the rug next to him.

"What are they doing?"

"Having a meeting."

They watched as Jeremy lifted his mug of chocolate and stared at it for a moment before turning to Carlos. He looked, Aubrey thought, worried.

"Carlos, I think that you'd better go first. How did Casper find out that Harold was called Aaron? Was it when he was looking in his office?"

Carlos nodded and dipped his head to his mug.

"He found a secret drawer and there was a passport in it. A passport with Aaron's photograph in it."

"Why didn't you tell the police?"

"We were going to, honestly." Carlos bit his bottom lip. "But Teddy and Casper, they wanted to do some detecting first."

Jeremy was silent for a moment. When he spoke, his tone was flat.

"I see. So what have they detected so far?"

Carlos shrugged.

"Nothing."

"Honestly?"

"Honestly."

Jeremy sat back and looked thoughtful. Even though Carlos had used the word 'honestly', he was inclined to think that he was telling the truth this time. Aubrey watched as he scratched his right eyebrow. If he was going to tell Molly everything that Morris had said last night then he was probably going to have to tell Carlos, too. He could hardly ask him to leave the room now.

"Carlos," Jeremy spoke slowly and leaned forward. "Morris told me some things last night that are quite serious." He paused. "Very serious. But if I tell you then you must promise me not to tell anybody else. Not even Teddy and Casper. Not yet, anyway. It's really important that you don't say anything. There's a danger that some people might get hurt. So not a word. At least, not until we've decided what we're going to do about it. If anything."

"I promise, Jeremy."

Jeremy nodded.

"Ok. Remember Carlos, I'm trusting you with this. Lips absolutely sealed, right?"

Carlos sat up straighter and squared his shoulders. His gaze was direct and his expression suddenly earnest. Aubrey's heart smote him. Carlos was being treated like an adult and he was rising to the occasion as best he knew how. His mother would have been proud of him.

"Last night," continued Jeremy, "when Quentin was here, he told us that Lucinda is Harold's second wife. His first wife, Charlotte, had died. She was murdered," he added.

He hesitated and took a sip of his hot chocolate, his eyes never leaving Carlos's face. He was treading carefully, Aubrey could see. Murder wasn't a word that was used lightly in the Goodman household. Following the death of his mother, murder was a reality that Carlos was only too aware of and it was compounded now by their close proximity to the death of Harold.

Jeremy placed his mug back down on the coffee table and glanced briefly across at Molly before leaning forward, fingers steepled together.

"Quentin told us that Harold's first wife was murdered by a woman called Josie. Harold and his wife used to run a business together and Josie worked for them. Josie developed a sort of fixation, like a crush, on Harold."

He paused. He was wondering, Aubrey could see, if Carlos had any idea what he was talking about. Did teenagers still use the word crush?

"What, you mean like stalking?" asked Carlos. "Following him around and that?"

In spite of the gravity of the discussion, Aubrey tucked his head under his paw and smiled. Carlos had clearly understood what Jeremy was saying and from the incredulous look on his face it was also clear that the concept of anybody being fixated on Harold was almost beyond comprehension. And, to be fair, he did have a point. Even on a good day Harold looked like a cross between a creased and balding mole and the kind of stuffed toy that no child in its right mind would ever choose to play with. Hardly love's young dream. Or anybody else's, for that matter. Although, it had to be said, counting Lucinda, he had managed to attract at least three women so he must have had something going for him.

"Yes, that's right," said Jeremy. "Only more serious than just following him around. According to Quentin she was totally deluded. Quentin worked part-time at Harold and Charlotte's factory when he was at school. He told us that he actually heard Josie threatening Harold that she was going to do something drastic if he didn't leave his wife and go away with her, and he had to give evidence at her trial. But last night, Morris, well, Morris told me a different story." He took a deep breath. "Morris told me that Josie hadn't been deluded at all. He said that it was true, that she and Harold had been having an affair and that Harold had promised her that he would leave his wife."

"Then why did Josie kill Charlotte?" Molly asked. "What was the point?"

"According to Morris, it wasn't Josie that killed Charlotte even though she said that she did." He paused for a moment and then continued. "It was Harold."

CHAPTER THIRTY-SEVEN

AUBREY WATCHED AS Carlos and Molly absorbed what Jeremy had just said. It was Molly who spoke first.

"So what happened? Did Morris tell you?"

Jeremy nodded.

"Josie told him that Harold asked her to come to the house that evening and that Charlotte was already dead when she arrived."

Carlos looked from one to the other.

"I don't get it. Why did she say that she killed her if she didn't?"

"Money," said Jeremy, flatly.

"What, he paid her to say it?"

Jeremy shook his head.

"No. Harold's wife was a wealthy woman. The business that they ran together was built on her money, Quentin told us that. And Harold had expensive tastes."

Molly suddenly sat up.

"Of course. If he was convicted of her murder then he couldn't inherit her money. It's called forfeit or something. I remember some of the trainees talking about it at Donoghue's. It was a question that had come up in some exam."

For a moment the three of them sat in silence.

"I still don't get why this Josie said that she did it." Carlos furrowed his brow, suddenly looking older than his years. "I mean, like, Harold was going to get the money, not her."

"It wasn't about the money. Not for Josie. According to Morris, Harold told Josie that it had been an accident, but said that the police would never believe him. He said that Charlotte had got angry when he told her about Josie and then threatened him with a knife. His story was that he tried to take the knife from her but she fought back and in the general scuffle she got stabbed. He persuaded Josie to take the blame."

"But if it was an accident…" Carlos looked puzzled.

"Harold told Josie that the police wouldn't believe him and that if he was convicted then he couldn't inherit her money and that wouldn't be fair, given that it was an accident."

Carlos stared at Jeremy.

"So she just agreed to it?"

Jeremy shrugged.

"Looks like it. Harold told her that if she said that she did it, but it was an accident, then they might believe her although they wouldn't believe him. He said that he would have to deny their affair or suspicion might fall on him and the prosecution would suspect that they were in it together."

"That's probably true," said Molly. "They're always going to look at who has the most to gain, which in this case is obviously Harold. God, to think that we sat and had dinner with him."

"This Harold geezer, he had it all worked out," said Carlos, frowning.

"I think he did," said Jeremy. "He told Josie that although he was going to deny their affair, she'd have to insist that he did have feelings for her, otherwise there wouldn't have been any reason for her coming to the house that evening."

"So she'd have to pretend to be deluded?" asked Molly.

Jeremy nodded.

"That's right."

"And she still went along with it?"

"Let's face it Moll, if you're standing in a kitchen with your lover and his wife is lying dead on the floor with a knife through her heart, you're probably not thinking that straight."

"No, but afterwards. Surely she must have thought about it afterwards?"

"According to Morris, Harold told Josie that it was the only way. He was a powerful figure, don't forget. He was not only her boss; he and his wife owned the factory. He must have managed to convince her that a jury almost certainly wouldn't convict her but, on the remotest off chance that they did, he would wait for her and, as soon as she was released, they could start a new life together."

"What, she still wanted to be with him, even though he'd just killed his wife?" Carlos looked genuinely shocked. Aubrey sighed. He'd seen some of the games that Carlos played on his computer. Apparently he had no difficulty in wholesale massacre at the click of a mouse, but faced with the reality of human behaviour it was more than he could comprehend.

"She trusted him," said Jeremy. "And she wanted to believe him. By her own admission to Morris, she would have done anything for him. Morris reckons Howard saw her coming."

"What do you mean?" asked Molly.

"Think about it. Morris and Josie were both children who had spent time in care. For Josie, she had been in one institution or another practically since she was a baby—it was all the life she had known. I'm not saying they weren't well looked after in terms of physical needs and so on, the state would see to that, but there was never the same kind of love and affection, the kind of attention, that you might get in a normal family relationship. Morris said that for all their bravado, they were all sitting targets for anyone that came along and made a fuss of them." Jeremy paused and took a mouthful of hot chocolate before continuing, his tone thoughtful. "I mean, you only have to look at some of these dreadful grooming cases to see how that happens. The children start bunking off school and hanging around outside cafes and shopping centres. Then some bloke rolls up in a flash car, gives them a packet of fags and buys them a bag of chips and they think they're in love. As soon as someone pays them some attention, they'll practically eat out of their hand."

Eat out of their hand is about right, thought Aubrey. He thought back to some of the poor pathetic creatures that he had known. Abused and neglected by their owners, still they remained with them. Always going back for more and always pathetically grateful for any scrap of affection, even when it was followed by a kick to the ribs. Although life had been tough for him after Raj died, really he had been one of the lucky ones, although to some extent he had made his own luck. He had been careful. More than once he had been tempted to adopt a new owner, the lure of a comfortable home and regular meals being strong, but at the last minute he had always taken a swerve. The sudden death of Raj had unnerved him. He didn't want to be in that position again. And he hadn't been. Well, not until he was banged up in Sunny Banks rescue centre, and even that hadn't been his fault. He was just in the wrong place at the wrong time. Found before he was lost. But luckily for him it had worked out. He had been chosen by Molly and Jeremy, and better owners a cat never had.

He suddenly remembered Brucie. Poor Brucie. A big affectionate mongrel with soft brown eyes and wayward ears, he had been kicked and beaten and thrown out into the back garden almost every day. He and Vincent had witnessed the heart-rending spectacle of Brucie waiting outside for the back door to open again, shivering on the step in the coldest and wettest of weather. They had often gone to check on him, watching as he grew thinner and more pathetic, the pleading look in his big eyes was difficult to ignore. He never made a sound. When they could, they had taken him food. Scraps stolen from bins and crusts of bread put out for the birds, they had persuaded some of the other cats to do it too. One day Brucie had simply gone. Vanished. They never saw him again. They had tried to persuade each other that Brucie had gone to a new owner. A good owner. But in their heart of hearts they didn't believe it. Not really.

"Jeremy," Carlos spoke slowly, his eyes on the floor, his face suddenly blank and his narrow shoulders tense. "Am I one of them?"

"One of what?"

"One of them kids, like you said. One of them sitting target kids."

Molly jumped up and sat next to him on the sofa.

"Of course not, Carlos." She picked up his thin hand and stroked it. "Your mother loved you very much. She would never have left you if she hadn't been… well, she would never have left you."

"Josie and Morris were very different to you." Jeremy's voice was gentle. "They didn't have parents who loved them."

Carlos looked up from the floor.

"My dad didn't love me."

"Well, we don't know that." Jeremy paused. Aubrey could see that he was choosing his words. "Alcohol gets a grip on some people and makes them behave differently. It's an illness. But your mother—your mother did love you. Very much. And she would be very proud of you now."

Carlos smiled suddenly; his shoulders relaxed. He picked up his mug again and took a huge gulp, leaving a smudge of chocolate across his top lip.

"I still don't really get why this Josie said she did it though." He frowned. "I mean, why did she take the blame?"

"She loved him," said Jeremy, simply.

Both Molly and Jeremy watched as Carlos absorbed what Jeremy had just said. Before the advent of Teddy in his life, these would have been just words. Now they had meaning. He would, he knew, do anything for Teddy. If she'd asked him to abseil down the Post Office tower with a mug of tea balanced on his head, he wouldn't hesitate for a second. Even though he was afraid of heights.

"But," Carlos paused slightly as his thoughts shifted reluctantly away from Teddy and back to Josie. "Wouldn't there have been, like, DNA evidence and that?"

"My guess is that Harold persuaded Josie to hold the knife. Something like that, anyway. At the trial, Harold said that he had taken the knife away from her and that was how it had his fingerprints on it. But in any event, all this happened at his house. There was no reason why the knife, or anything else in his home, shouldn't have his fingerprints or DNA on it."

Carlos nodded and took another gulp of his hot chocolate.

"So what happened? How come he married Lucinda?"

"Quentin told us that Harold sold the business and moved away. Eventually, he came here, to this village. I think that he never intended to wait for Josie. He'd got what he wanted. He had the money as well as the freedom to do what he liked. And then he met Lucinda. Who also had money. I suspect that Harold was a very greedy man."

"So he got lucky?" asked Carlos.

"Well, not that lucky. He *is* dead," pointed out Molly.

"Do you think that this Josie woman killed him?" Carlos leaned forward. "You know, like found out where he was living and came after him, for revenge and that when he let her down?"

Jeremy shrugged.

"I suppose it's possible. We know that she's been in the village."

"What about the evidence that Quentin gave at the trial?" asked Molly. "He actually overheard Josie making threats, he told us."

"He didn't overhear anything." Jeremy looked grim. "According to Morris, Harold paid him to say it, although obviously he didn't tell Josie that. It was to make his story seem more genuine. I mean, look about you." He waved his arm around. "All this lot must have come from somewhere. But," he added, "What we don't know is, if this story of Morris's is true."

"Why would Morris lie?" asked Molly.

"It might not be Morris who is lying," said Jeremy.

All four of them jumped as the strident ringing of the landline burst out into the room. For a moment none of them moved and then the answerphone kicked in. Lucinda's voice, small and anxious, filtered across the room.

CHAPTER THIRTY-EIGHT

FOUR SETS OF eyes fixed on Carlos. The cosy, intimate atmosphere in which they had been sitting had suddenly evaporated, leaving a distinct chill in its wake.

"Well?" said Jeremy. His tone was sharp, a note of irritation ticking just below the surface. "You heard what Lucinda said. Where are they? And don't say you don't know."

For a moment Carlos sat perfectly still, his body frozen into immobility. He licked his lips and swallowed. He looked from Jeremy to Molly and back again. Aubrey inched slightly closer to him, followed by Maudie. This was an aspect of Jeremy that they hadn't seen before.

"They didn't want to be sent home." Carlos shrank into himself, as though to distance himself from the scene. His voice was low and miserable. "They said that once their parents knew what had happened to Harold, they would have to leave and go to another school and they wanted to stay here. They didn't just go." His eyes were pleading. "They did leave a note."

"Where are they?" Jeremy repeated, his voice angry now, his eyes hard.

"Camping in the spinney."

"What?"

"Camping in the spinney," repeated Carlos. He looked away, unable to meet Jeremy's eye.

"Right." Jeremy stood up. "We can talk about the whys and wherefores later. Let's go and get them. Carlos, get some clothes on. And Carlos," he said, as Carlos rose to go upstairs, "don't even think about calling or texting them. Molly, as soon as I know if they're safe, I'll ring you and then you can let Lucinda know."

AUBREY RAN THROUGH the back gardens, racing across the lawns, and up the lane to the spinney. It was much quicker this way although obviously Jeremy and Carlos couldn't go tramping across everyone's flowerbeds. Above him flew Maudie, the ruffles on her petticoat catching on the breeze. His pace slowed as they approached the small copse of trees. From nearby he could hear Teddy's voice. Moving slowly he made his way forward. In the clearing stood a two-man tent and next to it a small folding table. As he watched, Casper emerged blinking, fully-clothed, his hands pushing back the tent flaps. Behind him came Teddy, her hair tousled and her T-shirt rumpled. Creeping behind the nearest bush he settled down to watch them. Maudie flew upwards and caught the branch of a tree, hanging suspended by one hand before dropping down again to join him.

"What did we do with the matches?"

Teddy dropped the rucksack that she had been rummaging in and looked around her as she spoke, the morning sunlight catching on the coloured glass beads of the necklace threaded around her neck.

Casper shrugged.

"You had them last."

"No I didn't. You did. You were lighting the candles."

Casper yawned and felt in his pockets.

"Here." He thrust a small box towards her.

"Oh, Casper. You've slept on them. They're all squashed."

A tiny sound, like the cracking of a twig, rustled the air. Turning his head, Aubrey watched as Edyth wriggled out from under a pile of leaves. Close behind her came Gnasher and Jethro.

"Morning Aubrey," said Jethro. "Morning Maudie."

"What are you lot doing here?" asked Aubrey.

"Just been checking the bus stop and then we came on over here," explained Edyth. "Just to make sure that they're okay." She nodded towards where Teddy and Casper were now trying, with notable lack of success, to light a fire. "Dino spotted them last night. He saw the light from the candles."

"Anything to report on the bus stop?" asked Maudie.

Edyth shook her head.

"No. That half-wit nephew of Bradley's got off the bus, but that was about it."

Maudie paused in the plaiting together of blades of grass and looked up.

"Was he carrying anything?"

"Only his usual back pack type thing. He…" she stopped and turned her head at the sound of people approaching. Striding forward, came Jeremy. Following behind, and panting slightly, came Carlos. Teddy dropped the matches.

"Oh, Carlos." The reproach in her tone was unmistakeable.

"Sorry." He spread his hands palm up in front of him, his expression one of tragic devastation. "I had to. I didn't have a choice. When Lucinda found you were missing she rang the police. I had to tell them."

Jeremy strode towards them and waved his hand towards the tent.

"Ok, get this lot packed up. And don't argue," he added, as Casper opened his mouth to speak.

From behind a bush, the cats watched in silence as Teddy and Casper gathered together their belongings and pushed them into a large plastic bin bag.

Keeping one eye on Teddy and Casper, Jeremy pulled his phone from his pocket.

"Moll, it's ok. They're fine. Can you let Lucinda know?" He paused as he listened to Molly's response. "Yes, I'll bring them straight back to the cottage."

He slid his thumb over the screen and ended the call. His expression was grim as he looked at each of the teenagers in turn.

"Did it not occur to any of you that Lucinda might be out of her mind with worry? Don't you think that she's had enough to put up with? And there is such a thing as wasting police time. Like they haven't got anything better to do than chase around after a couple of thoughtless kids. In case you hadn't noticed, there's been a murder in the village and somebody else was attacked last night."

"We're sorry, Mr Goodman." Teddy looked directly at him. "Really." She did sound genuinely contrite. "We were only going to stay away for a couple of nights."

"And we did leave a note," said Casper. "We told Lucinda not to worry."

"Oh well, that's all right then." Jeremy's voice was heavy with sarcasm. "Come on, get a move on. And you Carlos," he turned to where Carlos stood helplessly watching them. "Don't think that you're off the hook. That tent looks very familiar."

THE POLICE WOMAN flipped shut her notebook.

"Right, well, as long as you're both safe and sound. I don't suppose that there's any real harm done." She reached down and stroked Aubrey, who had parked himself next to her so as not to miss anything. On the window sill, Maudie tried to balance on one leg.

Lucinda suddenly exhaled heavily and closed her eyes, pressing her hands briefly together. She opened her eyes again and looked directly at Teddy and Casper. Her gaze lingered for a moment longer on Teddy and then flickered away.

"It was really very naughty of you both." Her blue eyes looked large and tear-shaped. "Very naughty indeed. I would have thought that the two of you would have had more sense. What on earth were you thinking? Anything could have happened to you out there. Anything." She shuddered slightly. "What would I have said to your parents? They trusted you to my care."

"We're sorry, Lucinda," said Teddy. Casper remained silent. Teddy nudged him with her elbow.

"Sorry, Lucinda," murmured Casper. He didn't, thought Aubrey, look very sorry.

"And of course, I shall have to let your parents know," she continued.

"Can't we…" began Teddy.

"No," said Jeremy. "You cannot. Lucinda has enough to contend with. If Lucinda agrees," he looked across at her, "you will both stay here tonight, where Molly and I can keep an eye on you. Casper, you can bunk in with Carlos. I'll make up a bed on the floor. Teddy, you can sleep in the spare room. We'll get your things and arrange for your parents to collect you as soon as possible."

"Right, well I'll be off now," said the police woman, stuffing her notebook back into her pocket and moving towards the back door. She stopped suddenly and stared at Teddy's neck.

"That necklace." She moved forward and peered more closely at it, her brow crinkling. "Where did you get it?"

Teddy reached up and touched her throat, her small fingers running across the coloured glass and stopping at the small ruby coloured heart-shaped pendant suspended in the middle.

"I found it."

"Where did you find it?" The police woman's tone was sharp.

Teddy looked across at Carlos and then at Casper, her expression confused.

"In the place where we were storing things for our…" she hesitated, searching for the right words, and then continued brightly, "For our camping trip."

You had to hand it to her, thought Aubrey, she made it sound like a jolly little holiday. The girl definitely had a future, although as what he didn't know. The police woman looked thoughtful.

"Right. And where was this place that you were storing things?"

"The ladybird house."

"The what?"

"The ladybird house," repeated Teddy.

CHAPTER THIRTY-NINE

FOR A MOMENT nobody spoke. Pausing in her balancing act, Maudie toppled over and fell into the sink. The sound of the big antique clock tick-tocked its way into the silence.

"I didn't steal it. It was just there and I put it on." Teddy suddenly burst out, her face flushed and the words tumbling before her. She turned to Lucinda. "I didn't steal it, honestly Lucinda. I just borrowed it. I was going to put it back. I didn't think that you'd mind."

Lucinda stared wordlessly back at her; her expression blank. The police woman moved forward and touched Teddy's arm.

"Was there anything else in this ladybird house?" she asked Teddy.

Teddy nodded and looked over at Casper.

"Show her, Casp."

Reluctantly, Casper thrust his hand into the pocket of his jeans and drew out a small silver penknife scratched with the initial L. He held it forward on the palm of his hand.

Lucinda rose suddenly, wrapping her long silky scarf more tightly around her as she looked around her for her handbag.

"I think, if you don't need me for anything else, I must go home. I've got the most dreadful headache. I really do need to lie down for a while."

"Of course," said Molly. "Do you want me to run you back?"

Lucinda turned to Molly and nodded.

"Yes, please Molly. That's very kind of you."

"I'll get my car keys. And I can collect some of Teddy and Casper's things while I'm there."

The police woman moved forward, partially blocking her way.

"Not yet, Mrs Goodman." She turned to Jeremy. "I think, if you don't mind, we would prefer it if you all remained here for the present. Just for a short time."

Without waiting for a response, she stepped into the garden and closed the back door behind her. The little group remained in tense silence as the buzzing sound of her voice speaking into her radio filtered through. They all looked up as she re-entered the room.

"One of my colleagues will be here shortly." She smiled a tight smile that stretched her mouth but didn't reach her eyes. "There are a couple of things that we need to ask you about. Just a few questions, that's all."

Casper rushed forward, his voice trembling.

"We didn't steal them. Honestly. We were just borrowing them; we were going to put them back." He turned to Jeremy; his cheeks flushed. "Tell them, Mr Goodman. We didn't steal them," he repeated.

"It's true." Carlos instinctively reached for Teddy's arm and gripped it hard, his eyes shining. "They would never steal anything. They're not like that."

Teddy, her bottom lip wobbling slightly, clasped her small hands together. "Tell them, Mr Goodman. Please."

"I'll make some coffee," said Molly.

THE TWO POLICE officers stood facing the little group in front of them. On the work surface behind them sat a plastic folder that the second officer had brought with him. He turned towards Lucinda who stood between Molly and Jeremy.

"Could you tell us, Mrs Fairchild, exactly what this ladybird house is?"

"Well, I don't know really." She gave a slight shrug of her shoulders and fiddled for a moment with a lock of her hair, twirling it between her fingers as she thought. "It's like a little wooden structure. A sort of shelter for animals. Small creatures, not lions and tigers," she added, with a light laugh.

The policeman nodded; his face remained serious.

"Do you know when it was built? Did you build it yourself?"

"It's been there for years." Lucinda thought for a moment. "I think that my uncle built it."

Beneath the table Aubrey and Maudie sat huddled together, Maudie with her knees drawn up under her chin, one arm draped around Aubrey's neck. They looked at each other.

"She's lying," said Maudie.

"What?"

"She's lying. She built the ladybird house. I watched her doing it. She made it from some old wood that was lying around and then she painted it. I was surprised. I thought she only did the fairy prancing stuff. I didn't know that she could build things."

"Why would she lie about it?"

Maudie shrugged.

"I don't know. Maybe she's scared or something." She tipped her head to one side and studied Lucinda more closely.

The police officer wrote something down in his notebook and looked across at Teddy and Casper.

"Can you tell us exactly how you came to find the necklace and the penknife? It's ok," he added and raised a hand slightly, as Casper's eyes shot suddenly towards the back door. "You're not in any trouble. We just need to know, that's all."

"We were looking for somewhere to store things, somewhere away from the Academy." Casper spoke slowly, his expression wary. "Matches and candles and tins of beans and stuff. Then we thought of the ladybird house."

"And the necklace and the penknife were in there?"

Casper nodded.

"What, just lying in there?"

"Sort of. They were in a little bag. We found it when we put our stuff in. We just looked inside the bag and there was this plastic bag and they were in there."

"What sort of bag was it?"

Casper thought for a moment.

"Like a kind of shoe bag?"

"What did you do with it?"

Casper shrugged and looked across at Teddy.

"I think it's still in there," she said. "I think that we just put it back. I don't really remember. We haven't got it now, anyway," she added.

"Could you tell us," said Jeremy, "what on earth this is all about? Why are you so interested in the ladybird house?"

He looked from one officer to the other. The female officer spoke first. She reached behind her and pulled forward the plastic folder. She held it gently in one hand as though weighing it, and then reached inside and drew out a set of coloured images.

"These pictures," she hesitated and looked at her colleague as though seeking confirmation before continuing. He nodded, almost imperceptibly. She cleared her throat and started again. "These pictures are connected with an old case. You may have heard of it. It was before I joined the force but it was in all the papers at the time. It concerned the murder of a young girl over in the spinney. The victim was fifteen years old. She was called Lisa Towner. The case was never solved. To this day, we still don't know who was responsible."

"She was horrible," said Maudie, turning to Aubrey. "She had one of those pinched in little faces and she used to bully the younger children and make them cry. And she was always making fun of people. Pretending to be their friend and then laughing at them."

Aubrey nodded. She sounded a bit like Oswald. The smallest cat in Sunny Banks, but definitely the nastiest. They'd all been grateful when he got picked. Their only fear had been that he might be returned once his new owners discovered his true nature.

The second officer took up the tale.

"When Harold Fairchild was murdered," he glanced apologetically at Lucinda, who bit her bottom lip and looked down at the floor. Molly threw her a worried glance and moved slightly closer. The officer continued. "We thought back to the previous murder. There have only been two murders in this village and, while we didn't think that they were connected, it made sense to have a quick look at the first case." He paused and took a breath. "That incudes going over the evidence. These pictures," he pointed to the top one and tensed his shoulders. "These pictures, show images of Lisa Towner and the boy who lived next door to her, William Garner. They grew up together, went to the same schools, and were often seen around together. They were pretty much like brother and sister. For a long time, William was the main suspect."

Everybody moved forward and stared at the sheet that the police officer was holding up. The image showed a young girl dressed in jeans and a cotton checked shirt, sleeves rolled up, smirking into the camera. Next to her stood a boy, slightly taller, side on, hands stuffed in his pockets, head tilted slightly backwards towards the sun. Standing under a garden tree, both looked as though they hadn't a care in the world.

"Lisa was strangled with some sort of ligature, fabric, but we never found out exactly what." The police officer waited a few seconds and then pointed his forefinger at the girl's neck. "You can see in this photograph that Lisa is wearing a necklace. It appears to be identical to the one that you are wearing." He looked directly at Teddy. "The necklace was unique. She made it herself from a jewellery kit that she had been given for her birthday. She was wearing it the afternoon she disappeared. The day that this photograph was taken. The last time that her parents saw her," he added.

CHAPTER FORTY

"BUT SURELY, ANYBODY could have put those things in there," said Molly. "Everybody knew about Lucinda's ladybird house. Even we knew and we've only been in the village five minutes."

Molly and Jeremy, sitting on the high-backed chairs, with elbows propped up on the breakfast bar and backs resting awkwardly against the stiff black leather, looked at each other. The cottage seemed very quiet now that the police officers had gone, followed shortly afterwards by Lucinda. Refusing Molly's renewed offer to drive her, she had decided to walk back. She needed, she said, to get some fresh air. By tacit consent, Carlos, Teddy and Casper had slipped up to Carlos's bedroom, followed by Aubrey and Maudie. For once, there was no sound of music pulsating through the ceiling.

"True." Jeremy looked thoughtful. "But she lied about building the ladybird house. Jo told me himself that she had built it. Why would she say that she didn't?"

"Oh, I don't know," Molly cried. She dropped her head in her hands. "Perhaps she was getting confused. Jeremy, I'm beginning to regret ever coming to this damned village."

Jeremy reached across and touched her gently on the arm.

"Sorry, Moll."

Molly sighed and raised her head again. She smiled slightly and rested her hand on top of Jeremy's.

"Don't be silly. It's not your fault. You didn't exactly have to twist my arm, it's what we both wanted." She looked around her, her eye running up to the big clock and back again to the expensive work surfaces. "When we first came here, I thought that all these things were amazing. I was actually a bit apologetic about Quentin having to swap all of this for our kitchen. Now, well, none of it seems quite so desirable anymore."

They both fell silent for a moment and then Molly said, "Talking of Quentin, it's odd, don't you think, that the police didn't say anything about him? I mean, they mentioned Harold but they didn't say anything about the attack last night. They must know that Quentin is Harold's nephew. Come to think of it, Lucinda didn't say anything either. I wonder how he is," she added. "I feel a bit guilty, given that we were the last people to see him. We ought to have at least phoned the hospital."

"I'll do it in a while," said Jeremy. "I don't feel like it right now."

They both turned at the sound of a tap on the back door.

"Can I come in?"

"Of course." Jeremy jumped up and pulled out one of the leather chairs. "I'll get the kettle on."

"I saw the squad car go past when I was in Bradley's," said Morris. "What did they want? Was it about Quentin?"

FROM THE TOP of the chest of drawers, Aubrey and Maudie watched with interest as Carlos, Teddy and Casper scrolled through their phones. On the bed sat Carlos and Teddy. Cross-legged on the floor, with his back jammed up against the radiator, sat Casper.

"Do you want this one?" said Carlos, holding up an image of Casper standing on his hands, his hair flopping forward over his face. Teddy nodded.

"Yes, I like that one. Makes you look almost normal, Casp."

Carlos continued flicking through his photos and then placed his phone down on the duvet. He looked thoughtful.

"That's strange."

"What is?" asked Teddy.

Carlos turned to face her.

"I was just looking at the pictures I took that day at the fete. The day that Harold got... well, you know, that day."

"What about them?" Casper asked.

"When we got home, afterwards, we were talking about what..." he swallowed. "About what happened and stuff, and what the police asked and, like, what we all said. I was a bit worried because of, like, my mum." He bit his bottom lip, his eyes fixed downward and his fingers plucking at the fabric of the duvet. "I was worried that the police might be more interested in me because of, you know, because of what happened to my mum and that."

He hesitated and glanced up at Teddy. She smiled at him; a great beam of a smile. It was, thought Aubrey, almost worthy of a cat. In fact, now he thought about it, there was something very cat-like about Teddy. It was something to do with the small, tidy neatness of her. He wouldn't be at all surprised if she had the proverbial nine lives.

"It's all right, Carlos. Casper knows about your mum. I thought that you wouldn't mind me telling him."

Carlos nodded and smiled back at her. Clearly, thought Aubrey, he was relieved that he wouldn't have to go through the whole story.

"Well," Carlos continued, "later that evening I was thinking about it again and sort of running it all through in my head. I was thinking about what happened and where everybody was when Harold collapsed in front of the band but it was all a bit blurred so I asked Molly. She said that most people were standing around listening to the music. So I asked her who was there and she said she wasn't completely sure but she was fairly certain that Bradley and Lucinda were, and some other people whose names I didn't know."

"And?" Casper looked up expectantly.

"I've just looked at the pictures again. You can just see Harold approaching the band; he's kind of clutching at his chest so it must have been just before he collapsed. And there's Bradley, standing on the edge. But she's not there."

"Who isn't?"

"Lucinda. She's not there."

"So?"

"But she was around earlier, I saw her. But she wasn't watching the band with everyone else."

He picked up his phone and turned it to show Casper and Teddy. The picture showed a group of people standing around the band, several of them holding drinks in their hand. Carlos bent his head and checked the date and time. "It was definitely taken just before Harold collapsed."

"Here, let's have a look."

Carlos passed the phone to Casper who held it up close to his face.

"That could be her," he said, pointing to the back of a head with long hair pinned into a glittery little clip.

"No." Carlos shook his head. "That's not her. Lucinda was wearing a bright yellow dress that day. I remembered it because it was my mum's favourite colour. I remember thinking that she would have loved it."

"She was probably in the beer tent," said Casper, passing the phone back to Carlos. "That raspberry cordial stuff she makes, that stuff she says is her herbal vitamin tonic," he turned to Teddy. "It's got vodka in it. I saw her pouring it in one afternoon when we were supposed to be in our rooms doing that meditation shit. It's just a way of getting rid of us for an hour," he added.

"Our parents drink vodka, too. And so do you, sometimes," said Teddy. "It's not a crime. At least," she added, "it is in your case."

"Yeah, but our parents don't go about pretending it's some health tonic. Neither do I," he added, his virtuous tone unmistakeable.

Teddy smiled.

"True. Are there any other photographs?" she asked, turning back to Carlos.

"Only of the animals and that, and a couple I took of the views from the paddock. I was thinking about my art project for school."

Teddy leaned across and peered down at the screen.

"Carlos, scroll back a bit."

Carlos obediently scrolled back.

"Stop there," Teddy said. "What's that?"

Carlos and Teddy peered down at the screen. One of the view shots showed a clear patch of bright yellow by the wall to Morris's garden.

CHAPTER FORTY-ONE

THE BRANCHES OF the trees threw a tracery of dappled shadow as the three teenagers ran lightly across the grass. Behind them stood the old garden wall of the Academy, the grey green of the lichen soft in the morning sunlight.

"What if the cloak cupboard window isn't open?"

Carlos looked anxiously across at Teddy. From his vantage point of the top of the oak rain barrel where he was sitting with Maudie, Aubrey could see that he was secretly hoping that it wouldn't be. Carlos was already in bad odour with Jeremy over the camping business. Being discovered breaking into the Academy was hardly going to improve matters. Especially as the three of them had told Jeremy that they were just going for a walk up to the memorial garden. If he discovered where they really were there would be hell to pay.

"It's always open," said Teddy. "The catch is broken. You just have to wiggle it around a bit."

"The pantry window's broken too, the frame's rotten and the bottom pane fell out years ago," said Maudie. "Harold kept saying that he was going to get it mended but he never did."

Together they waited until the teenagers were out of view and then slipped round the side of the house and in through the pantry.

Inside, the Academy was quiet. Usually echoing with the sounds of children and running feet, now the atmosphere felt as hushed and guarded as a secret. From the kitchen came the sound of Zofia singing, a light melodic tune that had been popular two or three years back. With one eye on her broad back, Aubrey and Maudie crept across the kitchen and out into the hallway. They watched from the shadow of the kitchen door as Casper, Carlos and Teddy tiptoed across the wooden floor. Outside Harold's study, Casper turned and put his finger over his lips. All three of them listened for a moment. The door stood slightly ajar. Pressing gently on it with the flat of his hand, Casper pushed it open.

"What are we looking for?" Carlos whispered, as he followed him in.

"Clues," said Casper.

Maudie looked at Aubrey and raised her eyebrows. She was, he could see, getting bored. Any minute now there was a danger that she'd flit away and then who knew when he would next see her. Sometimes she didn't turn up again for ages. He regarded her affectionately for a moment. He liked having her around. She was someone to talk to when it was raining and she was good company. He would miss her when they returned to the old house. He toyed briefly with the idea of persuading her to go back with them. Was that possible? Could ghosts travel or were they fixed where they were?

"Clues to what?" asked Carlos and then stiffened at the sound of footsteps on the parquet floor.

"Quick," hissed Teddy. "Behind here."

Without waiting for an answer she dived behind the large chesterfield sofa that stood along one wall. Squashed in next to her, knees drawn up to their chins, Carlos and Casper held their breath.

"What ..." Carlos began.

"Shh."

Teddy laid a hand on Carlos's arm as the door to Harold's study opened again and Lucinda came in, followed by Aubrey and Maudie. Catching sight of Aubrey as he slipped beneath the big wing-backed chair, Carlos opened his mouth to speak and then closed it again. Silently the three teenagers peered round the end of the sofa and watched as Lucinda settled herself at the large oak desk and began opening and closing drawers. The unmistakeable scent of the sweet floral perfume that she always wore wafted across to them. For several minutes there was the sound only of papers rustling and then Lucinda pulled out a small burgundy coloured booklet, tapping it lightly on the desk top before reaching across and picking up the house phone.

"Zofia, can you come to Harold's study please?"

IN THE MEMORIAL garden Casper strode around on the small patch of grass, hands in pockets and head bent in concentration. On the seat in the shelter Teddy and Carlos sat side by side watching him. Draped across the top of the shelter lay Aubrey. Maudie had drifted off again.

Teddy turned to Carlos.

"Did you think that Lucinda seemed strange this morning?" Carlos nodded.

"She was definitely weird. I mean, she was a bit tight on Zofia." He shuffled his feet slightly. Seeing an adult cry had made him uncomfortable. His mother had never cried, not even when somebody had stolen her purse with her week's wages in it and they'd lived off baked beans on toast and tinned soup for a week. True, she had threatened to hunt the culprit down and beat him to a pulp, but she hadn't cried.

"I know. I felt really sorry for Zofia," Teddy agreed. "She was always nice to us. Do you remember, Casp, that time she found us mucking about in the laundry room when we were supposed to be doing Elf Diaries?"

"Health Diaries?" queried Carlos.

"No. Elf Diaries. We were supposed to go into the garden and find an elf and then write its diary."

"Right." Carlos nodded, slightly non-plussed. Lucinda was even more bonkers that he'd thought.

"We did it for a bit, like, you know, pretending to find an elf and then writing about what it had for dinner last night, then Casper said that he was going to tell Lucinda that we found an elf but he accidentally trod on it so I thought we'd better go in. We were playing games on our iPads in the laundry room. We always used to go in there," she added. "It's warm and you can sort of sit around on the bags of washing." From the top of the shelter, Aubrey smiled. He was right about Teddy. She was definitely part cat.

"Isn't it warm in your rooms?" asked Carlos.

"We don't have heating on in our rooms. Harold said it was because central heating encourages germs or something. He was just too tight to switch it on. Anyway, that day Zofia came in and we thought we'd get told off but she just laughed and gave us some cake."

"Did you think that Lucinda looked different as well?" asked Casper, looking up. "I mean, different to how she usually looks?"

Teddy considered for a moment.

"Sort of. Usually she's all kind of rosy and smiley but this morning she looked, I don't know, sort of hard-faced. Like that maths teacher at our last school, do you remember Casp? The one that you said had a face like a bag of chisels."

Casper nodded.

"She looked older, too."

"How old do you think she is?" asked Teddy.

Casper shrugged.

"Don't know. Younger than Harold. Why do you think that she was sacking Zofia?"

"Maybe she needs to save money. What with Harold being gone and that," suggested Carlos.

"Perhaps she's going to sell the Academy," suggested Teddy. "But I don't see why she had to sack Zofia."

"It's not like she pays her much," said Casper.

"How do you know that?" Teddy frowned and then raised her hand, palm outward. "No, don't tell me, I don't think that I want to know. Casp, you've got to stop snooping. It'll get you into trouble."

"It's not snooping. It's detecting."

"Well stop it. At least until all this is over."

"That thing she had in her hand," said Carlos. "It was a passport, wasn't it?"

"Looked like it," agreed Casper.

"Do you think she's going away somewhere? Like, abroad?" Casper shrugged.

"Maybe."

All three of them turned at the sound of voices.

"Good. You're here." Jeremy gave a smile of grim satisfaction. Next to him Morris smiled at them.

"Of course we are, Mr Goodman." Teddy's tone was injured. "We said that we would be."

Jeremy looked from one to the other, clearly suspicious. As well he might be, thought Aubrey. Ten minutes earlier and he would have found neither sight nor sound of them. But Jeremy, he thought, was savvier than Teddy gave him credit for. There was no point in him phoning any of them, they could be anywhere, so he'd come down to check that they were where they said they'd be.

"Morris and myself are going up to the Academy to get some things for you." He indicated the empty holdall that he'd dropped by his feet. "Just overnight things and a change of clothes for tomorrow. We can pick up the rest of your stuff another time. Is there anything in particular that you want? Any books or anything? We'll ask Lucinda to get it from your rooms. And when you've finished here," he added, "I want you straight back home."

"Can we…" began Teddy.

"No," said Jeremy.

CHAPTER FORTY-TWO

ZOFIA PULLED OPEN the heavy oak door, her eyes clearly reddened from crying. She wiped her hands on her big cotton apron and looked up at them through damp lashes. The ready smile that she usually wore was nowhere to be seen.

"Mrs Fairchild? She is in Mr Fairchild's study."

She waved them along the hall and then, turning away, moved back towards the kitchen, her shoulders slumped. Jeremy and Morris began walking towards Harold's study and then stopped as the sound of Lucinda's voice filtered through the slightly open door.

"I don't give a fiddler's fuck how old you are. I've just told you; I don't need a gardener anymore. It's not like you do anything useful anyway. When was the last time you mowed the far lawn?"

Lucinda's voice had a hard, jagged edge to it. Jeremy and Morris looked at each other, aghast. It was definitely Lucinda talking, but not a Lucinda that they recognised.

"The mower isn't working properly. There's something wrong with the motor. I told Mr Fairchild weeks ago."

The voice was truculent, slightly defiant.

"A bad workman, George, always blames his tools. If you knew it wasn't working, why didn't you take it to get it fixed?"

There was a silence and then the man spoke again. The tone was placatory this time, almost pleading.

"Mrs Fairchild, you know that I haven't been well. And your uncle always promised me..."

The pleading note trailed away.

"In case you hadn't noticed George, uncle Charles is dead and has been for some time. And I don't care what he promised you. I've made my decision and there's an end to it."

"But…"

"George," Lucinda's voice dropped to a growl. "You are seriously starting to get on my nerves. Now just get your things and get out. I've told you I'll pay you for the week. If you hang around much longer I might change my mind."

The study door opened wide and an elderly man shuffled past them, his eyes on the floor. Jeremy hesitated and then, raising his hand, knocked tentatively on the door with his knuckles. Lucinda looked up from the desk and narrowed her eyes.

"Jeremy." She smiled suddenly, her voice now the familiar soft tone that they were accustomed to. "And Morris as well. Come on in. How lovely to see you both. What can I do for you?"

Jeremy shot a warning glance at Morris.

"We've come to pick some things up for Teddy and Casper. Their night clothes and something fresh to wear tomorrow." He indicated the large holdall he carried in his right hand. "Also, I wondered if you would like me to contact their parents and explain what's happened. Perhaps start making arrangements for them to return home. They're welcome to remain with us in the meantime. You must have so much to do. It would be one less thing for you to think about."

"That really is very kind of you, Jeremy. Yes, you're right. There is an awful lot to do." Sighing, she passed a hand over her face and then stood up. "I'll pop up to their rooms and get some things together. Shan't keep you waiting."

Jeremy and Morris stood in silence as she left the room. Morris turned to Jeremy.

"Blimey."

Jeremy nodded; his face worried.

"If I hadn't heard that little exchange with my own ears, I wouldn't have believed it."

"Why do you think she's letting staff go? I would have thought that she'd need more help at the moment, not less."

Jeremy shrugged.

"I have no idea."

THE PUB WAS quiet, the lunchtime drinkers had not yet arrived and a gentle hush lay over the room. Unlike the Academy, Jeremy reflected as he dropped the holdall under the seat by the window. At the Academy it had felt close, stultifying, almost threatening, like the air before a thunderstorm. He headed for the bar, relieved that Malcolm Dryden wasn't in yet. He could really do without that booming voice of his bouncing off the walls. He needed some peace and quiet in which to think. Lucinda's behaviour had been disturbing to say the least. Perhaps, he reflected, it was the stress of losing Harold. People did behave in peculiar ways when they were bereaved. Although why that should manifest itself in the brutal sacking of staff he had no idea.

He and Morris had waited in silence for her to return and, true to her word, she had been back downstairs with some garments for Teddy and Casper within moments. She had thrust the clothes towards them and then, obviously keen to see the back of them, almost pushed them towards the front door in her haste to get rid of them. On the way back, by unspoken agreement and with a mutual need to gulp in some fresh air, they had taken the longer route into the village, out past the spinney and down the old farm track, each with their own thoughts, but hardly exchanging a word.

Morris followed Jeremy to the bar, his hand already reaching into his pocket. Behind the bar, Jo finished his phone call and strolled towards them.

"Same as usual?"

The two men nodded and watched as Jo poured their pints. He pushed them across the bar and then leaned confidentially towards them. Glancing from right to left, he leaned on one elbow.

"Just had my cousin Terry on the phone. The one that works for the police."

Jeremy sipped at his pint and leaned in closer.

"Quentin Fairchild has regained consciousness," Jo continued.

"And?" Morris paused mid-sip and stared at Jo. "Does he remember what happened?"

Jo nodded.

"Most of it. He was walking up the lane, past your place," he nodded at Morris. "And he heard someone behind him. He started to turn round and just had time to see a face and then the next thing he knew he was in hospital."

"Who was it?" asked Jeremy.

Jo stood back and let out a great breath.

"He's trying to remember."

Morris opened his mouth to speak and then closed it again as the pub door opened and Carlos came in. He walked over to them.

"Jeremy, do you know how long Molly's going to be? Only I said that I would do lunch for us all. I tried ringing her but she's not answering."

"What do you mean? She's at the cottage, isn't she?"

Carlos shook his head.

"No, Lucinda rang and said that she wanted to talk to her about something so she drove up there. She said that she wouldn't be long but she's been gone ages."

CHAPTER FORTY-THREE

AUBREY SLIPPED THROUGH the pantry window for the second time that day. For once Zofia wasn't in the kitchen and he ran openly across the kitchen floor towards the sitting room where Lucinda and Molly sat side by side on the sofa. Nudging his way around the door he walked across to them.

"Aubrey!" Molly sounded astonished. "What on earth are you doing here?"

"Oh, it's your dear ickle pussy cat. He's come visiting." Lucinda moved across to stroke him as Molly leaned down to scoop him up.

"I'm so sorry, Lucinda. I'll put him out. If he found his way here, he can find his way back."

Dodging beneath Lucinda's outstretched arm, Aubrey jumped on to Molly's lap and settled himself firmly in place. Whatever else happened, he wasn't moving. He looked up into her innocent face. As soon as he'd heard that it was Lucinda on the phone his every instinct had been on high alert. The little incident that he'd witnessed with Zofia that morning had shown an entirely different side to Lucinda, and not one that he liked. He hoped that he was wrong, but he wasn't taking any chances. Pausing only to give instructions to Maudie, he had hot-pawed it up to the Academy, running all the way.

"Are you ok, Lucinda?" Molly spoke gently, her voice soft.

Lucinda reached down into her large handbag and drew out a packet of tissues. She dabbed lightly at her dry eyes.

"I think so." Her voice held a slight tremble. "It was so good of Jeremy to come and collect the children's things."

"He's glad to help. We both are," she added. "Did he get everything that they wanted?"

Lucinda's eyes narrowed slightly.

"So you haven't spoken to him yet?"

"No, why? He said that he might go for a pint with Morris afterwards so I expect that they're in the pub."

"Right." Lucinda looked at Molly, her expression thoughtful. The same sort of look, thought Aubrey, as a cat assessing a hamster cage. "The thing is Molly; I've decided to go away for a while."

"You know Lucinda, I think that's probably a good idea. It must be very lonely for you up here without Harold and it would do you good to have a break from everything." Molly patted her lightly on the arm. "But what about, well, you know, the arrangements?"

"Arrangements?"

"Harold's funeral? I mean, if there's anything that we can do…"

"Oh." She looked, thought Aubrey, as though the thought had never occurred to her. "The authorities haven't released his body yet. It could be ages before I can actually do anything."

"I see, yes, I hadn't thought of that. I suppose that while the investigation is still ongoing…" She trailed off, her face flushing slightly.

"I can't just sit around here waiting, jumping every time that the phone rings." Lucinda's long fingers twitched at the fringes of her scarf, running the light material across her palm and then pulling it tight. "I need a break." She paused. "I was wondering, as you've got your car with you, if you might drive me to the airport?"

"Well, I... what, you mean today?"

"Yes, today. As soon as I've packed."

"Well, I'll have to let Jeremy know, obviously..."

Molly looked bewildered. Lucinda stood up and looked down at her.

"Come and help me get some things together."

Molly rose reluctantly, letting Aubrey slide off her lap and on to the floor. He steadied himself and looked up. For the first time he realised how large Lucinda was compared to Molly. He had always thought of Lucinda as rather delicate, probably something to do with the floaty dresses and the sparkly things she wore in her hair as well as her general air of being, quite literally, away with the fairies. But looking up at her now, she didn't look delicate at all. In fact, compared to Molly she looked huge.

Lucinda made her way upstairs to her bedroom, with Molly trailing behind her. Aubrey hesitated for a second, struck by a sudden doubt. He was going into unknown territory here. He didn't know the layout of the house beyond the kitchen and a couple of rooms downstairs. What if he got stuck somewhere and couldn't get out? With Lucinda going away he could be trapped for days. Weeks. And what if he'd been wrong about all this anyway? It wouldn't be the first time that he'd got hold of the wrong end of the stick. He flicked his paw over his right ear and had a quick wash while he thought about it. There was nothing to stop him just slipping back out of the pantry window and returning home. It was a nice day out there and Edyth or Dino might be down at the memorial garden. Or he could call in and see how Trevor was doing, he hadn't been round there for a couple of days. He was probably jumping to conclusions about Lucinda. She just wanted some company, that was all.

But there was no denying, it had been a very ugly scene that they had witnessed that morning. It had upset Carlos, Teddy and Casper too. It was as if the slightly silly, smiley Lucinda that they knew and were mildly fond of, had been whisked away and her place taken by a gorgon. If she'd spotted them spying on her and turned them to stone it wouldn't have surprised him. When Zofia had started crying, far from comforting her as he would have expected her to do, Lucinda had told her to shut up and then threatened to report her to the authorities although for what, she hadn't specified. Zofia had said nothing, just cried harder, making her big plump shoulders shake and loosening the plastic combs that held her hair.

He wished that Jeremy was here. Just having Jeremy around always seemed to make things better. At the thought of Jeremy, he lifted his head and stiffened his resolve, ashamed at his momentary weakness. His time with Molly and Jeremy had been so far beyond anything that he could ever have imagined during those long dark nights in Sunny Banks rescue centre, that if Molly was in any sort of danger he owed it to both of them to at least do what he could. He jumped on to the first stair and started creeping up behind the two women, comforting himself that at least Maudie knew where he was if he did get trapped.

He reached the top of the stairs and slipped quickly past Molly and Lucinda, taking care not to brush against their legs. Breathing in, he squeezed himself under the small chintz covered easy chair in the corner of the room. Even if they spotted him, they'd have trouble getting him out. In fact, he might have trouble getting himself out. He lay on his stomach and peered out from beneath the frill of the chair cover.

"Lucinda, I…" said Molly, as Lucinda turned round to lock the door.

"Force of habit." Lucinda laughed as she said it but she didn't, Aubrey noticed with a sinking heart, unlock it again. "Too many nosy children around. Particularly that brat Casper, forever pushing his beak into things of no concern to him. Revolting child," she added, slipping the key into her skirt pocket.

Lucinda bent down and pulled a suitcase out from under the bed. She regarded it for a moment and then shoved it back. Reaching in further she withdrew a small nylon holdall. Crossing the room she pulled open a drawer and began stuffing underwear into it.

"Do you know, Molly, I always rather envied you and Jeremy." She kept her back to Molly while she talked, her tone conversational. "You seem such a nice couple. So ordinary."

Molly looked at her back, a slightly hurt expression on her face.

"Ordinary?"

Lucinda turned to face Molly and laughed; a short chortle with an unpleasant ring, like the scrape of an empty food bowl being rattled against the kitchen floor.

"Oh, sorry Molly. I didn't mean ordinary as in, well, ordinary."

What did you mean then, thought Aubrey. Ordinary as in not ordinary? It was dusty under the chair and he resisted the urge to lift his leg and scratch behind his left ear. He'd got this far; it wouldn't do now to alert them to his presence. He just hoped that Maudie would get a move on. It was quite difficult to breathe and he was starting to feel a bit uncomfortable.

"I mean ordinary in a good way." She gestured to the bed and waited until Molly had sat down. "Ordinary as compared to Harold and me. Did you know about his first wife? About what happened to her?"

Molly nodded.

"Quentin told us."

Lucinda sighed.

"Yes, well, he would. Did he tell you… well, never mind. I don't suppose that it matters now."

She looked down at the underwear that she was still clutching, a froth of lace and ribbons. She stared at it for a moment before pushing it back into the drawer and pulling out some more serviceable garments in navy cotton.

"Harold and I were always a little different, you know." She spoke softly, so that Aubrey had to strain to hear her. "Not quite like everybody else. We were both outsiders, in our own way. Not like you and Jeremy. You two would fit in anywhere." She looked up. "Harold told me that when he was growing up his father spent most of his time in and out of prison."

"Goodness." Molly sat up slightly straighter. "What for? Did he tell you?"

Lucinda nodded.

"Nothing violent. Mostly fraud and swindling, that kind of thing. Widows, charities and the generally vulnerable were his speciality, apparently. He can't have been very good at it though, because he was always getting caught. Harold said that from the age of about two, they were constantly on the move. His mother was always trying to escape the shame of it. But she always took him back. And everything would be all right for a while, but Harold said that he used to dread the sound of a knock on the door. It was usually the police."

"Poor Harold."

Molly sounded genuinely sorry. She seemed to have forgotten, thought Aubrey, Morris's story about how Harold's first wife had died. Although, to be fair, they still didn't know if that was true or not.

"My parents weren't criminals," said Lucinda. "At least not in the legal sense, but we weren't like other families."

"In what way?" Molly asked. She was, Aubrey could see, becoming interested. Good. It would take her mind off the locked door. And the longer they talked, the more time it would give Maudie to get here.

FORTY-FOUR

LUCINDA STARED BLANKLY at Molly as though, thought Aubrey, she had no idea how she had got there. When she spoke, her voice was low.

"My parents were much older than the parents of other children. They had me late in life, my mother was nearly fifty, and I suspect that they didn't quite know what to do with me. It was like they were constantly surprised that I was there. I was surprised myself, sometimes. It was like I'd been put down in the wrong family."

"What did they do for a living?"

"Nothing." She shrugged in a gesture of contempt. "They never worked, at least not that I was ever aware of. They may have done when they were younger, I don't know. My mother had a small annuity from her father and that was what they lived on. I always understood that her parents were quite well off, although I never met them. They died before I was born."

Molly nodded and smiled sympathetically. Lucinda carried on talking, the same faraway note in her voice. It was almost, thought Aubrey, as though she was talking to herself.

"We were sort of shut off from everyone else. Not literally, but we just never seemed to go outside. The only time my parents went out, it was for essentials, like shopping, and as soon as I was old enough they sent me for it. They never stepped past the front door if they could help it. Apart from the shopping, they didn't like it if I went out, either." She laughed suddenly, a light trickling noise, like the patter of raindrops on a window pane. "Every afternoon they had to have a little lie down. As though the effort of doing nothing all morning had worn them out." Her expression changed and she looked serious again, the light-hearted moment evaporating as quickly as it had arrived. "At the time I thought it was normal. I didn't know anything else."

"What about school?" asked Molly, glancing down at her watch. "You must have made some friends there?"

Lucinda shook her head.

"Not really. I went to the local schools but even there I was the odd one out." She gave a wry smile. "I was the kid that didn't get invited to other kids' parties. Not surprising, really. I never had one to invite them back to. I just sat at the back of the class, did as I was told and kept my mouth shut. Not much different to being at home. After about fourteen, I more or less stopped going. Nobody did anything about it, I doubt that anybody even noticed. Sometimes one of my parents would ask why I wasn't at school. I just used to say it was staff training or something. They weren't really interested. After a while they stopped asking."

"Didn't you get bored?" Molly asked.

"No, I didn't mind being on my own. I was used to it. There were some books lying about the house, and I used to read those. They were nearly all pretty old, a few encyclopaedias, an atlas, some of the classics, that sort of thing. I think they must have been some of my father's old school books. Anyway, in among them was a book about weird and wonderful things, including the Cottingley Fairies. Do you know about them?

Molly tipped her head to one side and frowned slightly.

"I think so. Wasn't it some story about children seeing fairies?"

"That's right." Lucinda threw her an approving smile, as though Molly were one of her pupils. "It happened in the early twentieth century. Two girls said that they had seen fairies in their garden and took photographs of them. I found out later that they admitted that they'd faked them. Except for the last picture. One of the girls, Frances, always said that one was real. Anyway, after seeing the pictures and reading about them, whenever I could, I would slip out into the garden to see if I could find any fairies of my own. I used to pretend to myself that I had sometimes. I used to draw them and give them names. They were my friends."

Molly was, Aubrey could see, struggling to find something to say. After all, what was there to say about a teenaged girl that was so lonely that she invented fairies to play with? Molly was more open-minded than most, but even by her standards, this wasn't exactly normal.

"When I wasn't reading or in the garden," Lucinda continued, "I was running around doing errands and all the odd little jobs that my parents wanted doing. You'd be amazed at how useful I can be." She smiled again, an impish grin this time that lit her face and made her look young. "I can put up a shelf with my eyes closed and a blocked sink is a piece of cake."

Aubrey looked at her with renewed interest. He would never have guessed. Lucinda looked like the sort of person who would have trouble opening a packet of cat food, never mind put up a shelf. But then, Maudie had said that she built the ladybird house by herself so clearly she had hidden talents.

"Funnily enough, although my parents didn't like me going out of the house, they didn't have a problem with me getting a job," she continued. "More money for them, I suppose. What I really wanted, more than anything, was to be an actress, but I would have had to go to drama school and there was no chance of that. But it didn't matter anyway. When it came to it, I didn't have much choice. No qualifications. I'm not sure that the school even entered me for any, if they did they never told me."

"I thought that you qualified as a nurse? Didn't you have to have GCSEs to start training?"

"I told people that I was a nurse but I wasn't really. I was what they used to call a ward maid. A cleaner," she added, her face hardening again. "And the occasional wiper of peoples' arses when the wards were busy. It was alright, at least it got me out of the house. By the time I was in my early twenties, my father had died and my mother had pretty much lost what little interest in life she'd ever had. She used to just sit in the same chair watching television all day and eating crisps. That damned chair was covered in crisp crumbs. I was forever shaking out the cushions."

"Was she ill?" asked Molly.

Lucinda shook her head.

"No, not physically. At least, I didn't think so at the time. But one day she died too. I came home from work and there she was. In her chair, surrounded by her crisp packets. Heart failure, the doctor said. She had one brother, uncle Charles, and out of the blue he asked me to come and house-keep for him. It turned out that he was ill as well, although he didn't tell me that at the time. It wouldn't have mattered though, if he had. I would still have gone."

"Didn't you want to stay in your home, in the place that you were used to?" asked Molly.

"Not really. Which was just as well, because as it turned out, I didn't have any choice there either. My mother had barely been dead for a week before I discovered that they didn't own the house we lived in, they rented it. They didn't even own the furniture. Anyway, I couldn't afford the rent on my own, not on what I was earning at the hospital. There was a little money in their accounts but not much and most of that went to paying for their funerals. I don't know why I bothered really. Nobody came except uncle Charles. I should have just put them out with the bins."

There was, thought Aubrey, something horribly practical about Lucinda.

CHAPTER FORTY-FIVE

FOR SEVERAL MINUTES the silence sat heavily in the room. From the hall downstairs the sombre chime of the grandfather clock struck twice, the sound echoing upwards and trembling in the air. Molly glanced at her watch again and frowned slightly.

"Lucinda, I…"

"To be honest, uncle Charles asking me to live with him was an absolute lifeline." Lucinda continued where she'd left off, as though Molly hadn't spoken. "He was offering free bed and board and what he called pocket money. It wasn't very much, but then I didn't have very much to spend it on."

She crossed the room and sat down on the bed next to Molly, just slightly too close. Aubrey watched as Molly inched away from her.

"I changed my name when I came here. I was torn between Melody and Lucinda. I chose Lucinda in the end. It's a name that I've always liked. It means 'light'."

"What's your real name?"

"Muriel. It was my grandmother's name. My father's mother. I never met her but I saw some photographs of her. I think that I look a bit like her. Same shaped face and eyes." She laughed, a brittle spike of a chuckle that held no humour. "Anyway, it saved my parents the trouble of thinking of a new name. God forbid that they should ever have had to make an effort with anything."

Molly was, Aubrey could see, struggling to imagine what such parents would be like to live with. Molly's own parents, who visited every few months, were warm generous people. So generous that they always brought several packets of cat treats with them in different flavours. In case, they said, Aubrey wasn't keen on one of them. While he didn't like to think of himself as shallow, he had taken to them immediately.

"Well, you look more like a Lucinda than a Muriel," Molly said at last.

"Thank you, Molly. I'd like to think so. Lucinda sounds so much freer, don't you think? Sort of romantic. Anyway, I liked it here. The house and the village. Right from the start. It felt like I could be whoever I wanted. I had more freedom here than I ever had at home. The house was big enough for me to have my own rooms and I didn't even have to do too much in the way of looking after uncle Charles. He wasn't very demanding. He got up late and went to bed early and his favourite meal was bacon and tinned tomatoes. Hardly a stretch of my culinary skills. After a few weeks I even made a friend. I found her running around in the grounds one day. I told her that she was trespassing but she just laughed and said that she didn't care. She was like that. Fun. She was younger than me, still at school, but it didn't matter. I'd never had a friend before. Not a proper one, only the other ward maids at the hospital and they were mostly older than I was. I didn't have much in common with them."

She fell silent and stared ahead of her, her expression suddenly morose. Molly's gaze flicked towards the locked door. Without turning, but as if sensing Molly's eye movement, Lucinda reached across and placed her strong fingers around Molly's wrist. Her touch was light but there was no mistaking the strength of the grip.

"My friend, I used to meet her in a secret place. She used to ask me to bring things."

"What sort of things?" asked Molly.

"Make up and stuff like that. I used to take wine, too. Uncle Charles had stacks of it. He never noticed if some went missing."

"Wasn't she too young to be drinking? I mean, if she was still at school?"

"I suppose so." Lucinda sounded disinterested. "But then, well, we quarrelled."

"What did you quarrel about?"

"I'd given her a present, a small... well, just a present. It was mine and I'd had it for years, I found it in our garden when I was little, but I gave it to her. So she said that she would make something for me, but then when it came to it, she wouldn't give it to me. She started making fun of me, she said some horrible things, she said, well..." She paused and tightened the corners of her mouth before continuing. "This thing she made me, she kept holding it in front of my face so I sort of grabbed it and we argued. I didn't see her again after that." said Lucinda, shortly. "Anyway, I thought about leaving the village. Going off and trying to start somewhere new. I reckoned that I could always get another job in a hospital. Maybe even join a local drama group or something like that. But, I don't know, time drifted on. And then Harold turned up. He had just sold his last house and was renting a house in the village while he looked around for somewhere else. I met him one day when I was out, buying uncle Charles's newspaper in Bradley's. We just started talking and he walked back up to the house with me."

Aubrey watched as Lucinda's fingers loosened slightly and flexed before taking hold of Molly's wrist again, tighter this time. Molly winced.

"Now, I know that Harold wasn't what you'd call conventionally good-looking," she paused and turned to Molly with a little tip-tilted smile.

You can say that again, thought Aubrey. In his opinion Harold had been what you'd call conventionally repellent.

"But that didn't matter because one thing that Harold was very good at," she continued, "very good indeed, was making a person feel special. He really did have that gift. It was something to do with the way he looked at you, the way he listened, as though you really were the only person in the world. He made me feel that I was fascinating, that I had interesting things to say. Not like my parents. If I ever so much as opened my mouth it would be, 'oh, do be quiet Muriel, stop prattling on, we're trying to watch this.' Usually some puerile game show," she added. "The sort where people have to make fools of themselves. They loved those programmes."

She pursed her lips as she spoke, and screwed her face up so that a sprinkling of crow's feet suddenly flashed around her big blue eyes.

"But after I met Harold, none of that mattered any more. Do you know, Molly, I think that I would have done anything for Harold. I'd never had a boyfriend, you see."

Molly muttered something that Aubrey couldn't quite catch.

"My parents had always told me that I was what they called plain," Lucinda continued. "But Harold said that was nonsense. He said I was beautiful." She smiled. "He was older than me, of course, but I didn't mind. I think, in a way, I liked it. It made me feel I could rely on him, that he would look after me. But in a good way, not like my parents."

Aubrey watched as Molly gently prised Lucinda's fingers from her wrist and glanced towards the locked door. She was, he thought, starting to look worried again now.

Lucinda carried on talking, serenely oblivious to Molly's anxiety.

"Harold used to wait by the gates for me and we would go for walks over to the spinney. He used to pick wild flowers and thread them through my hair." Lucinda reached up and touched her head as she spoke, as though she could still feel the petals woven into her curls. "And he bought me ribbons, too. He told me about his first wife, of course. How she'd died." She looked almost dazed now, thought Aubrey, as though she'd been drinking. Perhaps she had, he thought, suddenly remembering Casper's comments about the raspberry cordial and the vodka. That would explain a lot. "It was like something out of a film. The lonely girl. The tragic widower. He told me that I was one of life's true innocents. And so I was. To him." She smiled. "I've always been able to be whatever anybody wants me to be, I've always had that talent."

For a moment she fell silent again and then, as if remembering why she was there, she suddenly stood up. She crossed to the big oak wardrobe and reached inside. Clashing hangers together, she started to pull clothes down from the rails.

"Anyway, he persuaded me to stay in the village. He said that he needed me. Nobody had ever said that to me before." Her voice cracked slightly and for a moment she held herself perfectly still, her shoulders set, before continuing to tug at the clothes in the wardrobe. "He said that we had a future together. And then Uncle Charles died, rather sooner than expected."

Aubrey looked at her suspiciously. How convenient.

"So Harold and I got married. At the registry office in the town. Just us two and a couple of people who worked in the offices there as witnesses."

"Didn't you mind?" asked Molly.

"Mind what?"

"Well, not having more of a fuss I suppose. Something more traditional."

Lucinda shook her head.

"No, not really. It was enough that I had Harold. I would have just lived with him if he'd preferred, but he was keen for us to be married. He said that we would need to keep it low-key because if the press got hold of it, even though he'd changed his name, all the old stuff about his first wife would be dragged up again and he didn't want to put me through that. It's funny, I always thought of him as Harold, even when I knew that his real name was Aaron. Somehow, he didn't look like an Aaron."

She paused and looked around the room, her eye running from ceiling to floor and back again, a slightly puzzled expression on her face. Almost, thought Aubrey, as though she couldn't quite remember how she had got there. She took a deep breath and turned back to face Molly.

"It was Harold's idea to turn the house into a school," she continued. "He said that the house was in a pretty poor state of repair and too big for a regular family, even if they could get a mortgage on it. He said that we'd be lucky to find a buyer, but there was a lot of money in private education and we could do things our own way. And, do you know Molly, the more I thought about it, the more I liked the idea. For once, I would be in charge, I would be the one telling other people what to do. For the first time in my life, there was nobody to stop me from doing whatever I wanted. Harold didn't interfere with the teaching." She stood up slightly straighter and looked suddenly proud. "He said that I had a natural gift for it."

Of course he did, thought Aubrey. Just like he had a natural gift for sitting on his arse and thinking himself important.

"I know, of course, that there aren't really fairies." Lucinda tipped her head to one side and gave another of her impish smiles, as though inviting Molly to share the joke. "But, you know, it was such a lovely stretch of the imagination for the children. Especially the younger ones. And I don't believe that I did them any more harm than in any other school."

She was probably right there, thought Aubrey. At Sir Frank Wainwright's there had been bells or buzzers or something to tell the children when to change lessons. Jeremy had once said that it was a system designed to induce maximum hysteria. Just at the point where you'd got the kids interest and some of them were actually working, a sudden loud noise would get them leaping out of their seats, barging out of rooms and charging about all over the place. In an attempt to minimise the chaos, the Head had once tried a system where the teachers changed rooms instead of the pupils. Which had been fine until, left briefly without any supervision, some of the pupils had taken the opportunity to barricade themselves in. One enterprising group had even managed to grab a Year Seven and hold him hostage. After which the school had reverted back to the old system.

"Most of the children liked it here," said Lucinda. "They were all of them a bit different, too. They wouldn't have been here otherwise. We specialised in taking children who didn't fit into the mainstream." She paused and turned to gaze out of the bay window, her eye running over the long sweeping lawn and down towards the big double gates. "I know that half the village think I'm mad, but I don't care."

"What will you do now? Will you keep the school going?" asked Molly.

Lucinda laughed and turned back to face her.

"It would be a bit difficult with all the pupils gone. Anyway, once Harold found out that I didn't have any money, everything changed."

FORTY-SIX

MOLLY LOOKED PUZZLED.

"I thought that you inherited from your uncle?"

"Only the house and a few shares, and even that was by default really. I was uncle Charles only living relative, he didn't have anyone else to leave it to. But there was no money. Uncle Charles had a pretty good private pension but that died with him. The problem was, you see, Harold always assumed that I did have money. I suppose because of the size of the house and everything. Somehow, I never seemed to find the right moment to raise the subject. And anyway, I knew that he had inherited a lot of money from his first wife, so I didn't think that it mattered."

Her blue eyes gazed unblinking at Molly.

"But, surely, it wasn't important? I mean, if you loved each other…" Molly trailed off.

"It mattered to Harold." Lucinda's mouth twitched at the edges to form a tight, bitter smile. "He said that it wasn't the money itself, he said that it was an issue of trust." She clutched at the light floral dress that she was holding, her long fingers pulling at the fabric. "He said that he was disappointed in me, that I had deceived him."

"How did he find out about it?"

"Uncle Charles' will. I couldn't remember which companies the shares were with. I was hoping, you see, that they might have gone up in value. Harold had a habit of going through my things, he said it was to check that I was keeping up with all the school admin. So, I kept uncle Charles' will in my secret place."

"Where was that?" Molly asked.

"In the ladybird house. I keep all my important things there."

Molly tensed slightly and withdrew her mobile from her pocket.

"Lucinda, I think that I'd better let Jeremy know where I am. And the children, too. They'll be getting worried. They must be wondering what's happened to me."

Lucinda reached over. Gently pulling the mobile from Molly's grasp, she dropped it into her pocket along with the door key.

"Don't do that. Not now. I want to finish telling you."

She gave Molly a great beaming smile, looking suddenly like the old Lucinda. "It's so nice to have a friend again, and I've always felt that I could talk to you, Molly, even though we haven't known each other for very long. You're such a good listener."

Like she's got any choice, thought Aubrey. Nothing like a locked door to improve listening skills. He should know. When he was banged up in the rescue centre he'd even started to find old Rover's tales of life when he'd lived on a farm mildly interesting. And Rover was the most boring cat he'd ever come across.

"Anyway, after Harold found out about the money, at first everything seemed to carry on as usual. At least, on the surface. But then things began to change, I could feel it. He started to be cold towards me when we were on our own, going off on long walks without me and sometimes even staying away overnight. One evening, when it was obvious that he wasn't coming back that night, I looked on his computer. I knew all his passwords, of course. They didn't take a lot of working out." She looked

255

directly at Molly; her expression forlorn. "I know I shouldn't have done it. Afterwards I wished that I hadn't."

"Why?"

Molly's voice sounded hesitant, thought Aubrey. As though she had asked a question to which she didn't really want to know the answer. Like that time he had asked Vincent what he thought had happened to Clanger, the little Westie that had disappeared into the back of a van one quiet afternoon.

"He'd been looking at dating sites. More than looking. He'd earmarked a few profiles. Older women mostly. The sort that looked as though they had money. And there were other things too." She paused. "Other things that he'd been looking at."

For several minutes Lucinda fell silent, her long fingers still working the fabric of the dress she was holding, and then she said, "Suddenly, everything that I had was slipping away. I started to panic."

Molly nodded. She was trying, Aubrey could see, not to keep looking down at her watch.

"But I had to be sensible about it, you see Molly, I had to make a plan." Her blue eyes widened. "I mean, I could see that it was only a matter of time before Harold left and I needed to make sure that I'd be all right. Nobody else was going to. I didn't want to keep the school going on my own and even if I sold the house, it could take months and I'd have almost nothing to live on in the meantime. I did think about divorcing him but those things take time and a court wouldn't necessarily make him give me any money. So I'd be back at square one. Back to doing the kind of jobs that nobody else wants to do. Back to being invisible. Back to being nobody."

"Couldn't you have got a job as a teacher?"

Lucinda gave a short laugh.

"I'm not qualified."

"What about a teaching assistant? I've got some friends who do that and they…"

"Why should I?" Lucinda interrupted, her tone suddenly fierce and her eyes bright. "I don't want to be anybody's assistant. Anyway, you probably have to have qualifications for that too."

She fell silent again, her gaze wandering around the room. She leaned slightly forward and stared straight at the chintz chair. Aubrey's heart gave a great jolt. She'd seen him. No, it wasn't possible. Not unless she could see through the frill on the chair. He breathed more easily and shifted position to ease his aching back. Lying on your stomach for any length of time was, he had discovered, a lot less attractive than it sounded.

"I thought about it a lot." Lucinda drew in her breath and held it for a moment before letting it out slowly. "But I was going to lose him anyway so what did it matter how? And this way I would have something to live on."

Aubrey shuddered. That horrible practicality again.

"The more I thought about it, the more it seemed the obvious solution. But it had to be simple." She tipped her head to one side as though considering. "I've often thought that people over-complicate things. And that's when they go wrong. Then one day I saw that bitch hanging around the gates, I recognised her from her pictures in the press. I'd checked out all the old stories when Harold told me about his first wife. She hadn't changed much. And the more I thought about it, the more it seemed the perfect set-up."

She stood up straighter and shoved the dress into the holdall.

"Right. Must stop wasting time. I've got a plane to catch." She sounded brisk now. Reaching up into the wardrobe she pulled down more garments. "Let's get this lot in the car and I'll grab my handbag and passport and we can go. You can ring Jeremy from the airport."

Aubrey watched in alarm as Molly stood up and the two women left the room, Lucinda shutting the door firmly behind her. He ran across to the big bay window and jumped on to the sill.

Across the front lawn, Trevor ran ahead of the pack, his ears back and his fur flying as he picked up pace. Aubrey could see, even at this distance, that he was feeling the strain of his injury. The vet had done a good job in patching him up but he still wasn't entirely right. He hadn't let that stop him, though. Trevor, thought Aubrey, was a good mate. Not quite in the class of Vincent, but very nearly. Racing up behind Trevor came Gnasher, Jethro, Edyth and Dino. Of Maudie, there was no sign. Aubrey strained his eyes further. Where was she? Had she got bored and gone off somewhere? Just as the thought formed, a movement down by the gates caught his eye. Swerving in and up the driveway, going at a rate of knots, swarmed the tip cats, Maudie flying above them and Tubby struggling to bring up the rear, his short legs going as fast as his fat little body would allow.

Aubrey watched as the cats massed up on the front step, a great wall of fur clamped tightly together.

Suddenly the door swung open and Lucinda stood on the threshold, one hand clutching Molly's arm.

"What the…"

She stared down at the cats and made to move forward. A solid line barred her way. Moving to step across them she jumped back in fright as a Mexican wave of felines rose in front of her. Turning back, she ran across the hall and through to the kitchen, one hand pulling Molly behind her. Outside the back door came the unmistakeable sound of the tip cats growling.

In the distance the wail of police sirens floated towards them.

CHAPTER FORTY-SEVEN

IN THE PUB garden, the early evening air was calm and still, broken only by the sound of a pair of robins squabbling for territory. Molly and Morris sat on a wooden bench. Opposite them Carlos, Teddy and Casper bunched up together, elbows on the trestle table and all three of them slightly subdued. An hour earlier, Teddy and Casper's father had phoned Jeremy to say that he would collect them in the morning. Nearby in the children's play area, Maudie hung upside down on a climbing frame watched by Aubrey from the top of the slide.

They all looked up as Jeremy crossed the grass holding a tray. He angled the soft drinks towards the teenagers and pulled three packets of crisps from his trouser pockets.

"Here, help yourselves. Keep you till dinner."

Molly leaned over and picked the glass of wine from the tray. She looked at it for a moment and then put it down on the table.

"I know you all think I'm totally mad, but, I can't help it, I actually feel quite sorry for her."

"Don't be too sorry," said Morris, reaching for his pint. "If the police hadn't turned up when they did, who knows what might have happened." He glanced down at his watch. "I must keep an eye on the time. I'm meeting Josie off the bus later."

Molly looked thoughtful and picked up her wine glass again.

"You know, I don't think that anything would have happened. Honestly, I don't."

"I still don't get it, Molly," said Casper. She was Molly now to all of them, Aubrey noticed, not just Carlos. "Why did she want you to go to the airport with her? Why didn't she just go on her own?"

"Insurance," said Jeremy shortly. "She must have phoned the hospital and once she knew that Quentin had regained consciousness, she knew that it would only be a matter of time before he identified her. And there was that business with the things from the ladybird house. She must have known that there would be further questions about that. I think that her instinct was to get away while she had the chance. Having Molly with her, she had something to bargain with if she needed it."

"But she didn't though," said Molly. "She didn't say a thing, she just got in the squad car."

"But that's a measure of how clever she is," said Jeremy.

"What do you mean?" asked Molly.

"She knew that she had virtually no chance of getting away by then."

Molly sighed.

You know," she mused, "Even so, I think that she genuinely wanted somebody to talk to. She was very lonely. I got the feeling that nobody had ever really listened to her before."

"But why did she attack Quentin?" asked Teddy. "I thought that he had gone there to help her sort things out."

Jeremy looked thoughtful.

"I think that Quentin told her the truth about how Harold's first wife had died."

"So that made her want to attack him?"

"Not exactly. I think that he wanted money from her to keep quiet about it."

"I still don't get it," said Teddy. She looked at Carlos, her little heart-shaped face screwed up in concentration. "Do you?"

Carlos nodded.

"If Harold was guilty of his first wife's murder then the law says that he couldn't inherit her money. So if he didn't have her money then Lucinda couldn't have it either."

Molly smiled approvingly.

"Spoken like a true lawyer," she said.

Teddy turned to Jeremy.

"But Carlos told us that Quentin didn't know for sure that Harold had killed her, he only knew that Harold had paid him to tell lies."

"True," said Jeremy. "But what other reason would there be for Harold to have wanted Quentin to lie at Josie's trial? But whatever the truth of the matter, if Quentin went to the police it would be enough to throw doubt on Josie's conviction."

"But wouldn't he have got into trouble for that? I mean if he told the truth now?" said Teddy.

"Yes," agreed Jeremy. "But knowing Quentin, he would have a story worked out. Maybe that Harold threatened him or something like that. Remember that he was still only a teenager when it all happened. But my guess is that he was banking on Lucinda paying him to keep his mouth shut."

"But what if Lucinda tells the police that he tried to blackmail her?"

"I should think that he'd deny it. But I doubt that she will. There's no advantage to her. She's probably still hoping to get her hands on Harold's money. No, Lucinda's only mistake with Quentin is that she didn't hit him hard enough. He knows that he's in danger while she's still around, that's why he didn't hesitate to identify her as soon as he remembered what had happened."

"You all right now, Molly?"

They all looked up as Jo strolled across the grass towards them, pint in hand.

"Just been talking to my cousin Terry again," he said, sipping across the top of his pint. "Unbelievable." He shook his head and took another sip of his drink.

"Come and sit down with us," said Jeremy, shifting along the bench.

"Five minutes," said Jo, sitting down next to him. "Just wanted to give you the latest update and see how Molly is doing."

Molly smiled across at him.

"I'm fine, honestly. Lucinda didn't actually hurt me, you know. She didn't even threaten to hurt me."

"Well, I think that you had a narrow escape," said Jo. "Tel reckons that the officers interviewing her never saw such a cool character. Unbelievable," he repeated. "Apparently she's going 'no comment' all the way."

"So would I," said Casper stoutly. "I wouldn't say a thing. I'd just say 'no comment'.

"Well then, you would be saying a thing, wouldn't you?" said Teddy, poking her tongue out at him. "You'd be saying 'no comment'."

"Well, it's a bit pointless anyway, she's already pretty much confessed to Molly, and the police have got Molly's statement." said Morris.

"She didn't actually say that she did it," said Molly. "I mean, not specifically. I only told the police what she said."

"I still don't get how she managed it though," said Casper.

"She stabbed him," said Teddy, frowning. "You know that, Cas."

"I know, I mean why wasn't she covered in blood and that?"

"According to Terry" said Jo. "After the discovery of the necklace and the penknife," he nodded towards Teddy and

Casper, "the police started looking at her in a new light. They also checked Harold's computer."

The three teenagers looked across at him, interested.

"Well," Jo hesitated and glanced across at Jeremy. "There was some interesting stuff on it."

"What?" Casper leaned forward; his eyes bright. "What was on Harold's computer?"

"Never mind that now, Casper," said Jeremy. "Go on, Jo."

"One of the officers went back and checked everywhere that Lucinda had been after Harold was killed. Including the hospital."

"Did they find out anything?" asked Molly.

"The officer spoke to one of the nurses on the ward that Lucinda had been admitted to, asked her if anything unusual had happened while Lucinda had been there. Tel said that the officer didn't really know what she was looking for, she was just sort of digging around. Anyway, the nurse said no, nothing unusual had happened. Apart from when she saw Lucinda coming out from behind the area where they keep the bins."

"Why was a nurse hanging around the bins?" asked Teddy.

"Apparently it's the unofficial smoking area. Anyway, when the nurse asked her what she was doing there, Lucinda just said that she wanted a bit of fresh air. The nurse thought it was a bit odd, like, why would you hang around the bins if you wanted a bit of fresh air? But she didn't really think any more about it. So the officer went and looked and she found the poncho in one of the waste bins. It was spattered with blood. Interesting," he mused. "I wonder if a male officer would have recognised it. Ponchos aren't the sort of thing that blokes usually carry around."

Jo sat back and sipped at his pint, enjoying the moment.

"Poncho?" Casper looked confused. "What's a poncho?"

"It's a sort of cloak thing, Cas," explained Teddy.

"It was a rain poncho with a hood," said Jo. "One of those thin plastic ones that folds up. Clever, when you think about it. It's not like anybody would be surprised to find a blood-covered garment in a hospital bin. And they're not kept in an area where the public would normally go. It was unlucky for Lucinda that the bins weren't emptied that week because of a problem with the disposal company."

"But," Teddy paused as she thought it through, wrinkling her forehead in an effort of concentration. "She didn't know that she would be taken to hospital."

"No," agreed Jo. "But the opportunity presented itself and she took it. Just like she took the opportunity with Harold. She might have been carrying the knife around for ages, waiting for a chance. The fete must have seemed like a good opportunity."

"Why?" asked Casper. "There were loads of people there. She might have been seen."

"Look at it the other way," said Jeremy. "Loads of people means loads of suspects. All she had to do was keep her nerve. Which she clearly did," he added dryly.

"To get rid of the poncho thing" continued Jo, "all she had to do was shove it back into its pouch and wait for a chance to come along. She probably had plastic gloves as well. Those thin disposable ones, I should think."

"Well, what if she hadn't been taken to hospital? What would she have done then?" asked Teddy.

Jo shrugged.

"Put the poncho somewhere else, I guess. But that's not all."

He sat back and took a sip of his pint, enjoying the moment.

"What?" Casper leaned towards him, visibly holding his breath.

"The police are also questioning her about the necklace and the penknife."

"What's she saying about them?" asked Molly.

"She's admitted that she put them there but she's saying that she found them."

Carlos picked up his empty crisp packet and began methodically folding it into ever smaller squares.

"Jeremy, do you think that she's mad? You know, like, like…"

He trailed off and began smoothing out the crisp packet again with the flat of his hand. Aubrey slid down the slide on his back and ran towards him. When Carlos had been held captive in the barn by the pyscho that had killed his mother, only Aubrey and Vincent had witnessed how truly horrific that scene had been. Molly and Jeremy had no real idea of the ordeal that Carlos had faced. Even now, he still had nightmares. And, truth to tell, so did Aubrey. He parked himself on Carlos's right foot.

"I asked Terry that," said Jo. "The view of the police is that she knew very well what she was doing. And she might even have got away with it if the kids there hadn't found the necklace and penknife. That was what really got the police thinking. And there was the attack on Quentin, of course," he added.

"Yes, but…" began Molly.

"Molly," Jeremy reached across and put his hand over hers. "Please don't say again that you feel sorry for her."

"Well, she did have a rough start in life."

"So do lots of people."

"Anyway," said Jo, "According to Terry, it looks like she's going to be a tough nut to crack. One thing though," he paused and took another sip of his pint. "The police seem to think that she kept some sort of cattery up there. Apparently there were cats running about all over the place.

CHAPTER FORTY-EIGHT

MORRIS WALKED BRISKLY towards the bus stop. In the absence of anything better to do, Carlos, Teddy and Casper dawdled along behind him, each deep in their own thoughts. At a discreet distance followed Aubrey and Maudie, Maudie balancing on the garden walls.

They paused for a moment to watch Bradley who was taking in the newsstand and locking up, his ill-fitting greasy trousers slipping further as he leaned down, revealing two pale half-moons.

Aubrey turned to Maudie.

"What is it about him?"

Maudie shrugged.

"I don't know. He's just so… so…"

"Repulsive?" suggested Aubrey.

"Repulsive," agreed Maudie.

They trotted on in companionable silence and then Aubrey said, "That was good work you did with the tip cats, Maudie. How did you get them to agree?"

Maudie smiled.

"They didn't take much persuading. They owed me one."

Aubrey stopped and looked at her.

"What for?"

"Oh, it was ages ago. Some boy had got hold of Missy in the memorial garden. It was fireworks night. He'd caught her and was trying to tie some fireworks to her tail."

"What did you do?"

"I tapped him on the shoulder and said 'boo'." She laughed. "That kid could really run."

They looked up in alarm as a high-pitched agonised yowl suddenly split the air, shattering the rural peace. Without pausing they sped towards it, overtaking Morris, Carlos, Teddy and Casper who had also started to run. By the hedge next to the bus stop a youth had hold of a cat. In the lowering evening sun they caught the glint of a knife being pulled from a rucksack just as the bus pulled up and Josie alighted.

Heart in mouth, Aubrey quickened his pace, his heart thudding. In one great leap he jumped on the youth's back and dug his claws in. Running up behind him, Morris caught hold of the youth's parka and swung him round, Aubrey still hanging on.

"Got it."

Teddy held her phone high, showing the clear picture of the youth still clutching Edyth round the throat, knife in hand. Rushing towards him, Carlos pulled Edyth away and held her to his chest.

"It's ok, she's not harmed." He soothed his hand across the top of her small head until he felt her breathing steady.

The youth shook his body from side to side, violently trying to dislodge Aubrey who remained firmly attached.

"Get this bastard cat off me." His voice trembled with rage.

"I think that you've got some explaining to do, young man," said Morris.

CARLOS LEANED BACK and surveyed the tangle of shrubs and bushes.

"Morris's garden is in a right state," he said.

"Shh," said Teddy and nodded towards the open kitchen window through which they could see Morris and Josie talking, heads bent together. "He might hear you."

Casper looked up from his phone screen and towards the window.

"Shouldn't think so. They're more interested in each other." He bent over the screen again. "Were you surprised that it was Tyrone?"

Teddy shook her head.

"Not really. Were you, Carlos?"

"No. He goes to my school but I've never liked him. He bullies the younger boys. And the girls. He's been suspended twice."

"Why do you think he did it?" asked Casper, looking up again.

Teddy shrugged.

"No idea. Some people like hurting things, I suppose. Makes them feel powerful or something. I guess he's a sadist."

Casper nodded; his expression grave.

"I think you're right." He paused. "What's a sadist, anyway?"

"I was thinking," said Carlos, looking around him again, "that I might come over and give Morris a hand here. Just to tidy it up a bit, sort of thing."

Teddy smiled approvingly.

"That's a lovely idea." She sighed. "I wish I could be here to help you."

From the edge of the small stagnant pond where he and Maudie had been searching for non-existent fish, Aubrey could see the faint stain reddening Carlos's throat and flush its way up towards his face. He smiled and turned back to Maudie.

"I hope that Edyth is going to be all right."

"She'll be fine," said Maudie. "He didn't have time to do anything to her. She's a trooper. She'll be ok. And Dino and Gnasher will look after her."

Carlos stood up as Morris and Josie approached the garden table.

"We'd better be getting back now, Morris. Molly and Jeremy will be expecting us for dinner. And Teddy and Casper have to get their things sorted. They're going home tomorrow." He glanced over to Aubrey. "Come on Aubrey, you too."

Morris smiled. He looked different.

"Ok, Carlos. See you soon. And I hope to see you two again before too long as well."

He reached over to stroke Aubrey.

"Bye, Aubrey."

He paused and looked at the girl with the long curling hair and hopeful expression.

"Bye Maudie."

ACKNOWLEDGEMENTS

Grateful thanks to the Red Dog Team for their expert guidance and advice. Love and thanks also to John and Sarah for their encouragement and support.

ABOUT THE AUTHOR

I was born in London and spent my teenage years in Hertfordshire where I spent large amounts of time reading novels, watching daytime television and avoiding school.

Failing to gain any qualifications in science whatsoever, the dream of being a forensic scientist collided with reality when a careers teacher suggested that I might like to work in a shop. I don't think she meant Harrods.

Later studying law, I decided to teach rather than go into practice and have spent many years teaching mainly criminal law and criminology to young people and adults.

I enjoy reading crime novels, doing crosswords, and drinking wine. Not necessarily in that order.